As Grace wheeled her grocery cart through the pharmacy section, she saw the condoms.

Immediately her mind turned to fantasies of Mal Quarrels in various states of undress. Then a whole bunch of what-ifs suddenly crossed her mind, and she panicked.

If she actually had condoms in the house, what if she got Mal to kiss her again and things escalated from there? What if she just got out of bed, sleepwalked to Mal's, climbed in bed with him and ravished him—and he didn't stop her?

What if, indeed.

Dear Reader,

We've got one of our most irresistible lineups ever for you this month, and you'll know why as soon as I start talking about the very first book. With *The Return of Rafe MacKade, New York Times* bestseller Nora Roberts begins a new miniseries, The MacKade Brothers, that will move back and forth between Intimate Moments and Special Edition. Rafe is also our Heartbreaker for the month, so don't get your heart broken by missing this very special book!

Romantic Traditions continues with Patricia Coughlin's *Love in the First Degree,* a compelling spin on the "wrongly convicted" story line. For fans of our Spellbound titles, there's *Out-Of-This-World Marriage* by Maggie Shayne, a marriage-of-convenience story with a star-crossed—and I mean that literally!— twist. Finish the month with new titles from popular authors Terese Ramin with *A Certain Slant of Light,* Alexandra Sellers with *Dearest Enemy,* as well as *An Innocent Man* by an exciting new writer, Margaret Watson.

This month, and every month, when you're looking for exciting romantic reading, come to Silhouette Intimate Moments—and enjoy!

Yours,

Leslie J. Wainger
Senior Editor and Editorial Coordinator

Please address questions and book requests to:
Silhouette Reader Service
U.S.: 3010 Walden Ave., P.O. Box 1325, Buffalo, NY 14269
Canadian: P.O. Box 609, Fort Erie, Ont. L2A 5X3

A CERTAIN SLANT OF LIGHT

TERESE RAMIN

Published by Silhouette Books

America's Publisher of Contemporary Romance

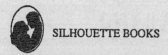 SILHOUETTE BOOKS

ISBN 0-373-07634-7

A CERTAIN SLANT OF LIGHT

Books by Terese Ramin

Silhouette Intimate Moments

Water from the Moon #279
Winter Beach #477
A Certain Slant of Light #634

Silhouette Special Edition

Accompanying Alice #656

TERESE RAMIN

lives in Michigan with her husband, two children, three dogs, three cats and an assortment of strays. When not writing romance novels, she writes chancel dramas, sings alto in the church choir, plays the guitar, yells at her children to pick up their rooms—even though she keeps telling herself that she won't—and responds with silence when they ask her where they should put their rooms after they've picked them up.

A full-fledged believer in dreams, the only thing she's ever wanted to do is write. After years of dreaming without doing anything about it, she finally wrote her first romance novel, *Water from the Moon,* which won a Romance Writers of America Golden Heart Award in 1987 and was published by Silhouette in 1989. Her subsequent books have appeared on the Waldenbooks romance bestseller lists. She is also the recipient of a 1991 *Romantic Times* Reviewer's Choice award. She hasn't dreamed without acting for a long time.

To Nathan and Brynna of the ever constant "Why?"
You make me crazy, but you're never boring, children.
I love you dearly.
Mom.

For Ann, who lends me Paul, and for Paul who
understands gobbledygook and can speak it with
computers: You can thank me later for giving you the
dog who broke your window and ate your couch.

And for Beep, who will always be one of life's main
characters whether I make her one or not.
Love you, kiddo!

My thanks to Nancy Humphreys of the
Property Shoppe, real-estate agent extraordinaire:
without her patience and energy in helping me
find an office with windows, this writing might not
have been possible. Thanks also to Melissa Senate,
Editor, for suggesting perhaps it was time to find a
different hero: this one's for you.

In the dark closet of my mind a phosphorescent
superball glows....
—tdr, 1971

Chapter 1

Southeastern Michigan,
Mid-May

The tip of the cigarette flushed red in the dusky light when Mal Quarrels inhaled.

Across KimSue Street near the corner of Auburn and Martin Luther King boulevards—someone had carefully spray-painted *Dr.* before the *Martin* on most of the street signs along the drive—at the outside edge of the area Pontiac residents once referred to as the Projects, a shadow passed in front of a window and someone turned on the lights in Our Lady of Roses Parish Center. Mal glanced at the face of the watch turned to the inside of his left wrist. Eight-fifteen. Shouldn't be long now.

"You know I did it, man, you know he in there, you know I found him, you know I always come through. You call, I jump, that the way it work, right, that the deal, so whatchyou need me hangin' around here for, waitin' for the dude to come out an' make me? Whatchyou need that for?''

"Insurance.'' Mal rolled the cigarette between thumb and forefinger, cupped his hand to protect the ash-end from the feeble wind; he was going through this butt fast enough, as it was. Jennifer had made him promise, no more than ten cigarettes a day this week, cut it down to eight next week and so on until he could clean the nicotine out of his lungs for good. Damn, what a man would do for his daughter.

He spared a wry half glance toward the Marlboro hardpack tucked into a roll of T-shirt over his left deltoid. *Intended* to do. He was halfway through his second pack today.

Another drag, another exhale and smoke curled white around his lips and nose. Beside him, Tigger danced on nervous feet, his skinny body jerking with the need to be elsewhere.

"Insurance? Man, what you talkin' 'bout? Who gonna touch you? You the man, right?''

Mal's lips thinned back without humor, tightening the smooth copper-rust skin along his jaw. Two hours back across the time zones—or was it three?—he could never remember—Jennifer would be getting home from cheer-leading practice in Murdo, South Dakota, about now. Maybe he should give her a call when he got done here, make his pack-and-a-half-today confession, let her chide him a bit, get him back on track. If her mother let her talk to him, that is. His ex-wife carried a big stick to beat back the snakes, where their daughter was concerned. Bitch— no heat behind the term, only a puzzled frustration and exasperated amusement; Livvi referred to herself as "the Bitch of South Dakota'' all the time considering him one of the biggest.

He glanced at the company he kept. Tigger's shaved head bounced to the rhythm of the nerves speeding his pulse and the rock of thin shoulders rolled in around his chest, hands jammed into baggy pockets holding his needle-scarred arms tight to his sides making him even thinner; his eyes showed a lot of white around their dark centers. Seventeen years old and wondering if he could make it through another day, scared out of his shorts to try. Could be Livvi had a point about Mal. Judging from the look of his sometime informant, Mal Quarrels was a give-you-the-screaming-willies, snakily scary kind of guy.

Mal's lips tightened into his cheeks a little more: in his line, the scariest guys stayed alive longest, in which case, scary suited him fine.

Bad to the bone, he thought derisively, and drew in more smoke. If Jennifer forgave him, he'd quit for good.

"I dunno, Tig-man, you tell me," Mal said aloud, letting the smoke go. "Last time I'm down here when you call, Mr. Drive-by happened along, tried to take me out. Lucky for you I got a paranoid gut and ducked. This time I figure I'll just take you to hell with me."

"Hell, *hell?* Man, whatchyou talkin' 'bout, takin' me where I already am, jive Native American honky, don' know where he standin'—"

Across the street at Our Lady of Roses, the sound of a solid door being pulled open in its frame clunked into the evening air. Mal felt the radar hair at the back of his neck stand up; the muscles in his arms tightened. He held out one finger and beside him, Tigger instantly hushed. Our Lady's screen door whined open and a slim, nondescript, bookish-looking man and a dress-for-success suit-shorts-clad, athletically attractive woman stepped onto the walk into the pool of bright yellow light from the lamp above the door. They paused together, the man, sandy hair, glasses, well-groomed, holding the screen door open while the woman, hair dark warm honey, features Irish-mixed-with-Scandinavian, from what Mal could see, pulled the inner door shut and locked it behind her. The man said something to her, teasing her about her difficulty with the door, probably. She looked up at him where she bent over the lock, her smile generous, laughter quick and relaxed.

Mal felt the huskiness of her laughter unexpectedly, in his gut where it didn't belong, and took his eyes off the man Tigger had called him down here to see long enough to give the woman a good hard once-over, more than the cursory memorize-the-face glance he'd given her already. Nothing remarkable that he could see from here, but something about her put his nerves on point clear down to his socks, shuffled along the edges of his libido poking it awake. He made a mental note to check her out—handy thing about being a U.S. marshal was he could do that just because his gut itched. Besides, if he had to justify it to himself, she obviously knew his quarry and maybe he could find a way to get close and stay close through her. A long minute passed before the woman finally got the door locked and the two of them turned face front into the light and started down the walk.

Mal's smile glittered grimly in his eyes when he ID'd the man. He dropped the feeble remains of his cigarette to the sidewalk, crushed it to ash beneath one heavy engineer boot.

Tigger rocked from foot to foot behind him. "It's him, ain't it, man, I told you, it's him."

Mal nodded and, without taking his eyes off the duo opposite, unrolled what was left of the crushproof pack from his sleeve and handed it to Tigger. "Beat it, kid."

"Man, I don't work for no half-empty pack o' butts. Five-oh, fifty, that's the deal, nothin' less. You got me down here riskin' my behind—"

Mal looked at him once; Tigger's Adam's apple convulsed in his throat and he shut up. "You owed me after last time—you don't get lost, I'll take payment out in hide."

Tigger held up his hands, backing away. "Hey, no sweat, man, didn't have nothin' to do with what you talkin' 'bout, but no problem, man, we square now, okay? Clean slate—"

Mal skewered him with a second glance and Tigger's mouth stopped working; he spun about on a pair of flashy new, three-hundred-dollar, pump basketball shoes and skittered away fast into the dusk. Able to hear the receding slap of rubber soles on pavement, Mal didn't waste time watching him go; he had other things to do.

He crossed the street, keeping distance, watching the man walk the woman to her rusty red Suburban, allowing himself an instant's luxury of watching the woman move. She strode cleanly, arms swinging, legs moving smoothly from the hip like an athlete's, a dancer's: loose, controlled, graceful, without a hint of any dishonest female-on-the-make come-hither sashay. He liked that.

Livvi had been full of sashay.

Again that stark sense of *want* made a foray into his gut, leaving him hungry without explanation.

Deliberately he switched his attention back to the man. Mal wasn't here to get hot; he was here, like the Mounties across the border, to get his man.

Or at least shadow him.

Well back, he waited while his quarry checked out the woman's truck, front to back, for possible waylayers before ushering her into it, then went to find his own vehicle, safely flooded by light in the unsafely darkening parking lot. The floodlight reconfirmed the man's identity, and Mal's mouth stretched wide again—not a smile exactly, but something far more primitive, predatory: a little older, a little tanner, a little thinner, a little blonder and sporting yellow-lensed aviator glasses, but still former deep-cover agent Angus "Gus" Abernathy in the flesh. Mal had asked the computer lab to run too many possible variations on the government's former star witness's appearance not to recognize him now.

He'd been chasing Abernathy for better than fifteen months to date, ever since Abernathy's safety and protection had been turned over to him just before the former G-man had, so to speak, gone over the wall, opting to look after himself rather than trust an imperfect system to cover his hiney any longer.

It was, of course, Abernathy's choice whether or not he stayed in the witness protection program. He'd committed no crime and was under no legal obligation to stay within the service's jurisdiction. But with the death of the third protected witness who'd testified before the grand jury against former Mafia honcho William Dunne, and with the discovery of an information conduit piped directly from the Marshal's Service to some of Dunne's former associates, Abernathy had become Mal's problem. And Mal Quarrels took his job—keeping the people he was assigned to protect alive—seriously, and no matter what kind of shadows Gus Abernathy had once lived in, they were still, in effect, brothers beneath the badge.

Departmental jurisdictions, gray areas, and interdepartmental disdain notwithstanding.

Finding Abernathy had begun as a matter of pride for Mal, who'd never lost a witness under his protection and didn't intend to begin with a former "fibbie" who'd never technically been under his supervision.

Finding Abernathy had also turned into a matter of necessity, like ferreting out the right valve in a plugged water line that would open a gusher straight back to the source of the original problem.

Damn, if he did say it himself, he was good.

It was no secret that he and his ego were on excellent terms.

Chuckling softly, Mal watched Abernathy move, assessing possible strengths and weaknesses. Abernathy's testimony before the grand jury that had indicted Dunne should have put Dunne away for life, but it hadn't. Instead, William Dunne had cut a deal with the U.S. Attorney's Office to deliver up his superiors and a good portion of the drug runners on the East Coast in exchange for a ridiculously reduced sentence and his own special version of government protection. Then the Mafia capo had done a bunk. Three attempted hits on Abernathy in twenty months of "witness protection and relocation" had been the result—obviously a leak sprung in the system. In self-defense, Abernathy, too, had disappeared.

It was relocating William Dunne and sealing the puncture in the protection pipes that were Marshal Quarrels's real purpose behind finding Abernathy. Cops protected their own.

Staying close to Abernathy could be a problem. Mal was the best tracker in the service—a phenom, a natural, they called him in the office, joking about the dominant Aztec-Cheyenne pieces of his heritage. But Abernathy had to have one hell of an effective friendly paranoia in order to have stayed alive and out of the way for so long. Mal would have to play this carefully, scout around, see what, if any, mistakes Abernathy made.

Angus was his key to the life-threatening trickle of information oozing out of a supposedly solid pipeline; you couldn't plug a security breach if you couldn't find it and Mal meant to find and plug both the source of the leak and its undoubted recipient: the only other missing witness protectee with an ax to grind against Angus Abernathy, one William Joseph Dunne.

Eyes never leaving Gus, Mal headed for the motorcycle chained to a tree at one end of the parking lot, pulled on his helmet, kicked the lock loose and got ready to roll. When Abernathy's Ford Taurus eased out of its slot and into the street, Mal was on him.

Jennifer's phone call would have to wait.

* * *

Seventeen miles west of Our Lady of Roses parking lot, in a still-rural White Lake Township subdivision, the dated red Suburban was just pulling into an oversize two-car garage, when Abernathy's navy Taurus turned onto the blacktop driveway and pulled in after it.

Well behind him, Mal watched Abernathy park the Taurus to one side of the garage and climb out. Sonofagun. Abernathy and the woman, together again. Curious. What little he'd seen of them together, he wouldn't have pegged them for one another's type. Too platonic, and from where Mal sat, whoever she was, this woman did not inspire platonic.

What the hell, huh? Wouldn't be the first time he'd misjudged a woman by her cover.

His jaw tightened, eyebrows lifted wryly under his helmet. Talking to himself again. Thought he'd gotten a handle on that. Solo surveillance inspired far too many silent conversations with absent people, induced him to place an excessive number of bets with himself—most of which he lost. Had to do something to keep himself alert and entertained.

Chastising himself for his latest wager, Mal geared down the Le Mans and drifted past the house, set deep on what he guesstimated to be a three-acre lot, and turned his bike around at the end of the dead-end road. Damn. Two streetlights and ten houses total—seven of 'em floodlit front and back—both sides of the road.

Land was being sold and developed at a breakneck pace throughout Oakland County, but Abernathy had managed to find one of the few spots where development was temporarily losing to environment, none of the houses were for sale or abandoned, neighbors knew each other by sight if not always by name and strangers were worthy of note. No place to simply sit and wait and watch without someone cuing the alarm, no woodwork to fade into—not that, according to Livvi, he'd ever faded into the wood-work very well, anyway. Still, he didn't want the local cops traipsing through here spooking Abernathy. Have to work out something else. Maybe there was a way in from the back. He'd take a look after they went inside.

He watched the woman climb out her truck, appreci-ated the way she bent back inside to retrieve something on the other side of the seat. Helluva berth Abernathy had picked out for himself—more ways than one.

Shut up, he told himself. Cop work first, then enjoy the scenery. Kick butt and take names.

Chaa, as Jennifer would say in her best laid-back Valley-surfer imitation, *like totally righteous idea, dude*.

Judas H. Priest, first talking to himself, now doing Jennifer imitations. Maybe his ex-partner, Tolski, was right, maybe he'd been without a partner so long that he'd finally lost his stinking mind.

Approaching forty—Jennifer had assured him dryly last week, diagnosing his restlessness from some com-ment he'd made about who-could-remember-what. She'd been fresh from a talk about "Male Mid-Life Crises" with Mal's sister, Sheila—whose husband, Bob, could cer-tainly double for the MMLC poster boy—while waiting for Mal to come to the phone. Kicking the tar out of the stall looking for his last hurrah just like Bob, Jennifer had said. Male menopause in the flesh.

Nuts, Mal thought, reaching for the pack of cigarettes he'd forgotten he'd given to Tigger. He was only thirty-eight, she was all of fifteen and he and her mother had been divorced for five years, so what the hell did she know?

Better question might be, what *didn't* she know?

After this assignment, he really had to get the time to go see her and find out. He took off his helmet, rubbed his eyes and wished for just one more cigarette.

Down the street, the woman's voice called "Good night," sending the same odd current her laughter had elicited earlier south along his spine. An instant later, the mechanism on the garage door whirred into action, descending. At the same time a light went on behind the wide vertical blinds in the wall-length picture window on the front of the house, Abernathy ducked out from under the closing garage door and mounted the steps on the side of the garage. A moment later, lights came on behind the horizontal miniblinds in a room over the garage.

Mal grinned. Score one for instinct. At least on the face of it, he'd been right about them, after all.

Cut the crap and get to work.

Pretending he'd lost something, Mal propped the Le Mans on its stand and hooked his helmet over the mirror, retrieved a penlight from the small compartment in the motorcycle's seat, aimed it at the ground and followed the road back toward the woman's house.

The May air was sharp and growing cool, tasted of spring barbecues and lawns cut after supper, with a spicy undercurrent of cedar and spruce, the sweet tang of lilacs, mulberry, apple and pear blossoms in the bushes and trees edging the yards. Up the canted lawn to his right, the rhythms of teenybop rap warred with the strains of the *Nick-at-Night* television theme; ahead and to his left, in a house set closer to the road, the clink of pots in a metal sink with water running into them melded with the chink of garage mechanics working on a car to the raucous strains of George Thorogood singing about drinking alone by himself. A few years back, for a mercifully brief period of his life, Mal had known exactly what Thorogood meant.

In between houses it was quiet except for the sound of crickets and tree frogs harmonizing in the darkness. A far cry from inner-city street noises, the song of people living too many and too close with hardly room to breathe between.

A tiny bat flapped silently out of the light and brushed past his head. Mal ducked, swearing softly, the hackles on his neck standing straight out against the involuntary chill that swept beneath the long, thick blanket of his hair.

One man's safety is another man's fright, someone had said to him once. He felt the uneasiness he always felt when he was someplace where trees outnumbered people and where crime, although present, took you by surprise, and knew that it was true. Give him either buildings and people or the empty dust of South Dakota over bat-harboring trees any day.

He stepped into the thick shadows provided by a black walnut tree opposite Abernathy's garage. A light went on upstairs in the house; the woman's silhouette passed in front of the curtained second-story window, moved away, then the light went off. Over the garage, the light at the front of Abernathy's apartment went out, exchanged for a softer light at the back.

Back downstairs in the house, a light went on front right and the woman appeared at the windows of what seemed to be her bedroom. She leaned her elbows on the window's high sill and put her chin in her hands, staring for a long minute into her floodlit front yard, and he felt that wary thing inside him stir again, less hormones this time, and far more personal: he wanted to know her name. Her expression was distant and wistful, tired. Mal watched her visibly shake off the wishes and pull herself erect as though however long her day had been, there were still things to do and it wasn't over yet. Then she pulled the blinds and unwittingly shut him out.

Sometimes peeping marshals saw more than they needed, or wanted, to see.

Growing up he'd witnessed that same unnamed longing a million times on his mother's face, then after they'd married and Jennifer was born, on Livvi's, most recently on his sister Sheila's. It was a woman's look, a mother's look: daylight gone, kids in bed, husband parked in his favorite chair, but she still had laundry to fold, a kitchen to clean up, cookies to wrap individually for the fifth grade's bake sale, thirty-two cupcakes to bake, frost and box for somebody's class birthday party and the bills to see to. Overtime with no time-and-a-half benefits to compensate for the lack of sleep.

For an instant, her connection to all the women he'd ever known well was bright and stinging, found a raw spot inside him and rubbed. He'd spent too many years observing and appreciating women not to be able to decipher the thoughts behind the look. Too many years disappointing the women he cared for most without being able to change what they needed and he lacked.

He was glad when the front yard floodlights suddenly went out at almost the same moment that Abernathy's apartment went dark, prompting him back to cases.

Taking advantage of the darkness, Mal quickly crossed the road, slipped into the blacker shadows of a line of spruce, hickory and maple edging the lot. The floods from the house next door—half an acre away—didn't quite reach the trees. Moving swiftly, he zigzagged his way up the lot line toward the back of the property. A chain-link fence he hadn't noticed from the road brought him up short for an instant; looking, he found the posts of a closed gate situated at the garage. The fence extended a hundred feet out from the garage, went back farther than he could see in the blackness, even with the help of the next-door floods. He edged along the fence until he was far enough away from the garage that Abernathy shouldn't hear the chain link rattle and vaulted into the yard.

He knew he'd made a mistake the instant the dogs began to bark.

He faded into the pickery cover of the impressive blue
spruce beside the fence just as the lights at the rear of the
house came up and three sets of floodlights were switched
on, illuminating the yard. The woman appeared behind
the glass doors onto the wooden deck that ran most of the
length of the back of the house. Mal barely had time to
swear out a prayer and heave himself back over the fence
before she slid open the doors and a massive flood of
hairy beasts poured out, growling and barking and headed
straight for him. Mother of God, she not only kept dogs,
she listened to them.

Even when they kept well-trained mutts strictly as guard
dogs, most people didn't listen; they knew the sounds of
their lives, didn't—usually couldn't—imagine the worst,
and simply told the dogs to shut up while they went back
to sleep. But not this woman.

Breathing hard, Mal lay in the weeds along the fence,
close enough to feel on his arms the hot puffs of air snuffled out by the dogs in their search for him. One of the
beasts snarled and jammed its nose beneath the fence,
catching Mal's T-shirt between its teeth, tearing. Eyes on
the woman who'd stepped outside and was peering at the
darkness beyond the floodlights, trying to discern what
the dogs thought was there, Mal rolled sideways, swearing to himself, trying to stay within the slim line of shadow
between the two yards and their lights. Damn. Soon as he
got finished here, he was going to find Tigger and kill the
little bastard for assuring him that trailing Gus would be
a cakewalk.

*"Do I know this guy? This who you lookin' for? Hey,
no problem, man, dude work at Our Lady, see him
sometimes down at Lighthouse, sometimes the rescue
mission. Think he got a place downtown Pontiac, easy
break-in."*

Easy break-in. Mal tried to breathe quietly with the dogs' humid breaths steaming white vapor into his face. *Nuts.*

"Grace?"

Mal looked up at the sound of a man's voice overhead. Barely visible through the light between them, Gus Abernathy stood in the darkness on the small balcony off his apartment.

"Everything all right?"

The woman—*Grace* fit her, somehow—lifted a shoulder, shrugged with her hands. "I don't know, John—"

John. Mal puffed out a shallow breath. Maybe losing his shirt and a portion of his self-esteem as a hunter to a smart lady with a pack of watchful pets wasn't going to be such a waste, after all. At least he knew more than he had before.

"—dogs heard something, but I don't see a thing. Probably a coon or that cat from down the street trying to get into the garbage again. I'll leave the dogs out a while to make sure."

"Keep one of 'em inside with you and the kids?"

Mal heard Grace laugh. "Keep the alarm armed?"

Gus-John chuckled in response. "Mmm. I want to know if anyone tries storming the castle from the front and you need help."

Grace pointed at the small wiener-shaped dog fiercely prepared to guard her feet. "Between Friar Tuck and my baseball bat I think we're set. If that fails—" She leaned down to pick up the tailless gray striped and speckled "cat" that suddenly stalked out the open door behind her and brushed against the backs of her legs. Its ears were sharp and tufted and it must have weighed forty pounds, easily twice the size of Friar Tuck. Good crud, Mal thought, staring. A damned bobcat—or as near a facsimile as he'd ever seen. What the hell was he getting into here? "—I'll just sic Fred on 'em."

Abernathy laughed again. "Good enough. There're days he's made me think twice about coming in."

"He has his moments." She patted her leg and the little dog, Friar Tuck, turned eagerly, showing Mal where the sun rose and set in his canine opinion. "David said something about making waffles for breakfast, if you're interested."

"He saw me come in with the strawberries?"

"You got it."

"I'll be down by seven-thirty."

"You're a good friend, John."

"He's a nice kid, Grace."

She nodded. "Usually." She slipped through the sliding doors. "Good night, John."

"G'night, Grace."

The glass doors slid shut.

For a long while, the man she called John, the one Mal knew had been born Angus Benjamin Abernathy, stood on his balcony watching the dogs, still rooting about along the fence to Mal's right. Unable to see Abernathy's face, Mal wondered what he was thinking, wondered about the innate paranoia that had kept the man alive for so long, concerned he'd triggered it, forcing Abernathy to pick up and run once again. Impossible to tell anything from where Mal lay except that Abernathy was either one lucky sonofagun, or a damn smart one. Not to mention that it would take a lot more than a little legwork and a lot of bad coffee to keep an eye on Abernathy now.

Overhead, Abernathy's door opened and closed, and except for the dogs, the bats, a distant owl, the crickets and the noise from Mal Quarrels's restless thoughts, the night was still.

At Mal's back, the neighbor's floodlights went out. Mal relaxed and lay silent while the dew settled and the dogs sniffed and occasionally howled in response to some far-

off, barely heard challenge. Helluva way to spend the
night.

The moon rose, a thin sliver of a smile against the clear
and present blackness of the sky.

At the midnight point, when the moon was nearly
halfway through its journey to find the sun, Grace slid
open the door and called her dogs inside. They thundered away across the grass, a herd of short buffalo re-
sponding to the migration instinct. The floodlights went
out, one by one, followed closely by the house lights, and
the night was complete.

For a while Mal continued to wait. The dew soaked
through his jeans and shirt, the dropping temperature
chilled his toes through the heavy leather of his boots, but
he knew the importance of stillness to the hunt, the ability to bide without moving—for days if need be—until he
was no more than part of the scenery.

He wondered if anyone had called the police to inves-
tigate the motorcycle he'd abandoned, but no roll bars
swung red arcs along the road, so he figured Abernathy
wasn't the only lucky guy out there tonight.

At last he rolled quietly away from the fence, found his
feet and did a quick tour of the perimeter of Abernathy's
landlady's yard. A run-down barnlike outbuilding with
glass windows and window boxes sat at one edge of the
acreage; looked like someone had tried to convert it to
living quarters at one time but never finished the project.
Woods bound the north property line outside a rusty sag-
ging fence stapled to rotted wood posts. The trees ran
north for fifty yards before opening out onto the unmowed pasture of a small horse farm. The east-west
boundaries opened up on neighboring lots. Not an easy
place to keep track of. Still, he was going to have to try.
Couldn't have a civilian wind up in the middle when
Dunne found where Abernathy was hiding. Especially not
a civilian with a kid. And if the size of the house and her

conversation with Abernathy was any indication, that probably translated to kids, plural. Which meant twenty-four-hour-a-day protection at the very least.

Duty got more complicated all the time.

Thoughtfully, Mal slouched back to the Le Mans through the shadows outside the floodlights of a yard two doors down from Abernathy's. Tigger had sworn Abernathy had digs in the city; Mal had followed him here. Tigger had also taken Mal sight-seeing at both the Lighthouse offices near downtown Pontiac and the Pontiac Rescue Mission a couple of miles away, before determining that Abernathy must be at Our Lady of Roses Parish Center. Interesting, particularly if Tigger was right and Abernathy frequented the other charities as well as Our Lady's, and had a place to crash in the city. Allow Abernathy to move around, vary his activities, keep his traffic random and hard to pin down, make it easier for him to spot a tail.

Eyes on the house down the street, Mal unstrapped a heavy denim jacket from the seat, slid into it and straddled the Moto Guzzi. *If* was a pretty small word on which to formulate a plan, but Mal had little else at the moment. And if Abernathy were as smart as he appeared, *if* seemed as good a place as any to put a little trust.

He kicked the motorcycle to life, revved the engine a bit and roared up the road. Tonight he'd go back to his sister's and get a little sleep, get up early, come back before Abernathy left and follow him to work. Then if things went the way he thought they might over the next couple days, he'd go see his childhood confessor, Father Rick, at Our Lady of Roses Catholic Church and lie through his teeth to get a job. After that he'd see what he could do about renting the lady's falling-down outbuilding.

Mal's teeth gleamed in the darkness.

Twenty-four-hour protection, darlin', at your service.

Chapter 2

Our Lady of Roses parking lot was dark except for the shadows provided by the floodlights, four of which had been doused one way or another since last night. Rocks, maybe, with slingshots, but most likely guns.

Grace Brannigan Witoczynski pressed her back against the chill orange brick of the porch wall and bent to the lock on the Parish Center and Food Depot, shivering inside the late-spring warmth, eyes slowly marking either side of the path she would have to travel between the center and her car, seventy-five yards away and parked beneath one of the dead lights. Damn. Couldn't keep track of everything no matter how hard you tried.

She hated being here by herself at night, hated the instinctive fear even more—enough to challenge it. Didn't have to challenge herself to walk out to the parking lot alone often, but about once a month she shut down the center by herself. Usually John drove over from wherever he'd worked that day and walked her out to her car—or picked her up at the curb and drove her out to it—but he was working late himself tonight and she was on her own.

Resolutely, Grace stiffened her mouth and dealt with her fear. She'd been told often enough that her fair Scandinavian-Irish skin had no business in this part of the world—the city—alone after dark. She didn't know whether it was idealism, courage, stupidity or the stubborn desire to show her faith in Pontiac's efforts to reclaim the city that made her ignore the naysayers and keep the center open until its usual lock-up time when everyone else left early—whether she was required to or not. Neighborhood Watch patrols were up, crack house locations and drive-by shootings were down—at least within the radius of the parish environs—and parents made a concerted effort to know where their children were. Still, crime was leeching out of Detroit, climbing hard and fast in the suburbs, and *Afterdark* was its own world, with its own rules, invisible and frightening.

She sucked up a breath of pungent city air, dropped the center's keys into her belly pack and plucked out her car keys, wove them tightly between her fingers, tips out—her own version of spiked knuckles. Simple but effective, they'd told her in her self-defense class. She wasn't sure.

Another breath. She straightened and let the storm door slam behind her. Eyes roving the shadows, she took the first step toward the sidewalk, the second, then she was down, moving quickly, arms swinging, legs striding fast when she cut across the parish's newly landscaped patch of lawn, stepped over a concrete parking tie and met the parking lot: the confident, aggressive New York strut worked equally well thirty miles northwest of Detroit.

At least so far.

Knock on wood, knock on wood, knock on . . .

Ten feet from her truck, still striding, she fixed her eyes on the dull gleam from the Suburban's windshield and unwound the keys from her knuckles, got ready to slide the round key into the driver's door lock. Wishing herself behind the wheel, doors locked, engine turned over, transmission in drive, cellular phone at the ready.

Pebbles skidded over the rough blacktop to one side of her and she started, jerking to look. The light from the three remaining floodlights at the back of the lot revealed nothing; she distributed her weight equally on the balls of her feet, tried to breathe herself calm the way she'd been taught and jammed her key at the lock.

The scrape came again, closer this time; yelling, Grace swung away from the truck, not wanting to be taken from behind, raking high with the key. She heard the grunt and curse of a male voice before someone grabbed at her wrist, attempted to body-block her against the truck. Eyes gleamed in the dark, somehow shiny and dead at the same time, here on a mission. Grace yanked her arm back and dropped the keys, opened her hand and jabbed the heel upward hard, just beneath the gleam of his eyes, jamming his nose up toward his forehead. Cartilage crunched and cracked, the sound at once repellent and satisfying. He swore and grabbed his beak, giving her room and time to bring up her knee. When he doubled over, she yelled again and kicked him hard, once, in the face: *don't mess with me.* He sat down, keeled slowly sideways, groaning in the shadowy light. Something metallic fell out of his hand.

Shaking, Grace looked down at him.

In class she'd been told to stomp and kick her attacker again, make sure he couldn't follow—finish him—then get the hell away. But, God, he looked so young, skinny, malnourished, she didn't want to; she'd already committed more violence than she'd known she was capable of. She wanted to pick up her keys and get somewhere she could wash it off, soak it away, start to believe it was only a dream.

Nervous, she dragged her foot slowly over the ground beside the truck, feeling for her keys without taking her eyes off her attacker. Couldn't find 'em. She glanced earthward, not quite panicked; they should be right *there.* They weren't. Only the dull sheen of a mud puddle off to her right. No keys.

Anxiety rose. She took her eyes off the man groaning on the ground and stooped, scrabbling around the beat-up blacktop underneath the Suburban, sliding her hand forward and back, along behind each tire, searching.

Nothing, *nothing.*

Panic climbed the walls of her belly, inching toward her throat, along her limbs; she fought herself to control it. She'd dropped the keys straight down, she hadn't kicked them; they *had* to be here.

Down on the other side of the mud puddle, her attacker suddenly heaved himself up, grabbed the shiny thing on the pavement next to his hand and threw himself her way.

Off balance and weaponless, Grace screamed—a real scream this time, high and piercing and frightened, not just a yell—and dropped, tried to roll away, wound up soaking up mud puddle with her clothes while her keys, buried in the middle of it, bit into her hand; the knife blade swept down where she'd been, hit the parking lot near her left hip and snapped. Then he was over her.

"No!" The word was in her mind and shrieking from her throat, the only thought she had.

She grabbed her keys and swiped up, kicked high, hammering the air and him, anything she could connect with. Whatever the outcome, she would not give it up: she would claw and bite, kick and scream and damage, but she would *not* go passively into any good night, however poetically correct it might prove.

She heard him grunt with exertion, felt his hand grab for her throat, then suddenly he was gone. Something banged against the Suburban, thudded hollowly into a door, bumped hard against glass, slumped like a sack of meal to the pavement. There was the sound of metal slapping flesh and clicking—the way handcuffs sounded closing on TV—before the bright beam from a heavy flashlight caught her in the face, blinding. A hard, rough hand engulfed hers and tugged; a low male voice spoke to her, but whatever he said was lost in fog.

Oh, God, another one.

Exhausted and terrified, tight, barely articulate but thoroughly definite no's issuing from her throat, Grace dug her heels in at the ridge of the puddle and tried to shove herself away. The hand wrapped around hers didn't budge, but the flashlight shifted a bit to the right of her eyes; she felt someone big squat next to her. His shin was a solid mass along the back of her hip.

"Are you all right?"

She looked at him uncomprehending; he was behind the light, she couldn't see much. He sighed and dropped the light farther. Grace gathered every last bit of strength she could find into her fist with her keys and punched him hard where she figured the side of his head, the vulnerability of an unprotected ear, should be.

"Damn!"

Mal looked at her, surprised, hand automatically going up to rub his ear. Unbelievable. But he didn't let go of her hand.

She hit him again, lower this time, in the side of his neck beneath his ear where the self-defense instructor said it was "soft"; there was almost as much give to it as there'd been to the side of his head. Didn't stop her; she continued to punch at him one-handed, connecting with his cheek, his nose, his shoulder, his jaw, until he dropped the flashlight and caught at her wrist; then she bit him. Or tried to, anyway.

"Whoa, hey!"

He straddled her legs so she couldn't kick him, tried to pin her arms so she couldn't hurt either one of them. She butted at his nose with her head, a direct hit.

"Ow! Damn."

Mal backed up, caught both her wrists in one hand and shoved them over her head, touched his nose; his fingers came away bloody. He stared at his fingers, at her, disbelieving and respectful. She tried to bring her knee out from under him, attempting to mash his groin. He sat back on her legs. Hard.

"Judas Priest, woman, knock it off. The bad guy's down. I'm the shining knight. This the way you always greet him when he comes to your rescue?"

Grace caught her breath, locked down on her terror. "The knight in shining does *not* sit on the distressed damsel, preventing her from kneeing him in the crotch and making a clean getaway, which makes you just another *jerk* who I don't know attacking me in the dark."

Mal unknotted the bandanna tied like a sweatband around his head and pressed it to his nose, glanced at the unconscious sack of flesh and bones reposing beside her truck.

"Hardly clean," he assured her, but released her hands, picked up the flashlight and eased himself carefully out of range of her feet. "You got a nice technique, darlin', but no follow-through. Always finish what you start. Give the bad guys time to recover and you just make 'em mad. Kinda like a wounded elephant. Brings mayhem to mind."

"I'll remember that as long as you remember that *darlin'* is my eight-year-old daughter, not me. I'm Mrs. Witoczynski." Keys at the ready, Grace slid away from him and got to her feet, declining the hand he offered her by ignoring it.

Chuckling, Mal withdrew the offer. "Mrs. Witoczynski, gotcha. Father Rick said you were something. Now I know what he meant."

"Father *Rick?*" Grace snorted. Oh, yeah, Father Enrico Guillean thought she was something, all right, something that ought to be done away with. *Father Rick.* Right. No one called the short, conservative, iron-haired, seventy-year-old priest anything so informal—at least to his face. He wouldn't stand for it, thought it was disrespectful. Thought women in any aspect of church ministry outside of dusting the vestry or teaching religious education classes was disrespectful, too, and thought nuns ought to be flogged for letting their hair show. Our Lady of Roses' congregation loved him.

Grace looked at what she could see of the man who referred to the irascible Father Guillean as though he knew something about her employer of eight years that she didn't, saw only a huge hulking shape with teeth that gleamed even in the darkness. The thought rose nonsensically to mind, *The better to eat you with, my dear....* She flicked it away.

"Do I know you?" she asked.

"Not formally." He turned the flashlight toward his face, tucked the bandanna in a hip pocket, and a hand big enough to palm a basketball came out of the night toward her. "Mal Quarrels. I started at the center last week."

She didn't ignore his hand this time exactly, it was more like she skitted away from it, wary. "The laid-off cop? Deliveries and odd jobs, maintenance? From Wyoming, right?"

Mal withdrew his hand again, nodded. The would-be mugger near his feet moaned; Mal nudged him with a toe. Couldn't blame her for being skittish. "South Dakota. I grew up around here and knew Father Rick before he turned into Father Guillean."

The image of a wide, high-boned, sharp-jawed face and long, sleek black hair seen through the windshield of the parish's blue 1964 Chevy pickup faded before it quite formed. "Ah."

"I delivered the beds and refrigerator to Mrs. Ortiz day before yesterday."

She peered up at him, trying to pick out his features, but all the flashlight he'd aimed at his face did was make him appear big and ghoulish. "Okay."

"You don't remember."

Grace's attacker rolled sideways and tried to sit up; the lump on his head and the handcuffs imprisoning his wrists behind his back impeded his progress and he cursed. Mal snapped the side of the man's head with a hard finger, both a silent reprimand for the curse and a reminder of who was in charge, and the mugger subsided.

Grace swallowed. There was an element about her rescuer that made him seem more of a threat to her well-being than the kid who'd assaulted her. "In this light?" She rubbed her arms, looked him up and down. At an easy six-four, two hundred ten pounds, give or take an ounce, he would hardly be unnoticeable, even in this culturally diverse section of town. "Who could tell?"

Cool, grimy water puddled in the cuffs of her best white skort, ran in muddy rivers down the backs of her legs and pooled in her moccasins. The June night was warm, but reaction sent chill settling bone-deep. If she didn't sit down soon, her legs would shake right out from under her. Her teeth chattered. "I'm sorry. Maybe the shock...or sometimes when I'm working, if I don't look up..."

Before her eyes, the darkness became a tunnel, closing in. She shook her head trying to clear her vision. "I probably *should* remember you—" Something was wrong. All of a sudden she couldn't stop shaking. Her head was too light and on fire at the same time, and it felt as though somebody had exchanged her real knees for a set made of rubber. She put out a hand toward the Suburban to steady herself. "You don't seem like a fade-into-the-woodwork kind of guy, but there we are."

Mal took a step forward. "Are you all right?"

"No," Grace said and sagged.

Mal caught her. "Grace?"

"Don't worry," she assured him—or maybe it was herself. "It's all right, it's not the end of the world, just the reality part."

"Grace."

"You know my name."

"It's on your desk. Come on, darlin', stay with me."

"Don't call me darlin'," Grace snapped groggily. "I'm not. And I'm not fainting." She flapped a hand at his arm, trying to push herself erect. *"Not."*

"Say the alphabet." Mal slipped an arm beneath her shoulder and pried her keys from her hand. "Concentrate."

"Able, Bravo, Charlie, Delta, Edward, Frances, Oscar—"

Mal fitted the keys to her lock, pulled open the driver's door of the Suburban. "Pardon?"

"—the Grouch—"

"What?"

Grace tried to push back onto her feet when Mal tried to sit her on the Suburban's running board and push her head between her knees. "From "Sesame Street," aren't you paying attention? You know. You told me to say the alphabet. It's harder when you spell it."

"What?" He held her down on the running board by leaning on her shoulders. "Sit. If you get up right now, you'll fall down."

"Can't sit." Grace shoved at his hands. "Have to call the police, make a report, press charges so he can't do this to anyone else for as long as it takes for a judge to set bail

and him to make it, go home 'n' see my kids and he—"
She swung a flaccid fist in the direction of her attacker
and the man ducked. "He might need a doctor. I think I
hurt him. And anyway—" she brought her fist back to her
lap in a wobbly arc that made Mal jump back "—I
thought you were a cop. You spell license plates, don't
you?"

"Did you hit your head?"

"Just yours." Grace chortled. "And his. Made you
both take notice."

Unable to help himself, Mal laughed. "That's true."

"Is it all right? Did I break it?"

"No, I think it's only sprained."

"Your head?"

"My nose."

"Oh, good." Her laughter was giggly and shrill. With
a sudden twist, she propelled herself out from under Mal's
hands and lurched to her feet. "You won't need crutches
then. Ohf—" She reeled drunkenly against the truck's
door. "Have to get going now, my kids—" She slumped,
grabbing for the door handle. "Oh, damn," she whispered and pitched face first into Mal's arms.

Concerned, amused, perplexed, Mal looked down at
the unconscious face with the slightly crooked nose
mashed into his chest. He'd learned a lot about Grace
Brannigan Witoczynski in the eighteen days since he'd
begun shadowing Gus Abernathy's movements and discovered that the only thing he could count on was that
Abernathy always made his way back to his apartment at
her house eventually, and that if Abernathy made a
promise to her he kept it. But no credit history, school
yearbooks, employment vitae, medical, dental, marital or
family records covered this.

He glanced at the perp she'd laid out, then refused to
finish off.

Something, Father Rick had called her, bemused, as though no other word in the priest's vocabulary came close to describing her.

So nice, the pastoral minister had enthused. *She takes in and finds homes for all the strays that come around here,* he'd said, leaving Mal with the impression of a woman as a faded, well-used doormat who didn't have sense enough to say no when *NO!* was required.

Stubborn bitch, was the center's maintenance chief's resentfully respectful, grudgingly fond assessment; she told him exactly what she wanted and how she wanted it done at the center, said no to him regularly and without argument whenever he tried to reassure her that there was a shortcut he could take that would require a great deal less work on his part, and okay, so maybe whatever it was *would* need repair again sooner, but...

And Angus Abernathy, aka John Roth, Our Lady of Roses' current free-lance, volunteer bookkeeper, simply called her *terrific.*

Looking at her now, Mal himself was inclined to think they were all absolutely right and positively wrong, that the real person behind Grace Witoczynski's various reputations was someone who would astound them all. He'd seen her places some of them never had: in her weekend capacity as arborealist consultant in residence for Bordine's Better Blooms, a local nursery; as coach to Our Lady's third- and fourth-grade girls' softball team—twelve highly individualistic preadolescents whose attention span and attitudes would have proved the undoing of anyone; and as the woman who stood looking wistfully at the moon from her bedroom window most nights before she went alone to bed. And he was just supposed to see and do his job and not care which was either.

But after studying her—perhaps a little more closely than he really needed to in order to keep track of Abernathy—for eighteen puzzling days, he did care.

A lot more than was healthy.

Sighing, he hoisted Grace up his chest until he could turn her and get one arm under her shoulders and the other beneath her knees, and picked her up. He'd been trying to figure a way to get closer to Abernathy, but now that opportunity had, so to speak, bitten him in the butt, as Sheila would say, he found himself reluctant to use it—her. But he also didn't see where he had a lot of choice. Not if he was going to find Dunne.

"Don't move," he said with such menace that the man on the ground simply nodded, frightened, and scooted up tight against the Suburban's rear tire. Then Mal carried Grace around and tucked her into her truck's passenger seat, belted her in and closed the door. Her head lolled sideways at an awkward angle. Blowing out his cheeks on a damn-it-all breath, Mal rooted through the back of her truck until he found a pillow and a soft blanket, returned to prop her up more carefully. Her skin was cold and clammy against the backs of his hands—faint producing the proverbial cold sweat—her eyelids white and blue-veined, translucent in the Suburban's overhead light.

How odd to find her beautiful.

And how unfortunate.

He turned his hand over, touched one pale cheek with his fingertips the way he'd wanted to since he'd watched her at her window the first time.

"I'm sorry," he said quietly.

He went back around the truck and released Grace Witoczynksi's attacker with the threat of great bodily damage if he or any other crim in the area ever came near her again. Then he pulled the day's last cigarette—only number ten, keeping his promise to Jennifer, no matter how much it killed him—out of his pocket, lit it and took his time smoking it before he climbed into the Suburban, fitted her keys into the transmission and drove the woman he was about to use, to further his investigations, home.

* * *

"*. . . listening to W-4 Country, 106.7 FM. The weather in a word—variety. Low temperature tonight forty-six degrees; high tomorrow ninety! Rain mixed with sunshine—a real Michigan day. Michelle Wright up next . . .*"

Grace roused to the sound of someone singing country under his breath and the rush of wind across her ears, the dotting of a light, near-summer mist on her face; taillights winked red beyond the windshield in front of her.

She blinked and rolled her head sideways, trying to put sense to circumstance. When she did, her heart jerked, charged with panic, and she snapped alert, stamped on phantom brakes before she realized that she hadn't fallen asleep behind the wheel of a moving vehicle.

"Whoa. Whoa, it's all right."

She blinked, swallowing panic. *"Whoa, hey! I'm the shining knight . . ."* It was okay, she knew the voice. Its name was Mal.

"Where are you taking me?" she asked. A little alarm at having been unconscious and at this man's mercy, but not too much; the evening's events were fuzzy in her mind but they existed.

"Home. Yours. You couldn't drive."

"But how—"

"Your registration's in the glove compartment, found a county map in the door."

"Oh." She looked at her lap, breathed deep cleansing breaths through her nose, trying to relax. "I'm sorry. I don't faint—I never faint, well, except for once right after my first son was born. The nurses got me up to go to the bathroom and I guess—" She moistened her mouth. That wasn't a story she wanted to share with a stranger. Particularly a man. "I hate fainting, but nothing like . . . like that's ever happened—nobody's ever—I've never . . . hurt anybody like that—" She swallowed. "What happened to—"

"I let him go." She looked at him. Mal shrugged. "You weren't in any shape to file a report and I recognized him. He's been into the food kitchen a couple of times since I started at the parish—gotta be from the neighborhood. Shouldn't be hard to locate if you want to file with the police in the morning."

She shook her head, not a no, merely a momentary uncertainty induced by grogginess. Later she would think about it, come to herself, get angry and decide to press charges, do her best to make sure that scuzz-bucket could never pull his stinking routine on her daughters—or her sons—or anybody else's daughters or sons or mothers or anyone. But right now...

Awash in leftover muzziness, she simply looked at his hand on her arm. His fingers were wide and flat, harsh from a lifetime of not asking someone else to push the broom, wield the shovel or handle the nightstick for him. Bemused, she peered down at them through the doodle-like patterns created by car lights, street lamps and night shadows, and tried to place their familiarity to her skin, the faint buzz that went with it. She glanced at the man they were attached to, the man she didn't quite remember: the loose, sleek black hair tucked behind his ears, hanging over his shoulders almost to his chest; the high, flat cheekbones, prominent jawline and hawklike features of his face; the dark T-shirt fitted nicely across a well-defined chest; the soft, faded jeans defining the bunched muscles of his right thigh.

Memory glittered, unkempt and awkward, just beneath the surface of her mind.

"How you doin'?" Mal asked, concerned. "You going to stay with me?"

"Mmmhmm." Grace met his eyes, suddenly not trusting herself to speak. A guilty chuckle fluttered in the back of her throat. Oh, yeah. Mal Quarrels, the Men at Work Fantasy. Now she remembered.

Her sister, Twink—thirty-eight, happily married, two kids—dropping a load of household appliances at the center the day before yesterday, had also dropped an oh-my-gawd-he's-gorgeous-introduce-me jaw to the floor when the center's newest employee, wearing well-fitting jeans and a tight white T-shirt under a faded denim jacket, had passed Grace's office door, a hefty case of canned peas on either shoulder. She and Twink had gone to lunch, where Twink had been playfully full of indecent suggestions about Mal's bad-boy-in-black look—the motorcycle-riding man in black leather with the dread secret past only one woman could tame—and the fact that after three years of widowhood with four headed-for-adolescence kids, Grace could use a little adult male companionship to remind her of what she was fighting for. And also, bearing in mind tool belts, plentiful closets and the Men at Work Fantasy—particularly this man at Grace's work—perhaps Grace should pick up some condoms and keep one in her pocket....

Embarrassed, laughing and outraged at once, Grace had crammed a wad of cheese-covered French bread at her older sister's open mouth and left Twink to pick up the check, returned to work and shut her office door so she wouldn't embarrass either Mal Quarrels or herself if he walked by again. Then she'd spent the rest of the afternoon trying her darnedest not to envision Mal every way Twink had suggested—and a few ways Twink hadn't. After all, my God, she was a leader of people, an influencer of children, she worked for a Catholic parish with priests and nuns and people who believed in innuendo and leave it at that, rather than in blatant suggestions that fertilized the imagination.

No wonder she hadn't remembered Mal in the parking lot. Between Twink and the circumstances, she'd probably forgotten him on purpose.

Mal rubbed a thumb over the back of her hand. "Sure you're all right?"

"Mmm." Grace bit her lip, leaned her head back and tried not to laugh out loud. Lord, if it took her last breath to do it, one of these days she was going to get Twink good. "I think I remember you now."

"Must be good, the way you're choking on it," Mal observed dryly. "But I don't think I've done anything that memorable since I've been back in Pontiac. Except for rescuing you tonight, of course."

Grace inclined her head, lips twitching. "Of course."

The Suburban dipped and bounced over the ruts of Cooley Lake Road; spring rain had turned driving into an adventure throughout the unpaved portion of the county. Some of the paved, too. Mal peered through the windshield at the unlighted trail, found the turn that would take them to Grace's driveway and took it.

"You going to tell me what suddenly jogged your memory?"

"It's personal."

"Ah."

"What does that mean?"

"Nothing. Just *ah*. It's a generic term implying understanding of an unexplained situation whether the understanding actually exists or not."

Grace cast him a cockeyed look. The vertigo she'd experienced earlier was gone, distracted by his nonsense. It had been a long time since she'd carried on this kind of conversation with...anyone...who wasn't related to her. And with four kids, six sisters, a concurrent number of brothers-in-law, plus nieces, nephews and assorted relatives best left unmentioned, she had a mess of relations. But this was different.

She felt the same faint tick in her pulse that she'd experienced during her, er, luncheon conversation with Twink two days ago, the same embarrassed but distinctive shimmy of anticipation up her spine. Yes, Mal Quarrels was infinitely different from her multifarious relations who raised her blood pressure instead of her pulse. "Which planet did you say you were from?"

Mal grinned.

"All right." Grace sighed. "You win. I suppose I owe you...something—which covers a lot of territory, so don't even *think* of taking advantage."

"Never," Mal returned promptly. Angelically.

Devilishly.

Grace rolled her eyes. "Yeah, right, anyway... My sister—"

"Brunette?" Mal interrupted. "Attractive, mid-thirties, five-seven, a hundred twenty pounds, green eyes, gap between her front teeth, looks like you?"

Grace looked at him.

He shrugged. "Sorry. Used to be a cop. Habit."

"You want to hear this?"

His teeth gleamed in the darkness. "Shoot."

Grace rolled her eyes and deliberately ignored his sad attempt at cop humor. "My sister was in my office the day before yesterday when you were unloading that minivan load of canned goods for the depot and she—"

"Took one look at my rugged muscular physique and turned me into a side of beef, which embarrassed you too much to let you remember me."

"Pardon me?"

Mal snorted. "I've seen reruns of "Designing Women" and "The Golden Girls," I have a mother and a sister. I know how normally sane women can turn any reasonably healthy man into a side order of steak tartare and dissect his *attributes* until they rot right out from under him and Robert Bly be damned."

Grace stared at him, flabbergasted. "You have to be the most arrogant, full-of-it human being I have ever met."

He grinned, unrepentant. "Called it in one, didn't I?"

Diligently not acknowledging his claim to the title, Grace rolled down her window and stuck her head out. "There's my driveway. It rained this morning. Watch out for the—"

The truck's front passenger side wheel went down hard in a particularly deep gully cut across the edge of the driveway and Mal swore.

"—hole," she finished.

She folded her hands primly in her lap while her body strained slightly against her shoulder harness from the cockeyed angle of the truck.

"Thanks," she said mildly. "I was looking for something to fill this ditch."

Chapter 3

With a single rolled-eye snort in Grace's direction, Mal reached down between the seats, pulled the four-wheel-drive lever and backed the Suburban out of the rain gully.

"Show-off," Grace muttered, disgusted.

Mal grinned. Nothing like a little one-on-one upmanship to keep a man mentally fit in the boy-girl wars.

He glanced sideways at Grace's decidedly provocative adult-woman, un"girlish" profile. Without warning, heat flushed his belly. The curiously primitive pulse thudding subtly, seductively through him since the first time he'd laid eyes on her burst its traces and sent the blood-rush-tattoo pounding through his veins.

He sat back waiting for the beat to dull, glad of the shadows, one-upped by his own body. No, Grace Brannigan Witoczynski did not particularly resemble a "girl." No, of course not. That would have made this whole undercover *far* too easy, and what was a hero without a challenge, particularly one provided by his own perfidious libido?

No matter how often he dressed the entity down, like the fourteen-year-old boy it remained, on most occasions it refused to listen, attacking him when it was least convenient and most likely to cause grief, leading him around by the proverbial, er, nose-only-lower—his mother's oft-stated assertion that an adult was merely a child wearing layers of experience proven once again.

Sometimes, as his sister so exasperatedly put it when referring to her perpetually pheromone-stoned fifteen-year-old son, being "vitally alive" was a pain in the butt.

Beside him, Grace lifted an arm near his face to touch the button on the garage remote clipped to the sun visor. The musky scent of leftover fear teased the edges of his nostrils and mixed potently with the heat of some subliminal subtext to which his hopped-up hormones responded in spades, pretzeling the adult in him to agonizing contortions of conscience. His body tightened, taut as it could get without exploding from frustration or hypertension; blood flushed eagerly inward to pool in combustible quantities where he needed it least at the moment.

The reaction was as ridiculous as it was extreme and unexpected: not even Livvi had ever wrung this response from him, and he'd been a teenager with Livvi, passionate, reckless and hard as a bone every time he'd thought of his ex-wife's extraordinarily well-endowed sweet-teen figure. But that experience was tepid and adolescent compared to this.

The door to the oversize two-car garage opened, the interior light flashed on and Grace dropped her arm; the backs of her fingers accidentally grazed Mal's hand as they slid past. Recognition heated the corpuscles beneath his skin, contracting them, urging response. His hand lifted away from the gearshift, drifted toward Grace all on its own. He clamped his fingers hard into a fist, pulling away, and replaced his palm over the H pattern imprinted on the ball of the lever. Lord God almighty, what had he done to deserve this?

Nothing, that was what, nothing at all.

At least not lately.

Except stay on the job Livvi had urged him to take, then screamed at him to quit until their marriage died. Except spend the last eighteen days getting to know Mrs. Witoczynski as well as distance, eyesight, and complete personal and medical records allowed. And, well, rescuing Grace and meeting her in person didn't help.

Oh, good. At last a scapegoat.

He grinned slightly and rubbed a thumb and forefinger along his nose: very few men in the universe Mal frequented had ever bothered to try to bust him up—it simply didn't pay—and no women that he could think of. He was too big, too easy on his feet, too—so they said—dangerous. But this woman, for the first time in his life since Sheila had last cold-cocked him for successfully warning off one of her boyfriends when he was fourteen and she was sixteen, had made a dent.

"Does it hurt?"

He looked at her, turned anxiously, apologetically toward him and stifled both a groan and a laugh. "Not as much as my pride would if I admitted it."

"Oh." Grace nodded thoughtfully. "Macho Nose Disorder. I understand. My twelve-year-old suffers from the same problem. We're working on it, but it's a tough one."

If laughter and need could strangle a man by getting stopped up in his throat at the same time, he was slowly dying. "How's that?"

"We have to ignore him and he hates that."

Mal nodded. "One of my best things is getting people to look at me."

Grace cocked her head and peered him up and down as she might over a pair of granny half-glasses. "I can see that," she agreed. "But does it have to do with your ego or your size? Or can we, perhaps, equate the two?"

"Pardon?"

"Nothing." Grace shrugged her mouth and shook her head. "Never mind. Just something I've always wanted to ask guys built like you, but it's probably too personal and likely to disillusion me if I get the wrong answer, so maybe it's better if I just let you sit there and look pretty and never mind."

The strangling pressure in Mal's lungs increased: laughter bent on doing him in. "Whatever."

"You can put it in the garage," Grace said.

"My ego?"

Grace cast him a reproving glance. "That too if it'll fit, but I meant the truck."

"Of course."

He swung the Suburban back into the driveway, wide of the ditch this time, and ran it forward, parked it under the light next to Gus Abernathy's Taurus. A familiar electric, Judas *zing!* booked passage through his veins, *I'm in!*, before he eased through the gears and switched off the Suburban's engine.

Beside him Grace released her seat belt and turned to him. "Thank you."

Mal waved an embarrassed hand and studied the steering wheel, guilt increasing. "No problem."

Damn, he needed a cigarette. Something to do with his hands.

"No, really." She touched his arm, made him look at her. He didn't meet her eyes. "Driving me home all the way out here is above and beyond, even for a knight-in-shining, and I appreciate—if there's anything—" She half smiled, catching the offer nearly made. "If there's anything within reason . . ."

It was the opening he'd been guiltily waiting for— shamefully reckoning on, truth be told, because that was the sort of person she was, and a goodly portion of his job was accurately sizing people up: the gratitude spot where he told her his story and she offered to help him and he hemmed and hawed, then accepted so—unbeknownst to her, of course—he could protect her. But now that they'd finally arrived at this point, the reason he was here eluded him. Seeing her in the pale, unreal light connected to the garage-door opener was a shock: it took a moment for the color of her blouse—a drying blood-soaked peach—to register. His lungs stilled, stomach cramped, fear set in. He reached for her, then didn't know where to touch, what to check first.

"Good God, woman, are you all right? I didn't think, I didn't even look. When you fainted—"

"What are you talking about?"

"You, your blouse, the blood..."

She looked down at herself then made a little *tcht-ing* sound against her teeth and rolled her eyes high. "I'm fine. You and that other creep bled all over me." She clicked open the door and stepped out of the truck. "I've got some bruises, but no scratches."

"You sure?" Mal clacked open his own door and climbed out after her. "Maybe you should have a doctor look at you." Not his usual métier, indecision felt odd coming out of his mouth, etching anxiety beneath his skin. "Maybe I should have taken you over to Osteopathic to get you checked out before I brought you home."

"No, just to the police station down the street from the parish so I could have filed a report."

"You'd have been a big hit at the police station, fainted and spelling the alphabet."

Grace stopped midway in her trek around the front of the Suburban and stared at him. "I *spelled* the alphabet?"

"Yeah. *G* is for Oscar."

Grace sniffed and resumed her trek. "If you think *G* is for Oscar, you didn't learn your alphabet very well."

"*I* didn't say *G* stands for Oscar, you—"

"And I still want to make a report, get that guy off the streets so he can't hurt anyone else—"

"Call and get 'em to send a patrol car out here. You make the complaint, I'll supply the description, but right now, go in the house, please, make sure you're not hurt someplace you don't know about ye—"

A half second before the garage-door-opener light went out, the inside garage door opened and Gus Abernathy followed by a gaggle of children and barking dogs burst through the breezeway and swarmed out of the house.

For a moment, confusion reigned. Growling and snapping, the dogs found Mal and treed him atop the hood of the Suburban.

"Hey," Mal yelped, scrabbling into the center of the hood, dogs leaping high. "I'm friendly."

If they heard, they didn't pay attention.

Grace commanded, "Enough!" and "Off!" and "Shame!," but was drowned out by a chorus of excited young voices each shouting something different.

"Mom, where are you?" Undeveloped, high-pitched, feminine. "Are you out here? Are you all right? Get out of my way, dogs!"

"Don't—" lower-pitched preadolescent male voice behind a hard-knuckled juvenile-feeling karate punch to Mal's thigh "—you—" another stiff poke, this time at his ribs "—hurt my—" jab, whack! at his forearm "—dogs!"

"*Ethan*, Mom said no hitting." Exasperated, agitated, sisterly. "She said we can't keep taking tae kwan do if we hit."

"Ethan!" Abernathy's voice, crisp and firm, but lost somewhere on the other side of the uproar. "It's all right. It's Mr. Quarrels from Our Lady—"

Barking dogs and insistent children drowned him out.

"We're not supposed to call our names in front of people we don't know, *Phoebe,*" Ethan snapped. "They might *take* our names and try to make us believe they know us when they really don't and try to get away with things like *us.* And anyway, Ma didn't say we couldn't hit strangers who kidnap her and try to hurt the dogs in our own garage. It's self—" energetic *Pow!* to the side of Mal's knee, fended off by the back of Mal's hand "—defense."

"That's—" Grace's voice, not quite loud enough to cut through the hubbub "—enough."

"It's still hitting—" Another youthful male voice, slightly older, but not yet at the cracking stage, above hands that grabbed the ones chopping at Mal and wrestled the chopper away from the truck. "—and I'll pound you good if she says we can't take the classes anymore because you hit!"

"Be *nice,*" the first little-girl voice advised its brother sanctimoniously, "until it's time to *not* be nice."

"Yeah, *Ethan.*" The Phoebe voice again, sending Ethan's name into danger deliberately and emphatically. Reminded Mal of Sheila's when Sheila was eleven: irritating as hell. "And *Mom* said she'd tell us when it was time to not be nice and she hasn't. Have you, Mom?"

Someone—probably Gus-John, who was near enough to reach it first—hit the light switch. The hundred-watt overhead came on to reveal Grace separating the boys who were doing their best to swat each other around her intervention. She shook first the taller one then the shorter one; and when she spoke this time, her voice was icy, provoked and tight, designed to reach clearly to the back of a good-size auditorium during Mardi Gras.

"That will be sufficient," she informed her children, then turned to their canine counterparts. "Dogs, *heel!*" she commanded.

Arrested in midsnarl, the herd of wild beasts—three, but it was a moment before he could count them, and it seemed like a lot more—desisted in their efforts to reach Mal long enough to look at her. She pointed a hard finger at them, then at her side and they took a last longing look at Mal before slinking meekly over to seat themselves in a row at her left knee. The first dog in the line, a hairy, silver-tipped black Bouvier-and-something, flipped its nose under her hand, urging forgiveness. She ignored it, returning her attention to the short human mob.

"Children, bed."

"But, Mom—"

"Don't 'but Mom' me, you know the rules. You've still got school for the next two days. Bedtime was forty-five minutes ago. Give me kisses and hugs and scram. I'll be up shortly to tuck you in. Oh, and put the dogs out."

"Put the dogs out, *please,*" the taller of her two sons—Mal recognized the boy from his research as the almost-a-teenager David—smart-assed.

Grace looked at him. "Don't," she suggested calmly.

David thought about it, a defiant how-far-can-I-push-it speculation printed plainly on his face.

"Love means frequently not having to say please and thank-you," his shortest sister—Erin, if Mal was not mistaken—she of the "be nice" statement, said. Quoting someone, no doubt.

"Shut up," David replied.

"*Go,*" Grace said firmly, herding them back toward the door into the breezeway.

Phoebe, the taller of her daughters and the one who most resembled her physically, balked, staring round-eyed at Grace's blouse. "You have blood all over you, Mom."

"Grace, are you all right?" Abernathy, alarmed, turned back from shepherding children and dogs into the house.

"It's not mine. Mr. Quarrels, please get your boots off my truck. It's got enough scratches as it is."

"Uh . . ."

"The dogs won't bother you, I've told them not to."

Mal gave her silent disbelief.

Grace sighed. "David, put them out."

"Why is it always me?" David queried rebelliously, but he went.

"Whose blood is it then, Mom?" Erin stood in front of Grace biting her lip, worried.

"Mostly his." Grace gestured a thumb at Mal.

Abernathy looked from Grace to Mal, eyebrows raised. "Who does the rest belong to?"

"She punched me," Mal said, enlightening no one. "I was trying to help her."

"With what?" Abernathy asked.

Mal had no chance to respond before the fledgling interrogation unit took over again.

"You're not supposed to touch other people's blood, Ma," Ethan stated emphatically. "They keep telling us that in school before recess and our coaches say it and nobody's supposed to touch anybody else's blood or throw-up or dirty tissues or anything because you don't know where they've been and some germs can live for a week in dried blood and in fresh blood if you have a cut or anything."

Erin nodded. "That's what you tell us at softball—if somebody gets hurt, don't touch anything, come get you and wear rubber gloves."

Grace gaped at her daughter, at Mal, at her daughter, at Mal again. Her hands moved, independent of her mouth, inadequately attempting shocked apology unaided by words.

Although he'd never willingly admit it, Mal was a trifle astonished himself. Concerns about infectious diseases—especially blood-related ones—were an increasing part of law enforcement life; a respect for simple on-the-job precautions was not only prudent but, in some instances, mandatory. Still, he'd never had the subject presented to him quite like this. At least not where he was the subject in question.

He eased himself off the Suburban, careful to keep his boots off the finish.

Grace shut her mouth, hands continuing to describe her loss of language. What the dickens could she say, anyway? She hadn't quite yet decided how to deal with the rampant paranoia of this brave new world she was raising her kids in. Or how not to be infected by it.

Or what to say if she was asked.

As head coach for each of her daughter's school softball teams, she'd been hard put enough to accept the countless liability precautions that included hepatitis B vaccinations, signing waivers, heavy rubber surgical gloves, instructions on how to sterile-seal anything used to clean up a bloody nose or vomit and dispose of it in a special container that would then be disposed of by a hospital, and instructions on how *not* to deal with the above situations, should they arise.

On the other hand, for barely a millisec of an instant, she also considered her chest and stomach, anyplace the blood might have touched, mentally taking stock of possible broken skin, scratched-open mosquito bites and any other epidermal imperfections she could think of. Not because of Mal, she told herself, not her Knight-in-Shining, but because of the other guy: who knew where his blood had been, or what he'd put into it? Came up clean as far as she was aware. Still, a quick, hot, soapy scrub followed by some sort of sterilizing afterbath couldn't hurt.

Lordy, lordy, lordy, the things your kids forced you to think about.

And what a pain to find her adult self still at the mercy of a child's "innocent" badgering the same way she'd always been at the mercy of her older sisters' pronouncements when she'd been a child. Did grown-up women ever stop being little girls and get it all together the way their own mothers had always seemed to have it?

She looked at Mal, color rising in her face. Not exactly the most opportune timing for her thoughts, especially given the tone and nature of her fantasies about him in the office.

"I, uh, I . . . I . . . I don't know what to say. Ah . . ."

"Me, neither," Mal agreed, and had the grace to look it.

The children stared from one to the other, apparently gathering breath for their next onslaught. Grace cast them a warning scowl and, angels all, they released a collective breath and offered her *who-me?* innocence.

Unconvinced, Grace turned to Abernathy, intent on circumvention.

He gave her a wry grin and held up his hands in silent explanation: *"Can't help, sorry. They're your kids. You're on your own."*

"Thanks loads," she told him.

"No problem," Gus replied.

Grace glared at him, one harried mother to her children's most instigative honorary uncle. "You brought 'em out here, you put 'em back to bed or I'll send that cat in to wake you in the morning."

Gus clutched his heart, giving her high drama. "Oh, no, not that!"

"Bet on it."

He grinned at her, clearly unrepentant. "I'll get 'em out of your hair as long as you tell me what happened afterward."

"Just so you know it'll cast you in a very unfavorable light."

"Always does." Gus shrugged, unabashed, and turned to Grace's children. "Troops, march."

"Aw, John, but you said—"

"Later," Gus suggested with a meaningful look from them to their mother and back.

As if at some prearranged signal, they all subsided and unwillingly preceded him through the breezeway and into the house.

Grace narrowed her eyes, studying their wake thoughtfully for a moment before returning her attention to Mal. Bore investigation, but not while she still had gratitude to express and Mal's bloody, possibly broken nose to think about.

"I'm sorry about that."

"Reminds me of home," Mal said truthfully, reminded of Sheila's most recent sex - can - kill - you - if - you - don't - play - it - safe - and - the - best - way - to - play - it - safe - is - not - to - play - at - all chat with his nephew: no longer morals, but life and death. "And they're right, as far as it goes. You do have to be careful—"

"Seems more like paranoid to me," Grace interrupted.

Mal shrugged. "Sometimes that's safest."

"Safe, but inhuman—or maybe that's inhumane, I'm not sure. And besides, isn't paranoia considered a symptom of several different chemical imbalances by the mental health community? Isn't there a treatment available for it?"

"You mean like twelve-step programs, psychotherapy, light therapy, group therapy, chemical therapy, Prozac, Lithium, Wellbutrin or shock therapy?"

"I wouldn't put it so crassly—or sound so smug simply reciting the jargon that can really mean the difference between existing and living to more and more people every day—but something like that.''

Mal's mouth twitched. Woman said what was on her mind, no doubt about it. Father Rick's *something else* was definitely the pigeonhole she'd never fit into. ''I apologize for impugning the mental, spiritual and physical health needs of mankin—''

Grace frowned at him.

Mal paused, thought about what he was saying, backtracked and amended. ''*Hu*mankind, excuse me. I've never managed to be politically correct when it comes to editing sexist terminology out of my everyday speech. And speaking of paranoia...''

Another look, this one withering, accompanied by foot-tapping and hands on hips.

Mal grinned, point made. Enjoying himself. Not a good sign. ''Sensitivities aside—''

''Are you?'' Grace asked.

''Am I what?'' Interesting the way she changed subjects without signaling. Downright dangerous the way he followed her digressions without batting an eye.

''Sensitive.''

''Personally or toward others?''

''Certainly not toward others, judging from this discussion.''

''Personally then.'' He considered himself for a moment. ''Judging by my lack of reaction to your insensitive pokes, not particularly.''

''Thought not.'' Grace nodded, confirming something she already knew. Pleased by the verification. Not sure why she was so pleased. She motioned toward the door. ''Would you like to come in and I'll see what other damage I can do cleaning up your nose?''

Mal followed her into the breezeway, once again distracted by the view. ''Now who's being sexist? Just because I'm a man doesn't mean I'm incapable of cleaning up my own boo-boos.''

"Just because I'm a mother doesn't mean I yearn to nurture the universe, either,'' Grace retorted tartly, opening the door into her living room and shoving three big noses and two short ones out of her way at the same time, "So you can get over that nonsense right now."

"Hey, I didn't—"

"But you were thinking."

"Tell me there aren't traditional roles men and women automatically assume—"

Mal stepped into Grace's living room warily, but as she'd told him they would, the dogs merely sniffed him over, shoved polite noses into his crotch in greeting and left him alone. To his right, Gus Abernathy appeared in a doorway, bowl of ice in one hand, washcloth in the other. Mal closed the door behind him.

God forgive his conniving heart, he was in.

Chapter 4

Even bloodied and bruised, he had a very nice nose.

Feeling infinitely more herself in fresh bicycle shorts and a cutoff, mostly white sweatshirt minus its sleeves and neckband—children at last all kissed, hugged, admonished, tucked up and settled for the night—Grace surveyed her handiwork on Mal's admirable proboscis. Bent but not broken, fortunately—and the bend was natural: God's workmanship, not hers.

Wouldn't be any hardship to spend a night and morning or two looking at that nose.

She stifled a restless mental snort of self-derision and surreptitiously eyed the fill of his black T-shirt. Wouldn't be too difficult spending time inspecting the rest of him, either. Sculpting a bit of this, molding a bit of that...

The snort hit the back of her throat and nearly choked her when she stifled it. *Get a grip, Witoczynski,* she advised herself. *The man has better fish to fry than a plump-thighed mother of four, so just get over that fantasy right now.*

Especially right now when he was close enough she could feel his breath tickling the inside of her forearm or look straight down into warm black eyes that were just a little crossed with trying to focus on what she was doing to his nose. Like he wasn't sure if he quite trusted her not to belt him in it again.

Oh, fine way to ruin a nice fancy.

Offering a wry chuckle to the keeper of her thoughts, she took one last gentle swipe along the bridge with a cool washcloth before handing Mal a bag of ice. "Tilt your head back and put this on your nose—keep it from bleeding again."

"It won't bleed again," Mal assured her, but he took the bag from her, anyway, caught by the laughter she didn't try to hide. Ruefully hoping it wasn't directed at him.

The sides of their forefingers scraped, more sensitive than either of them might have guessed or wished, and current crackled between them: awareness and surprise mixed with consternation for Grace; awareness and acknowledgment mixed with an uncomfortable sense of inevitability for Mal. He already knew what effect she had on him, advantage his after nearly three weeks of spying on her.

What he hadn't known was that he'd have the same effect on her.

He'd thought she was too smart for that.

He watched her flinch and blink, her eyes shedding hazel light on guilty secret longings, and felt ashamed.

He shouldn't be here.

He had to be here.

Carefully he set the ice pack on the dining-room table, fumbled in his pockets for a smoke. Came up with a bent one long ago hidden deep in the pocket of his T-shirt in case of emergencies. He straightened the cigarette, calling himself the sorriest bastard in the universe for being

so addicted to the nicotine that even a stale butt appealed
to him. He missed the uncrushable pack he'd forever
managed to have on hand since he was sixteen, but he
couldn't even pretend to keep his promise to Jennifer if he
carried it with him now. Too many butts, too great a
temptation, too anemic a desire to quit.

"Mind if I smoke?" he asked, fitting the cigarette between his lips and digging for a lighter.

"Yes." She made a face without thinking, fantasy interrupted by the sudden image of soggy cigarette butts
filling the bottom of a not quite empty disposable coffee
cup on the center's kitchen table.

Lighter flame wavered at the end of the cigarette. The
question was rhetorical; he hadn't expected her to say no.
Mal looked at her, released the wheel to douse the flame.
"Oh."

Grace flushed. She'd learned long ago that keeping an
opinion to herself made her uncomfortable, but sometimes speaking her mind without editing first was just as
bad. "I mean, I mind if you smoke in here—well, actually, I mind if you smoke anywhere, it's not good for you,
but you are a grown man and you can make your own
decisions even if they're bad ones—but you're welcome to
smoke out on the deck." She indicated the double glass
and screen doors beyond the end of the dining-room table. "Just don't blow the smoke through any open windows."

Disbelieving laughter rose from deep in Mal's chest.
The woman was a trove of things he'd never have thought
she'd be. "Okay." He eyed her for a moment while she
squirmed, embarrassed but sticking to her principles. "Do
you always say what you think?"

"Have to." Grace shrugged. "I've got four kids, six
older sisters and a mother who thinks on her feet. If I
don't say what I think when it occurs to me, then it
doesn't get said or somebody else takes credit for think-

ing it first." Again the shrug, described by her hands. "And I learned a long time ago that suffering in silence is a crock and martyrdom is for people who have nothing better to occupy their time."

Mal grinned at her, teasing because it felt natural to do so. Because something comfortable about her invited it. "So you speak your mind as if you've got one."

"I do have one," Grace corrected firmly.

Mal grinned, his craving for nicotine momentarily sidetracked. "Touché," he conceded. "And a most interesting mind it is, too."

They eyed each other, hazel eyes to black, and what had begun as simple banter in a flash became a surprisingly dangerous admission. Uneasily, they courted silence, Grace discomfited, Mal looking for ways to verbally backpedal and correct a balance he suddenly felt he was about to lose.

At about the same time the silence reached do-or-die proportions, Gus came through the door from the kitchen carrying a tray holding a steaming kettle, a jar of instant coffee—decaf, in deference to the hour—a dish of assorted herbal tea bags and a host of company trappings Grace invariably forgot to offer when she was playing hostess.

"Thanks," Mal said quickly before he was asked. "Nothing for me." He dumped his cigarette and lighter back into his T-shirt pocket and rose. "It's late, I should go."

"Yes. All right." Grace dropped the washcloth on the table and scrubbed her hands dry on her shorts. "You'll need a ride. Where did you put my keys? John—"

She looked at Gus. Mal thought he detected a hint of pain in Abernathy's nod of acknowledgment, a trace of *I wish* mixed with a desire to have this woman know the truth. But maybe it was only Mal's own guilty conscience wanting Grace to know *his* truth.

"Will you stay with the kids while I drive Mal—"

Mal came back to reality with a crash. "No." He shook his head. There wasn't a chance in hell he was going to spend more time with her than he absolutely had to in order to keep track of Abernathy and make sure she and her kids were around-the-clock protected. She had conflict of interest written all over her—his conflict because she was head to toe, and every place in between, of interest.

He dared a glance at her, the form-hugging shorts, the legs that definitely went all the way up, the cutoff sweatshirt with the hint of bra straps showing at the torn neck and her bare midriff peek-a-booing along the bottom.

And stimulating.

He eyed her face, the small full mouth, determined jaw—the dare-me glint in her eyes.

And downright provoking.

"No." He shook his head again. "You won't drive me anywhere." *Especially over the edge.* "Not at this hour." He fished the lighter out of his T-shirt pocket, fiddled wishfully with it a second, then grabbed control of himself and jammed it forcefully into the corner of his left hip pocket. "Definitely not."

"Excuse me," Grace said tartly, balance regained in feminist indignation. So, he was a smoker and arrogant, to boot. Took all the pressure off her finding him so impossibly... cute. And sexy. And... really, really *male.* "You're not the boss of me, so I don't think it's up to you to tell me what I can or can't do."

"Hey, after dark, back at the same place, shot-out parking-lot lights and all—I don't feel up to rescuing you again tonight. Or rescuing anyone from you, for that matter. Not to mention you got kids you need to be home with. I'll hitch."

"Or you could—" Gus began, but nobody was listening.

"Oh, sure." Grace snorted. "Like somebody's going to stop at this time of night and give you a ride twenty miles downtown looking the way you look."

"Oh? And how is it I look?"

"Like you took on the Incredible Hulk and lost."

Mal sucked patience between his teeth and looked at Gus.

Gus shrugged. "It's not quite that bad, but you don't look real tame, either."

"She's not driving me back to Our Lady right now."

"No argument here," Gus agreed. "And there is another option—one where no one drives anyone anywhere. Yet."

It was Grace's turn to look at him.

"He can sack out on my couch for the night. You can drive him to Our Lady with you in the morning."

Continued silence—with a glower.

"I'm going in the opposite direction," Gus said. "I've got to leave early and be in Ann Arbor all day."

Grace threw up a hand in a gesture of frustration. Great. Already tomorrow with four crazed kids in the Suburban for seventeen miles through madhouse morning traffic on the second to last day of school, and John added a six-foot-four-inch two-hundred-ten pound hunk of a smoker who made her blood boil. For several reasons. Clearly, this was not to her advantage.

But she did owe him.

A little.

She eyed Mal—*the ball's in your court*—and puffed acquiescence. Never let her mother—or her sisters—say of her that she lacked the appearance of Christian charity in a strange situation. Of course, Twink would undoubtedly call it "finally giving in to the opportunity to keep company with a cute guy when it bit her in the butt."

Most days, Grace could really do without Twink.

Gus grinned and turned to Mal. "How 'bout it?"

Mal studied Abernathy. A faint warning buzz skirted the perimeter of his omnipresent skepticism. Friendly, outgoing, hospitable. What was wrong with this picture? *Too easy,* it shouted at him. But then, it had always been almost too easy with Abernathy.

Fifteen months Mal had looked for him, then suddenly, there Abernathy was, barely disguised, working in Mal's old hometown neighborhood under Mal's Detroit-stationed nose. If Mal were paranoid—which he was when it paid to be—he might think he was being set up for something. Because the only lie Mal had told anyone in order to get close to Abernathy was that he was a laid-off cop from South Dakota with family in the Pontiac area. And ninety-five percent of that was true, anyway.

Still, anyone with the right computer connections and a little know-how—and by all accounts, Gus Abernathy was chock-full of know-how—could check Mal's story within a few hours. It would take longer to break Mal's cover, but a former *FiBbIe* like Gus, who was also a hacker bang-up enough to steal money from William Dunne, could undoubtedly do it.

If he wanted to.

But even if he didn't, a guy as urgently trying to stay out of harm's way as Abernathy should have run a mile—or a thousand—from any kind of cop, former or otherwise. Cops smelled fear, dealt in it much of the time. But Abernathy was relaxed. Jovial. Comfortable. Sure of himself.

Unafraid.

The hackles on Mal's neck stood up straight. Hell on a hatpin, what had he overlooked? He didn't like what he was sensing, but he was in it now. Worked damned hard to get here, too. Couldn't back up yet.

All right, so sue him. Grace was right about his machismo, after all. Probably wouldn't have the sense to back out of a game of single-lane mountain-road chicken, either—if you caught him on the wrong day.

He peered sideways at Grace. The whitish cast of strain showed in the set of her mouth, the muscles around her eyes, the almost-checked slump of her shoulders. She looked as if she were about to fold up again, exhausted as though what had happened to her in the parking lot had caught its second wind and was about to emotionally smack her about. He didn't know what he could do to redirect the reaction, but he *liked* Grace Witoczynski, damn it. And, as Sheila often snippily reminded him, he was bullheaded enough to try everything once—whether he should or not.

Ah, hell, he thought moodily, somebody shoot me. It was definitely the wrong day.

"So," Gus repeated, "you wanna hitch, call a cab or sack out on my couch?"

Mal shrugged. "Couch," he agreed. "Sure. Thanks. Why not?"

Grace threw up her hands again. "Great," she said, irritated. "Fine." She picked up Mal's unused ice pack and tossed it through the kitchen doorway. It hit the edge of the stainless-steel sink a resounding *thunk* and dropped to the floor, spilling its contents. The washcloth slapped down after it. "Just dandy."

She stalked to the doorwall, glared out at the night. She shouldn't be so snippily ungrateful toward the man who'd possibly saved her life, but...well...

But nothing, she told herself firmly. There was no excuse for rudeness.

She'd been raised to be neighborly, to trust people—at least as far as she could throw them—but for some odd reason, she'd reacted like David confronted with the girls who'd begun to tell him how beautiful they thought his hair; he'd reacted by immediately going to Fantastic Sam's and getting it buzzed. She didn't want to grow up any more than she'd already grown up, change the fragile status quo. And Mal Quarrels, every square solid inch and muscular pound of him, threatened her and everything she held dear: her children, her heart, her independence.

And not necessarily in that order.

He represented a danger of distracting proportions, and so she reacted like a Peter Panning twelve-year-old instead of the sure-of-herself grown-up she'd supposedly become. Because on top of everything else, finding him...attractive and...impossibly desirable was simply too much.

And so knowledge didn't transform irritation into apology. Instead, with a troubled, heart-wrenched glance of *I-don't-know-what's-happening-to-me* over her shoulder, Grace yanked open the screen and went out into the darkness of the deck. An enthusiastic horde of dogs and their single feline counterpart went with her. The door crashed shut, bounced open, slid violently closed and stayed there.

Mal and Gus stared after her.

"What happened?" Gus asked. "She wouldn't tell me in front of her kids."

"She got mugged in the parking lot. Took the guy down but didn't finish him. I came along and hauled him off and she punched me, too. We sorted out who I was and she fainted. I found her address, a county map and drove her home. Been a wild night."

"You didn't report it?"

Mal shook his head. "Figured it'd be better to get her home."

"Ah." Gus nodded, as though that explained everything.

Mal stepped to the deck door, searching the darkness for Grace, turned and slid a wordless, troubled, involuntarily revealing question at Gus.

Gus viewed him thoughtfully for a moment, seemed to find something that elicited an odd, almost bitter smile and made an offhand, you-can't-fight-it motion in the air with a hand. "She runs on a stiff set of principles, and she takes not living up to her own expectations pretty hard."

"She didn't do anything wrong."

"Not in your book or mine, either." Gus shrugged. "But our rules don't apply to Grace—nobody's rules apply to Grace. She's got her own, and one of 'em is that all crimes should be reported and that the criminal justice system needs to be served notice when it protects law-breakers better than it protects victims and treats witnesses like criminals. She has the kids study martial arts because she wants them to grow up with both the courage and the know-how to stand up for themselves, the discipline to understand when to walk away instead of fight. Above all, she wants them to learn not to knuckle under to pressure, not to run from their fears and never to be afraid to take a risk for something they believe in. Mostly she feels that she ought to be able to take care of herself and her kids and live equably with everybody. Apart from that, she can't stand statistics, especially when she's one of 'em, and most days she's not wild about reality."

"I don't blame her," Mal said. "It bites." Then, resigned, "Should've called the cops from her car phone." Statement, not a question.

"Probably." Gus nodded. "For what it's worth, I'd have brought her home, too."

"Great." Somehow, knowing that a man with Gus Abernathy's background would have behaved exactly as he had himself didn't make Mal feel better. "I recognized the guy, seen him around the soup kitchen the last few days. Gave me an antsy feeling, but the courts say gut's not enough."

Gus nodded: been there, done that. "Sometimes proof's not, either."

Mal eyed the patio doors, first with indecision, then defeat. "Ah, hell," he said and stepped to the door.

"That, too," Gus agreed.

They eyed each other: two men cut from similar cloth of differing patterns, each housing within himself a capacity for violence, in doubt over one stubborn everyday woman who, for different reasons, embodied the potential to bring them each to their knees. The silence lasted hardly a moment. Mal put a hand on the screen preparing to slide it open; Gus turned the other way.

"I'll be in my apartment," he said. "Steps are around the other side of the garage. Come up when you're ready."

Mal nodded once, turned off the dining-room light and stood in the sudden darkness waiting for his eyes to adjust and find Grace.

He was going to make her feel better if it killed him.

The night was dark and warm, cloudless, the moon a Cheshire-cat sliver of a smile amid a faint scattering of stars.

Grace hugged her arms about herself, cold despite the almost-summer temperature, and wandered across the deck, stepped off into the yard. A surge of insect voices chorused the night, conducted by the cadence of a single loud cricket somewhere on the deck behind her. She breathed deep, hoping to find some kind of emotional footing in the act, but serenity eluded her, lost in post-trauma jitters and in some new and far more threatening awakening.

When the man attacked her in the parking lot, he'd stolen a sense of safety integral to her psyche, violated her dignity and self-respect—bruised her body and her ego and turned her into one more damned statistic in a universe that adored statistics more than life. She hated becoming just another number on a list for some scientist, politician or poll-taker to manipulate in the guise of "telling it like it is," but she hated the way she felt now even more: fragile, apprehensive, rebellious—unwillingly self-conscious about the mother-mature spread of her hips and the heft of her thighs.

When Mal Quarrels came to her rescue, statistics changed, jeopardy increased instead of lessened.

In a moment, he'd gone from being a bit of titillating fantasy deployed by imagination to entertain her when work became too repetitive and mundane to being a person with a voice, a physicality, a sense of humor. He became both a sexually and emotionally appealing man whose eyes and face had told her more than once tonight that he found something in her equally... sexual, equally... tempting. And with two boys headed immediately and mutinously toward puberty and in the midst of everything else she was currently involved in, an interesting, *interested* man was something she did not need.

Or want.

Men were a lot of work, no two ways about it. They demanded care and compromise, support and pampering—and sometimes forgot to return the favor. No matter how much she missed Phil, and despite the added responsibility of raising the kids by herself, there was also a freedom in not having to answer to another adult—especially a man—a relief in not having to consult someone else over every financial decision she made. A tranquillity in not having to be the one always in charge of making sure the relationship, partnership, marriage stayed strong and that the sun never set on anger.

She shut her eyes, ashamed of the unfamiliar bitterness of her thoughts. She hadn't realized until this instant that she'd ever felt put upon with Phil.

By Phil.

But remorse changed nothing: she still wasn't in the market for new and provocative ways to complicate her life—especially when the potential complication came with the last name *Quarrels*. The *skirmish* omen in that was a little too blatant even for someone who didn't allow herself to be superstitious. Grace was already a world-class life-complicator all by herself.

But at least in thinking about Mal, she'd stopped thinking about the attack.

Rubbing her arms, she moved deeper into the yard. The whole thing still scared her—what she'd done, what she hadn't done, but particularly the things that might have happened and hadn't. She was okay, right? Nothing irreparable had taken place in the parking lot, she hadn't been hurt, raped or robbed. Oughtta be able to get up, walk away, move on, right? Don't look back, be strong, she thought. Forge ahead, deal with it and forget it.

Right?

Her lips trembled, trying to laugh at herself, failing miserably. Oh, yeah, right, just not in this lifetime.

She touched a finger to the corner of each stinging eye, scraped moisture across each temple and into her hair. Damn, crying, as if she had nothing better to do. Sometimes she felt like such an emotional bag lady: everything collected randomly into a stolen shopping cart and hoarded for dear life. Other times she was a sentient spendthrift, zealously depleting resources needed for herself and her children.

Sometimes—now—she was simply a mess.

An owl hooted, startling her. Grace jerked and clasped her arms tighter about herself, felt the burn of disquiet down the frayed nerves in the center of her back. Usually this was her favorite part of the night, home alone, kids in bed, peace vacationing for a short but intensely satisfying moment in her yard. Not tonight.

Shadows glutted the twilight beyond the perimeter of the illumination spilled by the house, cut deep edges into the dewing grass. Surrounded by the fabric of imagination, she clung to the boundary of light, too able to conjure trolls among the sinister, tenebrous trees, define beasts in the blackness out to steal her soul.

Some nights, when she stood in this exact spot and looked at these same trees beneath a silver moon, they were friends, warm, well-known intimates who shared her favorite dreams, took away her deepest fears. On those nights she was content, knowing of nowhere else she'd rather be—knowing that nowhere else could she find this peace. She knew that what she saw and the way she saw it depended solely upon the moment's mood and a certain slant of light. But tonight, what she knew didn't matter; she was lost in what she felt.

Confusing.

Out in the darkness, fireflies flashed mating signals among blossoming fruit trees and June-richening grasses. Inside the house, male voices rose and fell in thanks and good-nights; the breezeway door clicked and a minute later the old-fashioned wooden screen door on the garage apartment whined and slammed hard on too-tight springs; the light came on in the kitchen and the silhouette belonging to John crossed the room.

Unable to stop herself, Grace raised her head and concentrated, waiting to see if Mal would follow. Spying because he made her curious. Peeping because some indecent part of her wanted to know if the promise outlined by his T-shirt was all that was real. Even at thirty-three, she had a hard time leaving Christmas surprises unrattled, unprodded and unexamined.

She'd always preferred to stay well ahead of uncertainty rather than behind it—and then she kept vigil in the rearview mirror so it couldn't creep up on her unaware.

Behind her, the inside light went off. Grace had barely enough time to avert her avid, embarrassed gaze from the upper garage windows before the sliding screen slid open on its track and Mal stepped onto the deck.

He stood quietly for a moment, letting his eyes adjust, wondering what approach would best sidetrack this uncommon woman from the sleepless night she was sending herself to. Chose the most indirect route he could think of. Then he moved to the edge of the deck nearest Grace and sat down, dug the broken cigarette out of his pocket and stuck it in his mouth, found his lighter and flicked the Bic.

"I'm trying to cut back," he said, cupping his hands around the flame and bringing the cigarette down to it.

"Good for you." Grace's applause was genuine in a voice thick and wan with swallowed emotion, trying to avoid feelings she chose not to share.

With him.

Turning to look at her, something inside Mal unexpectedly wrenched. He'd come out here for reasons he'd rather not name, come to make her laugh, jolly her out of delayed shock and reaction—tick her off, make her mad, anything so she wouldn't have to think about the attack anymore. Anything so she could hide from herself, at least for tonight. But now that he was here, he didn't want her to hide herself from him, trying to make him comfortable despite her own...discomfort. Her own difficulties.

For an instant his hands wavered, making it tough to light his cigarette. Uncharacteristic. He was a rock, nothing affected him. He could find humor in anything.

Almost.

He shrugged away the essence of something softening inside him. Controlled his hands. Lit his cigarette and dragged deep. Oddly, the smoke tasted sour, didn't relax him the way it normally did. He blew it out. "Promised my daughter. She thinks quitting will be good for my heart, lungs and love life."

"Makes sense to me," Grace muttered, intrigued in spite of herself, her watery emotions and her long-held rule of not passing righteous judgment on people who couldn't help themselves.

Mal pretended to ignore her. Actually, ignoring Grace was growing impossible. "She's only fifteen, so I asked her, how does she know? She gives me this 'Oh-Dad-you-are-so-stupid' sigh and informs me she's kissed enough boys to know that for a woman who doesn't smoke, kissing a man who does is like licking out a dirty ashtray and you don't want to do that more than once and even once is too much."

"Good for her." Grace's chuckle was rough, drawn from the other side of a deep blue funk.

Mal eyed her darkly. *Women.* God-created from Adam's rib like it said in Genesis, his left big toe. Nothing like this had ever once been part of man. His ex-wife, his daughter, his sister, his mother and now Grace Brannigan Witoczynski, all of the same outspoken, unsought mind. And simply to distract her, he was about to encourage Grace further. He offered up a long-suffering mental sigh. What would-be heroes were bound to do for women.

"Not that I asked," he continued, "but she also says insurance policies on smokers aren't as good, so what woman wants a smoker who's going to die early and leave her in debt? Not to mention that she'll never forgive me if I die before the children who have become almost a glimmer in her eyes have a chance to meet me. I told her she'd better dim that glimmer until she's thirty, and then she'd better have a husband to glimmer with, or we'd see how well a smoker's lungs work."

He sighed, dragged deep and appreciatively on the cigarette, looked at it regretfully while the smoke curled around his lips and nose with his breath. "She laughed and hung up on me and I'm still tryin' to quit."

Grace looked over her shoulder at his bulk in the darkness. If there was a point to this announcement, she didn't see it. On the other hand, she had to admit to being vastly entertained.

Something else to hold against him. She already had an overly full life, four enormously energetic, monstrously colorful children, too many dogs and a cat who attacked intruders. She didn't have time to be bored, and so did not need—or want—to be further entertained.

Especially not by him.

In which case, why she said what she said next was completely beyond her. "She's right, you know."

Mal looked askance. "About what?"

"The kissing." Grace colored. Lord above, why could she never just keep her mouth shut. "My...late husband...smoked until I got pregnant with David, our oldest. I was too much in love before that to say so, but, if I remember right, a dirty ashtray is exactly what kissing a smoker tastes like."

Mal eyed her wryly. "And I had so many fantasies."

"Ha!" Grace laughed, disbelieving and self-conscious at once. "Dream on."

"I will."

Grace's turn to ignore him. "What's your daughter's name?"

"Jennifer—Jen. Just turned fifteen, and every time we talk, she's got more opinions."

"She doesn't live with you?" Sudden mortification. "I mean—I don't mean—I'm not—"

Mal grinned. Damn, she was cute when she let him get the better of her. *Enjoy it while you can,* he cautioned himself. He sincerely doubted Mrs. Witoczynski allowed anyone to get the better of her verbally very often.

"Jen lives with her mother in South Dakota," he said. "Livvi and I are divorced. With two households to keep up..." He shrugged, using the vestiges of truth as easily as he might a flat-out lie in his effort to get close to Grace. Every second he got to know her made protecting her and hers from the unease he felt over William Dunne's unknown whereabouts all the more urgent. Urgency made truth or lies a matter of splitting hairs in how you looked at them, made whatever worked fair game. "City cutbacks and layoffs hit hard, that's why I'm back here tryin' to keep up with ye olde alimony and child support. Old neighborhood, old friends, sister to stay with, people who knew me when..."

Hands on hips, Grace eyed him with blunt, all-telling skepticism, and Mal nearly choked. Oh, hell, he'd misjudged her vulnerability and laid it on too thick. Screwed himself good now. *Vulnerability,* he reminded himself, *is not synonymous with gullibility.*

"Too much?" he asked. "Not sad enough?"

"Oh, plenty sad enough," Grace said dryly. "But I've heard it before and it doesn't..." She hesitated. "*Fit* you. You want something, my guess is you either ask for it, or you take it and charm your way through the fallout later. You tell this story often?"

"It's true," Mal said sadly, determined not to give ground before he had to. "And it's only half of it." Then, eyeing her silhouette sideways, he offered her a self-deprecating grin and admitted, "And as often as I think it'll work."

"It didn't."

He shrugged, forever sure of himself. "Yeah, it did."

"No," Grace said evenly. "It didn't."

"You still mad at yourself for gettin' mugged and at me for finishing what you think you should have handled for yourself?"

Grace looked away from him, laughter gone. "It's not finished. I didn't turn him in. He's still out there."

"Oh, hey, don't." In one fluid motion, Mal exhaled smoke, stubbed out his cigarette, conscientiously stuck the butt in his pocket instead of littering her yard and crossed to Grace. "I didn't mean— Ah, nuts."

She ducked her face into her shoulder and turned when he reached her; he caught her arm and the telltale glitter of emotion gave her away. He dragged an incongruously white hankie out of a stained back pocket and handed it to her.

"I'm sorry. I didn't mean—I meant to distract you, make you laugh. Guess that's a bust."

"Yeah." Grace snuffled loudly into the hankie, blew her nose hard twice and folded the small square of cloth into increasingly smaller squares. "This sort of thing's never happened to me before. I mean, I've lived or worked in the city most of my life and no one's ever—"

"Don't," Mal urged again. He'd dealt with the recriminations experienced by hundreds of victims and witnesses and had never felt helpless. He was helpless now.

"It's..." She swallowed, groped for what *it* was. "Maybe you begin to believe the best, that what you learned in kindergarten about the golden rule is true. You think not that it can't or won't happen to you, but that somehow maybe because you treat people the way you want to be treated that maybe you're blessed, maybe you've found the secret to living a violence-free life, or maybe just that your guardian angel is the best in the business—and then it happens, and you can't stop it, you can't control it, you can hardly even control yourself."

"Let it go," Mal said gently. "Dwelling won't get you past it."

She looked up at him, face troubled in the starlight. "It has to be done, don't you see? Now or later, I have to look at it. Now is when it's here."

"It'll be here later, too."

"Not like now. Not where I can touch it. It's like that damned horse people tell you to get right back up on. I have to go in there tomorrow. That guy may come into the center and he'll know me, but will I know him?" She crumpled Mal's hankie into an anxious fist. "I have to talk to the police and my kids and warn the school principal and the other people who work late nights at the center. I don't like feeling out of control and I don't like feeling violated, but I have been. That guy didn't get my purse or my truck or—or—''

She shut her eyes and hesitated, dealing with the thought. ''Or anything else he might have been after, but he took me, my self-esteem and my control of the situation. He almost took control of the whole course of my life and that of my kids—and maybe in ways I don't even know about yet, he actually did. If he'd maimed me or killed me, what about them? How am I supposed to think about that? What am I supposed to say to my kids when I can't even explain why it happened? Don't trust anybody anymore? Don't trust themselves? Don't trust me because maybe I won't always be there for them the way I told them I'd be?''

''Teach them to depend on themselves first, anyone else a distant second.''

Grace snorted. ''That'd be great if I wanted to raise autonomous *Me-first* drones, but I don't. They should be independent enough to think for themselves without depending on anyone else to choose what's right or wrong for them, but if they can't learn to depend on one another in a pinch, learn that it's okay to need other people so long as they don't overdo it, let other people expect the best from them—teach them to expect the best from themselves—in any situation, then what's the point?''

''Survival,'' Mal suggested.

''Not enough,'' Grace said fiercely. ''Not even *half* enough.''

''How about a balanced paranoia then? Trusting, but not at any expense.''

She looked up at him, face full of wistful shadows, eyes a dark, fathomless well without reflection. ''You know how to teach that?''

Mal swallowed with difficulty, looked away. Somewhere back a way he'd crossed a line he never should have had to draw. As far as he could see, she was, without a doubt, the most intriguing woman he'd ever laid eyes on and he was out of his depth here, big-time.

He touched her hair because he couldn't stop himself. It was an intimate gesture that said he knew and understood her far better than the shortness of their acquaintance allowed, but he wasn't a man full of restraint; he was a man full of physicality and passion. A man who sometimes acted first and thought better of it later. "I know how to learn it."

Without meaning to, Grace leaned her head into his touch. She shouldn't trust him; he wasn't trustworthy. He was a big old playful tomcat who had the nerve to play tiddledywinks in her bloodstream without being invited. He looked at her the way Phil used to look at her when they were twenty, only more so. Grown-up so. Hot and knowing so. Recognizing opportunity *and* responsibility when he saw it so.

And touching, anyway.

A reckless combination, if ever there was one.

Run, the sensible part of her brain cried. But the other part, locked firmly with intuition and instinct, stubborn from generations of careful breeding for the trait that had created her tigress heart, stood its ground.

Like a she-cat anticipating a confrontation with the streetwise old tom she'd compared him to, Grace was curious.

It was the curiosity, more than anything else, that made her turn and walk deeper into the night, away from him.

Chapter 5

It took Mal a moment to realize she'd gone.

He blinked, unsteady and amazed. One instant the silkiness of her hair had graced the hardness of his palm and her face was so close he'd tasted the sweetness of her breath with each intake of his, the next he was alone with only the breeze on bare skin, leftover sensation and a longing so deep it created an ache.

The fact that he wanted to kiss her didn't surprise him as much as the list of absolutes surrounding his desire: he *needed* to kiss her, he *required* her taste, he *craved* a knowledge of her he had no right to have.

Something about her made him think of hot sun and haylofts, tranquillity, the scent of sweet grasses and clover—of lovemaking, hot and earthy, clean and erotic: explosive. Spoke to the springtime impulse—the human passion—to sow for later reaping. To plant and nourish and propagate.

To replenish the earth.

And feed himself.

He breathed, sucking great drafts of reality through the fog of phantasm.

It had been...forever...since a woman had made such an impression on him—if, indeed, a woman ever had. Certainly not Livvi.

His heart clutched with regret. Certainly not.

Out of the far reaches of the acreage, the herd of canines and cat thundered, barking, growling and *meowrowring*. Mal jerked; he'd forgotten about her animals and their protective propensities, but they simply dashed up, jammed negligent noses up his crotch in cursory inspection and turned anxiously to Grace.

"What?" she asked them.

They panted and nosed her hands, circling her, ruffs high. Along the back fenceline, a beam of light flashed among the trees, reflected off the windows on the outbuilding Mal had seen the night he'd first spotted Abernathy. Grace stiffened visibly and looked at the dogs. Glanced at Mal. Something uncertain and unreadable in the starlight crossed her features.

Tension drifted across Mal's shoulders, lifted the hair on his arms, fuzzed over the back of his neck; unease spiraled deep into his cop's gut, lay like so many of the flatfoot's proverbial greasy undigestible doughnuts. Before he could pick out the intuition and do something about it, however, Grace eyed the fragment of light again and her expression firmed, hardened. She turned to the dogs and pointed at the beam.

"Bring," she said softly.

Startled by her vehemence, Mal turned and stared. "Bring what?" he asked.

Grace shrugged. "Whatever."

She made a slight "go" motion with her hand, and without a sound the three largest dogs turned and melted into the shadows, one to each flank, one down the middle, hunting; the big cat, Fred, and the little dog she called

Friar Tuck backed up against her feet—either to protect her or have her protect their backs, Mal wasn't sure which—and sank to the ground, watching. The cat's nothing of a tail twitched and a low otherworldly growl quivered low in its throat. Mal viewed the animal grimly: protecting her, without a doubt.

And by all appearances, better than *he'd* managed to do so far, despite all the monitoring he'd done.

Without warning, the cat's growl changed and he dashed forward, after the dogs.

"What is it?" Mal asked.

"Probably fireflies."

Mal smiled grimly. "Too big."

Grace hesitated, formulating possibilities, considering the lies she'd told herself for the last two weeks. "Kids then, looking for privacy and conquest. The dogs find used..." She paused, trying to sound matter-of-fact and unruffled when she wasn't. "Used...condoms around the barn sometimes."

"Kids from out here would know better than to cross your fenceline because of your dogs."

"You dare a lot for possible sex when you're seventeen." She sounded as if she knew. Wistful. Apologetic. Concerned.

Mal studied her, wondering for a tick what she'd been like at seventeen, wishing even more briefly he'd been around to find out. But she still didn't convince him—or herself—that the flashlight flicker had anything to do with kids out looking for a place to score.

"Try again, Grace."

She looked at him. Hesitated. He was a stranger, barely known, and her problems were her problems, no need to share. But by his own admission and that of his employment record, he also used to be a cop. And he was younger than her brother-in-law, Gabriel Book, who used to be a Fed and had kept his connections. And he was bigger than

John who did the books for a local police charity and was friendly with the patrolmen who'd been driving by a lot more lately, and he'd helped her out once tonight already.

She eyed the back forty, listening for the dogs, watching the thin beam of light trace the fencing that she'd had to replace last week after someone had cut it and left poisoned meat for the dogs. Glanced once at Gus Abernathy's apartment. Eyed Mal. When it came down to it, he was here and nobody else was and she was tired of doing this alone.

"I don't know. Somebody's been poking around nights off and on for the past couple weeks. Some of the neighbor's pets have been poisoned. Mine have been taught not to touch anything the family doesn't feed them, but lately, almost every morning before the kids get up, I've found and buried a lot of dead squirrels, a couple skunks, some possums and coons, even a young fox. The kids don't know, so please..."

"I won't," Mal said. Then circumspectly, "Does *John* know?"

Grace's attention sharpened, caught by a violent edge in his voice she couldn't define. That he hadn't intended her to hear. "Yes, of course, John knows. And you know, and the police know, and my brother-in-law Gabriel, the ex-Fed, knows. A lot of men *know*, but it hasn't changed anything. Gabriel and John put in motion sensors and lights. The first night the lights were in, we had a power outage—not uncommon around here, but in the morning the lights were smashed and the power to them was cut. That happened twice. Now the dogs and I deal with it."

Mal stared at her. Funny, the sensation crawling into his gut, weaseling through the chinks in his ribs, strangling his lungs: protect, protect, protect...

"Don't you have any sense of self-preservation?"

"Nobody gets near my kids." Flat, emotionless: a statement to be believed.

The light flashed in their direction suddenly, bright and blinding. Without thought, Mal froze in position, shutting his eyes automatically so they wouldn't reflect the light; a seasoned stalker, he wore his watch on a flat black stretch band, face on the inside of his wrist for the same reason. Beside him, he felt Grace stoop and collect something. Before he could open his eyes and stop her, she moved forward out of his reach, hampered by some mother instinct, feet rubbing and catching in the unmowed grass, first slowly, then at speed.

Hopelessly outsized but unaware of it, Friar Tuck moved with her, his short legs working hard to keep him in front of his lady. At the same time, the other dogs issued harsh snarling challenges and converged on a section of the fence near the outbuilding. It banged and rattled under their onslaught, mingling with the sound of some savagely human epithets.

Muttering a profanity that would have delighted his daughter and shocked his mother but not Father Rick, Mal hiked up his right jeans leg, snatched his standard-issue .38 out of his boot and followed Grace at a dead run.

By the time he reached her, Friar Tuck had squeezed his little body through a hole under the fence, one of the other dogs had climbed it and she'd closed her hands over the top of the fence, preparing to vault it. Still running, he tucked his gun inside his belt at the middle of his back and hauled Grace off the fence before vaulting it himself and pursuing the crash of bodies through the underbrush and out onto the truck-width utility easement separating the lots.

In front of him, Grace's dogs barked, Tuck's voice high and fierce, the other bass and heavy. Alongside him, the other two dogs ran the length of the fence adding their vehement two cents to the tumult.

There was a sudden scream of pain and rage, a curse and a yowl, the crash of something sizable landing in the thicket. Then the creak of a vehicle door opening, slamming closed, and the roar of an engine. Mal barely had time to leap out of the way before a small, four-wheel-drive truck hurtled past, spraying mud from the recent rains in all directions.

Grace jogged up, stopping in the easement near Mal and wiping mud from her face. The baseball bat she'd picked up in the yard behind the deck dangled loosely from her right hand, an extension of her arm he had no doubt she knew how to use. "D' you get a license?"

Mal picked himself out of underbrush that made him itch and stared at her. This was the same woman who'd fainted after punching out a mugger less than half a night ago? She'd vaulted the fence even after he thought he'd stopped her and given chase anyway and she wasn't even breathing hard. "Did I what?"

"Get his license number."

Mal shoved hair out of his face, shook the mud that came with it off his hand. "When?"

"Now." Grace threw up a hand, disgusted. "Ah, damn, you didn't. I thought you were a cop."

"Laid-off," Mal said evenly. "And you know, I can get my chops busted somewhere else for a whole hell of a lot less trouble."

"Well, excuse me, but don't expect apologies," Grace returned tartly. "I've been chasing who I think is this same bastard off my fenceline almost every other night for the past week and you haul me off just when I finally have the chance to nail the turkey's license number and maybe get something done about him!"

"Look. I don't remember you filling me in on your plans before you took off—"

He stopped, struck by a sudden gut-deep wrench of guilt and fear. The last few days he'd arranged to have another marshal stick with Grace—out of sight, of course—while he'd hung closer to Abernathy.

Working at the center, it had gotten harder to be around her all the time—which was odd, since he hadn't even known her further than the person she was in some flat cryptic files that had nothing to do with her person, personality, her convictions. Was simply some type of inter-office from-afar schoolboy crush on a woman whose mere physical presence on the other side of a room had begun to make his senses reel. Disturbing. Distracting.

Dangerous.

Don't get involved here, Quarrels, he'd told himself. *Don't "come on," don't flirt. She's got the look, guilty-lonely-wounded-ready, you could take advantage of her, but women with big hearts are dangerous, too easy to use. Using always gets you into trouble. It's bad for the conscience and hard on the environment. You don't need the fallout and neither does she.*

And so he'd backed off, deliberately taken himself out of range of her appeal, concentrated harder on Abernathy. But maybe he'd stuck with Abernathy more than he'd thought when he should have been here, guarding her. Maybe...

Never trust someone else to do a thing as well as you'd do it yourself.

He stepped close and peered hard at her—or as hard as he could without light—aware of an anxiety he'd experienced only when he'd been afraid for Jennifer. "You've been chasing him off every other night for how long?"

"Well," Grace hedged, trying to back away. Mal caught her arm and held her still. She swallowed and looked down at his hand. The same unfamiliar awareness she'd felt at the merest touch of his fingers earlier caught in her throat, left her breathless. "Maybe it hasn't been *every* other night, but it's been a good three or four times at least in the last ten days."

"Same truck every time?" His mind clicked along, forming theories, discarding all but one: the outbuilding would be the perfect place for Dunne to sit and bide his moment to hit Gus.

And anyone else who got in the way. The dogs. The kids.

Grace.

His hand tightened on her arm. She made a small sound when he shook her.

"You're hurting me."

"Think, Grace. Is it the same truck?"

His urgency fed hers. "Never got a good look at it to be sure, but it's always a dark four-wheel-drive Jimmy-type truck, so I assume so. For what that's worth."

He thought it, but he didn't say it: Ass-U-Me. Particularly the *Me*. "What's he after?"

The question was addressed more to himself than to her. Hard. Musing. She answered, anyway.

"I don't know. It doesn't make sense. There's nothing here, just the barn—"

"What's in the barn?"

"Well, it's not really a barn—not for livestock, or anything. It's really just a huge shed on a slab, but it's structurally sound. I've been trying to turn it into a second income, but it's not—"

"Let me look at it."

"Please," she automatically prompted. Almost thirteen years of motherhood and a man's arrogantly peremptory demands did that to a woman.

"What?"

Embarrassment warmed her cheeks. Oh, blast, she'd done it again, and all he was trying to do was jump in headfirst without looking and help her. But she didn't give ground. Principles to uphold, you know, and a sense of equilibrium to maintain in the face of the fact that every minute she spent in his company, and the longer he held

her arm, the more difficult it became to catch her breath.
Her sister, Helen—still referred to as the Major despite
two promotions and an impending General-ship—would
be proud.

"Let me look at it, *please!*"

Mal gritted his teeth around a sigh of pure frustration.
"Will you *please* show it to me." Then, with more satis-
faction and admiration than he intended to feel, "There's
nothin' easy about you, is there?"

He'd never had any use for easy women. Or flimsy
ones, either. He felt the solidness of Grace's arm—arms
sturdy enough to hold a man secure in safe harbor and
never leave him adrift—the feminine strength buried under a veneer of softness and serenity.

That's enough, he told himself. *She's not for you. Stop
imagining it.*

"Like I tell the kids." Grace opened her hands in a
careless shrug, belying the pounding of her pulse. "Follow my rules and I'm the easiest person to get along with
you'll ever find."

"I'll believe that when I see it."

"Do you want to examine the thing or not?"

In spite of himself, Mal grinned and released her arm.
"Lead on, Mrs. Witoczynski."

It took her a minute to lead him anywhere. First she
called the dogs and Fred. Then she checked them over in
the dark, running her hands over their sides, legs, necks
looking for injuries. Aside from Friar Tuck's slight limp
in his left front leg—strain caused by his oversize partner, Boomer, the Bouvier-and-whatever, stepping on him
in an enthusiastic effort to love Grace up in return for her
checking him over—and a minor tear along the edge of
one of Fred's tufted ears, they were fine.

When they finally did go back along the fence, Tuck
and the cat scooted back through the hole they'd used
before, but Boomer—despite energetic urgings from his

left-behind canine cohorts—forgot how he'd gotten out of the yard in the first place. There was a gate farther down the fence near the outbuilding, but it was sturdy and locked and the key was three acres away hanging on a hook inside the kitchen door.

Sighing, Mal gave a protesting Grace an unnecessary boost over the fence—and enjoyed the contact with her a little too much, damn it and thank you—then squatted and cleaned and jerked the squirming one-hundred-twenty-five pound dog as effortlessly as he might the weights he worked out with daily, and lowered him over the fence as far as his arms would reach. From that point, Grace wrapped her arms around Boomer's middle, hefted him out of Mal's hands before that gentleman could stop her and set the beast gently on the ground.

Mal stared at her, scrambling to adjust his view of her for the sixty-seventh time this night. "You didn't have to—I could have—"

Grace viewed him with exasperation. "Who do you think takes him to the vet and lifts him onto the examining table every time he has to go?"

"I thought you had brothers-in-law."

"Puh-lease." She sniffed. "If I had to sit around and wait for a man to do things for me just because they're heavy I'd never get anything done. Besides, becoming a mother means turning into a packhorse for the first four or five years per child—especially when your kids are close together in age like mine. I mean, where do you think I learned to lift weights? A screaming toddler on each hip, plus my purse, a sack of groceries and their diaper bags. The dog is a piece of cake compared to that."

"What did your husband carry?" He asked because he couldn't stop himself, not because he didn't know the answer firsthand. "Didn't he help?"

"Oh, yeah." There was laughter in her voice, a note of *gotcha* teasing. "He carried his jacket. Came back for the bread. Just like you did with your daughter, huh?"

His voice was a shrug filled with a self-deprecating grin. Laughter warming the night. "Probably. Although whenever Livvi called me on it, at the time I was sure she was out of her mind."

"No doubt she was," Grace said mildly. "With good reason."

"Hmm." Mal grunted, then settled his hands and vaulted the fence.

A tree root hobbled his landing and he stumbled. Grace reached for him, steadying, hands at his waist; he braced himself, balancing, hands on her shoulders.

Close.

The top of her head brushed his chin; the scent of her filled his nostrils: warm and cool, spicy and sweet.

Tantalizing.

Beneath her hands, his T-shirt was worn and soft, the man beneath everything she'd tried for weeks not to imagine: rock-solid and yielding, muscular without being muscle-bound.

Inviting.

Between them there was *something:* rapport, rightness, a physical link, a biochemical wavelength that produced concert movement. As he lowered his head, she raised hers. When his hands grew firm and gentle on her shoulders, drawing her forward, her fingers spread and tightened on his sides, anchoring them together. Their breath matched, hearts thudded in unison, heat washed them both. They were no longer Mal and Grace, not Mom and any kind of cop, not watcher and watched, but man and woman: simply created, kinetically bound, connected in spirit, separated by nature—opposing forces drawn together by the elements. By nature and a thoughtless urge to join some piece of themselves and create a bridge to something new.

Too much for one night, for grown-ups with responsibilities to overcome, they both knew it.

This time it was Mal who stopped short of the fork leading to the irreversible course, Grace who was left blinking and bewildered, adrift in the moment, fuzzily aware of the dogs butting at her hands and legs to get her attention.

Swallowing hard, tasting the moistness of the mouth his hadn't touched, Mal pulled back, suddenly and acutely conscious of the inappropriateness of this situation. Of the dangers her mouth represented.

Of the potential hazards he posed to her, emotional, physical and sexual.

Divorce and the law enforcement service had a way of making a man wary of intimacy—even, and maybe particularly, of the wham-bam-I'm-on-my-way-ma'am variety. Grace was not a wham-bam sort of woman. She was the sort who made a man think twice about who he was and what he wanted before he even spoke to her the first time.

She was a woman who could love without thinking twice about who she was loving—that much was clear in the way she dealt with people at the center, in the way they reacted to her. A woman who gave easily, and didn't regret it later even if she should.

He felt something in his gut sink and yaw like an earthquake suddenly opening a cavern in the ground. Once again, not what he'd expected.

Stunned by a reaction he'd neither experienced nor thought himself capable of before and hampered by darkness, he looked at her from memory: the hazel eyes, the short, neatly styled autumn-wheat-colored hair, the heart-shaped but not delicate Irish-Scandinavian cut of her face—and yes, the leggy but hardly willowy, full-figured frame. A woman who a man would want to protect and harbor, but could hold tight without breaking, a woman who could take—who probably already had taken—a man's weight when needed, would share the load, accept the burden.

A woman who a man couldn't fool himself into believing he could get lightly involved with then leave—even if he had to—because, when it came right down to it, he wouldn't want to leave, would sell his soul to stay.

A woman, he reminded himself, who wore no wedding ring but who had children and was, therefore, out of the question. Whatever the question was.

He was a man making use of her nature and a night full of unanticipated circumstances to further his own ends. To do his job and get close to the man he intended to use to bait his hook and catch a killer the legal system had allowed to escape once before. To kiss her now would be just another lie—emotional means to a popular end—and he acted out too many lies to achieve his ends, as it was.

Hazard ahead. The sign blinked pink neon in front of his mind's eye. *Menace, danger, risk—EXPOSURE. Walk away.*

Troubled, he hauled himself together and pulled a small flashlight out of its leather sheath on his belt. Merely getting the job done had never before required so much thought on his part. He did what he had to do and that was that, no thought, no effort, no regrets, no nonsense.

No hint of emotional liability at all.

He twisted the flashlight to switch it on, aimed it at the outbuilding the intruder had apparently been attempting to get into.

"Come on," he said to Grace. "Show me."

It took her a minute to pull herself together and remember what he was talking about.

She'd always thought Phil was the only man in the world for her, that not only could no other man take his place, but that she really had no desire to have another man take his place—not to mention that even after three years it was hard to let go of the man she saw in her children's faces every morning—or fill the place her late husband had left absent. Or find a new spot, open it and lay the groundwork for another hole she'd one day have to plug in her emotions and those of her children.

She'd been wrong.

It was difficult to imagine sweating and moaning in the back seat of Phil's car when she looked at her oldest son, David, and saw puberty and rebellion staring her in the face. Difficult to remember when she'd been that carefree and irresponsible now that she was in the position of necessarily preaching responsibility and consequence, safety and the merits of abstinence to her own near-teens.

But she imagined it all with Mal. Couldn't help herself. Sweating and moaning. Gasping and pleasure. Search and discovery. Lust and sensation. Pure, sensual, erotic torment applied to body parts—his and hers—she hadn't even thought about in who knew when.

It was kind of like overdoing the first workout of a new exercise program and finding muscles you never knew you had. She certainly hadn't known this about herself. Hadn't known fantasy could stand in front of her and change everything in the space of a breath. Hadn't known she'd lacked for anything.

Hadn't known there was anything left for her to dream or want.

She'd thought that what was left of her belonged to the next generation, to her children and Phil's, product of their mingled genes, their ethics and moralities, their memories of who had gone before and left what they'd passed on with them. But apparently that wasn't so. Her oldest sister, Alice, had tried to tell her there might come a time...

But Grace knew how she'd felt, knew the struggles she'd been through that Alice—bless her for her own tribulations before she'd found her husband Gabriel Book—couldn't possibly imagine. Phil's death three years ago had not been a sudden thing, but long and drawn out over the course of two years, a slow withdrawal from physical contact, a learning to live and love without the necessity for consummation or intimacy. A learning to accept desire, but not to act on it.

A time of rearranging priorities and curbing impatience, a time to put the pieces of herself on hold in order to love and honor while death tore them apart.

There'd been time to settle affairs, put things in order, say goodbye, let go. But there'd been no time to *want,* no time to mourn—four kids didn't leave time. She missed Phil in the night—had started letting the dogs sleep on the bed with her just for the feel of something warm and solid at her back—but by day, life had kept her too busy. And gradually, she'd gotten used to the empty bed, the independence, to being the sole decider of her own future and her children's. Death was part of life, after all, wasn't that what wisdom said? Death made room, closed some doors, opened others...

And now there was Mal Quarrels, standing beside her huge, glorified shed, impatiently waiting for her to join him, open the door, show him around—as though the space of a single evening's intimacy due to his rescue of her gave him the right to know her well enough to be impatient with her.

As though it gave him any rights at all.

"Grace." Sharp, concerned—as though this wasn't the first time he'd said her name to get her attention—with an underlying current of come-on-hurry-up-let's-see-what's-going-on excitement.

She looked at him, feeling spacey and confused, unlike herself. Funny, the tricks light played in how you saw things, because she thought he looked . . . worried about her. Personally, not distantly, the way a stranger might be. Odd, how some part of her felt as though she owed him an explanation to ease that anxiety. As if she'd known him forever, when she'd really only seen him around for the last few weeks and, before tonight, spoken with him only in passing, if at all.

In the course of a whole lifetime, two weeks and a night were akin to less than five minutes real time, and that was nothing, *nothing* on which to base an almost kiss—two almost kisses—and an increasing awareness that despite a life filled with children, family, pets, the home she'd always wanted, two jobs she was happy with and a multitude of irreplaceable friendships something was missing.

In the course of a lifetime, in less than five minutes, she hadn't realized that before tonight.

"Grace?" Gentler this time, Mal approached her, hand extended.

She took a deep breath, let it out slowly, eyed his hand, then ignored it. It was all in her imagination, pure and simple, time to get over it. He hadn't meant to almost kiss her; it was the moment, the atmosphere, the light, that was all. He was too sexy, she was too long without, she wasn't his type, and reaction to the whole long night was making her crazy, and tomorrow everything would be different.

That was all.

She told herself.

"Grace?" Mal stopped in front of her, lifted a finger to her chin, paused uncertainly, withdrew it without touching her. "It's late and you've had a rough night. We could wait and I can look things over in the morning."

She wiped suddenly sweaty palms on her shorts and shook her head, trying to figure out what had happened to make her lose her breath simply because he was near.

"I'm coming," she said, "but the door's locked. I'll have to get the key."

Chapter 6

She was going crazy.

Grace shoved her hair away from her face and laid her forehead on the steering wheel, trying not to scream. As days from hell went, this one wore the look of a classic. The sign over the Speedway gas pump read: Gas Sales Monitored. Failure to Pay Will Result in Prosecution.

It was a simple statement, really, a threat clear and succinct, and Grace was simply and succinctly considering throttling her eleven-and-a-half-year-old daughter as she attempted to explain the sign to her for the hundred and tenth time in five minutes. The child had an IQ of 164, but the things she professed not to understand were legion.

"But what does it mean?" Phoebe asked.

"It means don't steal gas or they'll send you to jail."

"But how do they know? What if you're not the one who stole the gas and they think you are?"

"They try to read license plate numbers."

"But what does that mean? How do they know?"

"I don't know." Flummoxed and annoyed, Grace glared at her daughter. In a few years, Phoebe would make an interesting sixteen-year-old—if Grace let her live that long. "Maybe they have a television camera recording gas sales. Maybe it's just a threat to make people think twice about stealing gas. I don't know. It says what it says and that's it."

"But *how?*" Phoebe insisted. "How..."

The rest of the question was lost in a sudden self-righteous roar from the way-back seat.

"Those are *my* school papers," ten-year-old Ethan shouted. "If I wanted you to see what my grades are, I'd hand 'em to you and say 'look at my grades, Dave.' But I don't want you to look at them, so give 'em back! Mom, David took my papers."

"No I didn't," David, almost thirteen, said. "They were on the floor. I just picked them up. You're not supposed to leave them on the floor of the car, is he, Mom? Make it look like a pigsty. I'm really glad I don't have to share a room with you anymore since we moved—"

The need to scream rose in Grace like an out-of-control freight train blasting full tilt toward the end of a track hanging over the edge of a high cliff. God above, no blasphemy intended, she hated the last day of school.

Dear Lord, why now? she pleaded. With all the other things *somebody* had dumped on her plate today, she really didn't need bickering children on top of it. Peace and quiet, a deserted isle, a thoughtful massage—a grandmother in desperate need of four grandchildren to brighten her weekend: that would be nice; she could use that. But this...

She shut her eyes tight and swallowed, breathed deep through her nose and out through her mouth, slowly, three times, trying to calm the raging pound of the blood in her temples. The bickering mouths behind her belonged to her children and, she reminded herself, she loved her children dearly and heaven help anyone who tried to hurt them.

Children behaved this way occasionally, it was part of sibling rivalry and growing up and the kind of day-to-day familial familiarity that bred contempt—not permanent hatred, only a temporary disdain for the people you spent too much time with. *She'd* behaved this way with her six older sisters. Her mother reminded her of that often enough, and look at how well the seven of them got along—now that they were all over thirty.

Oh, God, Grace thought with a silent groan. She glanced at eight-and-three-quarters-year-old Erin, her youngest, belted safely into the front seat beside her. Only twenty-three more years to wait.

She switched on the engine and pulled away from the gas pump.

"Did you pay, Mom?" Erin asked.

Grace stiffened her jaw against a surge of irritation. Love meant never reaming out your children for asking questions when you were the one who'd spent their formative years encouraging them to ask. "Yes."

"I didn't see you."

"I paid after I pumped the gas and before I got back into the car."

"Are you sure?"

"Yes, Erin, I'm sure," Grace said evenly. She eyed the bright red Miata that purred up to the speedway exit beside her, fondly recalling the little two-seater M.G. she'd once owned that had no room for children, dogs, sports equipment, bags of cement, a seven-child car pool or the trappings of a three-hundred-address weekend paper route. But that had been B.K., B.I. and B.S.: Before Kids, Before Insanity, and Before Suburban. The good old days. The tranquil and boring days. The days of self-indulgence and romance.

She sighed, watching the Miata gun its way left into the City of Pontiac-Waterford Township junction of Dixie-at-Telegraph traffic, then turned the battered seven-year-old Suburban right at a more sedate pace. No regrets, she thought, nothing I'd have done differently, no changes I'd make even if I'd known Phil was going to die. They'd had a little better than nine years; the old saw, some time is better than no time, proven again.

"Mom," Ethan called, "why do worms come out in the rain?"

"I don't remember, Eth."

"*Disney Adventures* magazine says it's because their homes get flooded out."

"Then that must be why," Grace agreed.

"But if that's why," David argued, "then why do night crawlers come out at night when there's only dew? Their homes aren't flooded out then, are they?"

"It's cooler then," Phoebe said in her most pedantic voice. "They don't get sidewalk fried when they mate in the dark."

"How would you know?"

"I read about it, that's how—"

Stopping on the red at the next intersection, Grace gritted her teeth and stretched her neck to ease the tension. If Phil were here now, she'd wring his neck for dying and leaving her alone to keep track of four kids without him.

The light turned green; only twenty more minutes and she'd have them home. Grace stepped on the gas and guided the glorified truck around the corner. The urge to speed to get them there quicker overtook her like a drowning woman's need for air. She breathed deep, trying to distill it.

When it comes to children, her oldest sister, Alice, always said, *show no weakness, or they'll trample you in a minute.*

Which was, Grace thought, if she remembered right, exactly why God told Noah to fill the ark by twos: because that's what parenting took—two to make them, two to raise them.

Sperm banks notwithstanding.

Which brought her right back to the crux of her current stressed-out insanity: Mal Quarrels.

God bless his well-built not-so-little hide.

She didn't know how it had happened. One moment yesterday morning she'd been a marginally sane adult in a world full of children. The next she'd become a hormone-fluxing adolescent-woman on the verge of a nervous breakdown with a far too sexy man now firmly ensconced in her unrenovated outbuilding—which, by the way, wasn't even ready for tenants—at his suggestion. John Roth's enthusiastic concurrence with Mal's plan and her children's subsequent vociferous invitation—bless their too-generous, pea-picking little hearts for deciding they liked him *immensely* despite the fact that they'd been under the impression only the night before that he was kidnapping their mother out of their garage—had only added to her frustration. Of course, Mal's offer to help them build a Swiss Family Robinson-style tree-fort this summer if they helped him work on his apartment their first week out of school hadn't stacked that part of the deck in his favor in the least, disloyal little turkeys.

And it was all in the name of, as Mal had put it, mutual convenience: he needed a place to live so he could get out from under his sister's overcrowded feet, and Grace needed someone to guard her rear defenses.

Her own sisters were in seventh heaven.

"Oo-ooh, Grace," Helen had singsonged last night at their monthly family simply-for-the-hell-of-it get-together. *"Bringing a man home just like Alice. Did you find him at the side of a road, too?"*

"No," Grace had snapped, *"I did not. He found me in a parking lot."*

"In a parking lot, Grace?" Meg, second oldest of her *much* older sisters, had raised her eyebrows and eyed her youngest sister down the insignificant length of her interfering little nose. *"Is there something you haven't told us?"*

"I don't think so," Grace had said evenly.

"Well, be sure to let us know if you do," Sam had suggested sweetly. Age and a husband suffering from the slings and arrows of an outrageous case of midlife I'm-bored-and-should-have-done-anything-else-with-my-life were doing nothing to temper her fifth eldest sister's perennially prickly nature.

"He's not living in the house with you, is he?" Edith, worried. She was fourth in line to Grace's oldest sister, Alice, beautiful, dark-haired and green-eyed—and a disaster-monger of the highest order.

"No," Grace had assured her. *"He moved into the shed this afternoon."*

"But I didn't think it was ready. You said you hadn't gotten far enough on it to use it as an income yet."

"It's not ready." Grace had stood on the deck eyeing the place where Mal was visible unloading a box of belongings from the back of his motorcycle. Even at that distance, the flex and bulge of his musculature under the weight was irritatingly evident—or perhaps it was simply her overactive something or other supplying the needed incentive to imagine the flex and bulge of his musculature—sent excitement and an intoxicating sense of danger scurrying across the tips of every nerve in her body. *"He said he'd pay a reduced rent and finish the work in exchange for board and an occasional ride to work."*

"Hmm."

Grace didn't like the sound of Twink's calculated speculation one bit. Twink was only five years older than her, but since the day Grace was born, Twink had seemed to feel that Grace's welfare—and upbringing—was every bit her responsibility. Undoubtedly came from having so many older sisters looking after her before Grace-the-baby came along.

"*So,*" her second to the last sister mused out loud, "*he'll be eating in the house with you all the time, two or three meals a day, getting to know you . . . How 'bout I take the kids next week so they don't scare him off, hmm? Give you time to—*"

"*Shut up,*" Grace said.

Twink grinned.

Alice, big sister—well, oldest, anyway, and probably the shortest except for Meg—had pulled Grace aside while the others were collecting their dish-to-pass dishes and their youngsters. As was undoubtedly the case in many families, the Brannigan girls, Alice in the past and Grace in particular at present, had a long herstory—not *his*tory, but *hers*—of doing less than wise things for heart-felt reasons. Painful as it was, there was an unspoken rule among them that it was up to the other sisters—in their best do-what-I-say-not-what-I-do fashion—to point out the possible pitfalls on the wayward sister's path.

No mention here of how they each preferred to walk to one side of the beaten path rather than on it. Or of how they were each better at giving advice than taking it.

"*Look, Gracie,*" Alice had said, clearly concerned, "*I know you're old enough to look after yourself, but what do you know about this guy? Where's he from and everything?*"

"*According to him, he's from South Dakota by way of Pontiac—laid-off cop. He grew up around Our Lady of Roses, Father Guillean knew him as a kid. He's been working at the center a little over three weeks. The dogs like him, the kids like him and John seems to trust him.*"

"*How do you feel about him?*"

Grace shrugged. *"I don't know. He helped me out of a bad situation—"*

"Don't confuse gratitude with sentiment."

"I'm not—I don't—"

"What if I have Gabriel check him out the way he did John?"

"I don't think I want to know as much about him as I know about John. Makes me feel dirty. Like I spied and I'm not even the one who did it."

"It's for your own protection."

"Is it, Allie?" Grace had eyed her sister, troubled. *"Sometimes I truly don't see how. I mean, you think you see things so clearly, but you don't. You see them just like everyone else—relative to where you're standing. I can't run my life on what you think you see happening to me."*

"Yeah, but you're so close to what's happening to you at any given moment that maybe what I see is more to the point—"

"True, but it's my point, isn't it, Allie? My life. And since when have you worried about not accepting people at face value, anyway? You're the one who taught me that people are who they pretend to be. I learned from you to accept first and judge later. I mean, you're the one who brought Gabriel home when you didn't know him from Adam. All Mal's done is try to help."

"Still," Alice had said dubiously.

And that, in a nutshell, was entirely the point, Grace thought, that dubious *still* where the baby of the family was concerned. Never mind what they practiced, they—her sisters, every single one of them, from Alice to Sam—expected Grace to do what they said, not what they did. Twink only expected Grace to be absolutely happy by the moment and damn the consequences.

Of course, Alice had an excuse for what she said and how she felt. It wasn't a good excuse, but it was more than the others had, anyway. Alice had lived with Gabriel too long not to have let some of that man's ex-federal-agent-groomed and naturally suspicious nature rub off on her. And Gabriel himself had lived too long as Grace's oldest and most overprotective brother-in-law not to be suspicious of anyone who came around the family baby. However old and mature she'd become. However many babies of her own she had.

Not to mention that Grace herself was sometimes still insecure enough in her own adulthood where her sisters were concerned so that she gave credence to their naysaying rather than trust herself.

Which was, she realized, a very bad habit. She grimaced. Why was it always so easy to get rid of good habits and so difficult to forgo the bad?

Sighing, she turned the Suburban into her driveway. She'd been sighing a lot lately, over a multitude of things, mostly over which she had no control, and not the least of which was Mal—

There was a sudden preverbal eruption from the back: David and Ethan, still buckled behind their shoulder harnesses, pounding each other. Only the first half day of summer vacation and already their confrontations were getting physical. Hadn't even had time to get tired of each other yet.

Boys, her sister Edith, who had one age twenty-three, said. Adolescent pack animals jockeying for supremacy, if this were the animal kingdom, or a wolf pack—which, in fact, at the moment, it was.

"Hey!" Grace shouted, stamping on the brakes and getting the boys' attention when their belts snapped tight, forcing them apart.

"He started it." David, leading off the accusations.

"I did not. You said—" Ethan, countering.

"Oh, baloney." David, interrupting with a punch to Ethan's shoulder. "You don't know what you're talking—"

Pound! Smack! Slap!

"That's enough!" Grace switched off the engine, popped her seat belt and jerked open her door in a motion, went around to the side door, crawled in across Erin who exited in a rush, and grabbed a hunk of boy's shirt-front in each hand, hauling them physically apart. She had no idea how she'd handle them when they were finally bigger, stronger and more coordinated than she. "I said *enough*."

"But, Mom, he—"

"Oh, I did not, you big baby."

"You did—"

"Stop it," Grace said. "What's with you two?"

"Mom, he keeps bugging me and I'm too old for him." David. "He's getting on my nerves. He follows me around and he keeps copying me and he won't leave me alone."

"Everything bugs you lately, Dave. That's no reason to hit your brother."

"Yeah but—"

"No buts. You're bigger, you're stronger and you're older. He's young and delicate and you don't hit."

"I'm not delicate." Ethan, indignant.

"Fine. You're shorter, younger and more wiry, and you don't hit, either."

"But he—"

"I don't care what *he*," Grace said firmly. "No hitting. No tattling. No fighting. Period."

"But he's got—"

David reached under Grace's arm, socked Ethan in the side. "She said she didn't want to hear about it, Eth. You better not—"

Ethan kicked him in the shin. "Stop punching me."

David kicked him back and the battle raged anew. "I told you—"

"Quit—"

"You—"

"I said—"

Grace tried to haul them apart again, but their adrenaline had kicked in and her arms were weakening. "Boys—"

"If you ever—I'll—"

"Yeah? You and what army—"

"David! Ethan—"

An arm closed around Grace's waist, hauled her bodily out of the truck and set her to one side.

"Hey!" she exclaimed, taken aback.

With a sidelong wink in her direction, Mal reached into the back of the Suburban and lugged first one Witoczynski son then the other out over the seat and stood them in the driveway in front of their mother. Instead of focusing on her, they stared the whole long way up at him, speechless.

At last, Grace thought dourly, dealing with her own surprise at Mal's sudden appearance, her own defensiveness that he should feel the need to step between her and the boys. Someone who commanded their complete and silent attention. Chalk one up for the well-met—and towering—stranger.

A fiendish albeit reluctant chortle tickled the back of her throat; she corralled it. And they'd been so anxious for Mal Quarrels to move in and take up at least a summer's residence at the periphery of their lives. She'd tried to tell them be careful what they wanted, but did they listen?

She glanced at Phoebe and Erin, hovering anxiously— and exultantly—in the background. Never let it be said that they didn't enjoy seeing their beloved brothers in trouble from time to time. Or getting them in trouble, as the case may be.

On the other hand, also let it be said that family loyalty ran deep and Phoebe and Erin would fight to the death anyone else who tried to get David and Ethan in trouble. But this wasn't one of those times.

"What's the beef?" Mal asked.

David and Ethan looked at him, at their mother, at each other and clamped their mouths tight.

"Must have been good," Mal suggested idly, "for you not to hear your mom tellin' you to quit."

"Wouldn't have to be," Phoebe commented.

Erin nodded. "More 'n likely it was something stupid."

Grace eyed them daggers. The "two puppy" theory, her grandmother Josephine called having four kids, two of each gender: they could each, boys or girls, cause twice as much trouble together as they could alone.

"Shut up, Erin." Ethan.

"Nobody asked you, Erin." David gave her a light shove, off-balancing her into Phoebe. Uncalled-for, but predictable.

Grace caught his arm before Mal could. She might have needed his defense in the parking lot, but she didn't need him to get between her and her kids.

"David," she warned.

Her number-one son sent her a troubled, rebellious, almost pleading glance, but subsided. She looked at him, wishing she could figure out what was bothering him so much recently. Wishing he could be happier, less restive, rebellious, needy, and of late so in tune with his own grievances that he was unable to recognize anyone else's when they reared up and bit him on the nose.

Wishing she didn't recognize in him so much of herself at his age.

David was having a hard time giving up Santa Claus, but was also endlessly cynical about other things. Like his mother, he wanted to believe in magic, clung to the hope of miracles with all his might. And like her, no matter how badly he wanted to, he didn't believe in real magic at all.

She glanced at Mal, at the children, wondering what to say, how to say it—and to whom—and what to do. Whether or not it was important to *do* anything right now. Wondering if she could let this slide and deal with it another time. Parents were supposed to automatically know how to handle everything, when to discipline, when to turn a blind eye—or so she'd always thought as a child.

Before she could decide, Gabriel, Tim and Rob—husbands to her sisters Alice, Meg and Twink respectively—rounded the side of the garage looking for Mal.

Ah, good, she thought irritably. Someone new to glare at.

Around her the children came alive, metamorphosing from clones of Mr. Hyde to the saintly Dr. Jekyll in less than a heartbeat. "Uncle Gabriel, Uncle Tim, Uncle Rob!" Breaking discipline formation, they rushed to greet their uncles, looking for their cousins. "What are you doing here? Where are—"

Beside her she felt Mal turn and stiffen warily, recognized his tension for what it was: under the guise of helping him work on the outbuilding and move in, her brothers-in-law had been checking him out—and it probably wasn't even at her sisters' behest. No, they'd probably come up with this plan all on their own. They'd done the same thing when she'd rented out the garage apartment to John. And just as probably, their darling wives were close by, fixing food for the laboring troops "the way women were supposed to do."

Not.

Grace shut her eyes and gritted her teeth. Great. Just great. As though she wasn't capable of wiping her nose by herself. Interfering biddies. Never let it be said that family wasn't there when you needed them least. Damn it.

She jerked a thumb from the kids to the house. "Go see if the aunts are inside and get washed up for lunch. We'll finish this later."

Off the hook, sentencing temporarily commuted, they raced to obey.

Grace looked at her brothers-in-law, turned to Mal, felt the flush that rose every time she got near him spread warmth and color through her belly, flash into her chest, send heat along her throat. Hoped nobody noticed. Realized with sighing despair they undoubtedly did. She nodded toward her sisters' husbands, doggedly biting back self-consciousness in favor of dignity.

"They bothering you?" she asked quietly.

Not as much as you bother me, Mal thought, looking her over for the first time today. The pink of the mild sunburn she'd gotten working at the plant nursery this morning spoke of health, looked good on her; the blush of awareness that darkened her eyes when she met his for an instant made his belly burn and his jeans feel tight. Had to address this thing, whatever it was, with her soon, but not now.

She moistened her lips, swallowed, sipped a wary, shallow, too-aware-of-him breath and the unexpected surge of blood and heat through regions south nearly did him in. God almighty merciful, not now.

He shook his head, attempting a smile. Felt more like a grimace. "No more'n I can handle."

She nodded. "Let me know."

His lips twitched in a grin both conspiratorial and wry; he sketched her a two-finger salute. "Yes, boss. You got it, boss."

She grinned at him, a quick, shy, unwittingly flirtatious curve of the mouth that did impossibly erotic things to him in his dreams and he felt his composure drift, felt himself, for the fraction of an instant, get lost in an illusion of what might be if circumstances were different.

Across the hood of the Suburban, Gabriel, Tim and Rob offered up knowing looks in their direction. They recognized the symptoms: another member of their gen-

der had bitten the dust at a Brannigan girl's feet and there
was no help for him now except to surrender—then try to
convince the Brannigan in question that it was okay to do
the same. But life was hardly ever so straightforward with
Brannigans, and so they sighed in sympathy, empathy,
knowing there was no way to forewarn and forearm.

Whether or not Mal Quarrels deserved their support as
concerned his obvious interest in their baby sister-in-law
remained to be seen.

For her part, Grace viewed them with disgust, recognizing the look—having seen it on her brothers-in-law and
potential brothers-in-law before—and considered the
possibility of flipping a rude gesture at them. Discarded
the idea when they grinned at her all innocence, clearly
waiting for it. Stubbornly, she tilted her chin skyward and
issued the single clipped order "Lunch." Then she turned
her back on them and headed for the house.

With a hackle-raising premonition of misgiving, Mal
watched her go, uncharacteristically uncomfortable with
the role he'd chosen to represent in her life, for the first
time in recent years uneasy inside his own skin.

Troubled by the absence of Gus Abernathy—on whom
he knew he should be concentrating and wasn't—since the
night he'd spent on Abernathy's couch and wound up
helping Grace chase off her prowler.

Troubled by the look her brother-in-law, Gabriel Book,
gave him: tough, cynical, knowing—unconvinced.

An I've-got-your-number-and-I'll-use-it-if-you-screw-
up look.

Mal eyed him. Although a good twelve to fifteen years
younger than the bureau's legendary Gabriel Lucas Book,
Mal knew the man well by reputation. They'd also wound
up like ships passing on a couple of undercovers during
Mal's early years in law enforcement before Book had left
the bureau after fifteen years of deep cover. He'd come
out, some said, a shadow of himself, soiled if not dirt-

ied—a man who'd lived closely enough with monsters to have taken on a few of their characteristics.

At about the same time that Book left the FBI, Mal had transferred—at Livvi's insistence—to the reputedly safer Marshal's Service and had begun escorting prisoners, protecting witnesses and a few other things with the service's Special Operations Group that made Livvi too uncomfortable to stay with him, have Jennifer around him.

Be careful what you ask for, he'd told her at the time. But she'd thought she knew better.

Keep your guard up, he thought now. Only thing you're here to do is kick ass and take names. That's the way it works.

Yeah, right up to the moment it didn't anymore. Until someone like Book intervened in the name of protecting his sister-in-law.

But then, Grace Witoczynski being the sister-in-law in question, who could blame him?

Apparently oblivious to the tension between their wives' brother-in-law and their youngest sister-in-law's newest tenant, Rob and Tim headed for the house.

Deliberately lagging behind, Book smiled at Mal, a challenge, a warning—or was that Mal's imagination?

"Guess we should go in," Gabriel said, and motioned Mal ahead of him.

Mal shook his head, waved a too-polite hand toward the door. "You first."

"Oh, no," Book returned, guise of politeness wearing thin. "I insist. After you."

Mal's lips thinned grimly, but he acquiesced. Oh, hell yes. If he wasn't real careful, Gabriel Lucas Book could become a major-league problem.

Chapter 7

They stayed through dinner "to help him get settled," they said, to finish the renovations on his new abode, to "make him feel at home."

They stayed through dinner, he thought, to "get to know him," "check him out," judge whether or not he was a fit person to leave unguarded around their little sister-in-law and her children.

Mal twirled fetuccini around his fork and watched them gathered, laughing and teasing, around the big dining-room table where two nights ago he'd sat while Grace attended his nose, and he knew, truthfully, it was both: the chaos felt uncomfortably like home, and he was being inspected.

"Mal, Grace says you're a laid-off cop?" Gabriel, probing. "Where from?"

"Murdo, South Dakota."

"Long way from Pontiac."

"Mmm."

"I was out that direction a while back—"

"Years," Alice supplied pointedly.

Gabriel ignored her, attention on Mal. "Who'd you work with? Maybe I know 'em and can pull some strings, get you back to work—"

"*Gabriel.*" Alice, warning.

"So, Mal." Segue to Meg, sliding smoothly into the breach. "Is that your name? Mal, *M-A-L,* not Mel, *M-E-L?* Grace said I pronounced it wrong before."

"It's Mal."

"Is it?" Meg took a dainty bite of garlic toast. "Mal," she mused aloud. "That's different. Is it Native American?"

Mortified, Grace rolled her eyes at Mal: *You don't have to put up with this.* Ms. Mary Margaret Brannigan-Wheaton was always her most politically correct while being her most tactless.

Mal gave her a *don't sweat it* shrug, turned to Meg. "It's really Malcolm. My mother's step-grandfather came over from Scotland."

"You don't look Scottish." Twink, elbow on the table, chin in her palm, not accusing, simply interested. "Well, maybe around the ears—what I can see of 'em—in a sort of uncivilized way. Of course, there were Druids and Celts in Scotland at some point, weren't there? And the Celts, at least, were kind of barbaric—"

"That's it." Grace rose from the table, snatched Twink's plate out from under her fork and headed for the kitchen.

"Grace, what's wrong?" Twink, genuinely astonished by her youngest sister's lack of etiquette, swung around in her chair to stare at Grace.

Grace plopped Twink's plate on the counter, turned and glared at her. "I've had enough of you guys dissecting my non-family guests in my house like they were squashed onto a microscope slide or sitting in some petri dish instead of at my dinner table just because they're men. Any man who's been married to a Brannigan can tell you that it's the females in this family who are the deadlier of the species, so why you can't trust me to pick my own tenants regardless of their sex is beyond me.''

"But we do—"

"Bull," Grace snapped. She gestured at Alice's husband who was surreptitiously using a paper napkin to slide a stainless-steel dinner knife off the table. "Look at Gabriel trying to steal Mal's knife so he can take it someplace and check out the fingerprints."

As directed, they all looked.

Gabriel reddened. "I—" he said and stopped, unwilling and unable to deny the obvious. But he didn't put down the knife.

"Leave it," Grace told him. Reluctantly, Gabriel set the flatware on the table. "Honest to John, you're behaving the way that stupid dog—" she pointed at the wiry-haired yellow miniature wolfhound-looking mutt snoring heavily beneath the table, body pillowed across Mal's feet "—usually acts. Only this time, the dog likes him—" she waved a hand at Mal "—and he hasn't been wrong yet, so why—"

"Grace," Mal said gently.

She looked at him. Heavens to mercy, he had the most gorgeous eyes she'd ever seen on a man: thick-lashed, aeons deep and blacker than ink. A woman could get lost in them and never care whether she found her way out again or not.

Not that that was here or there at the moment. "What?"

"It's all right."

It was as though everyone else ceased to be, as though only the two of them were left in the room, their concentration on each other was so absolute.

"No, it's not." Her eyes on his face; his eyes on hers. No one else existed outside of them.

"Trust me, it is. My family does the same thing. Let it be."

"I'm tired of being treated like an infant." She didn't mean to sound whiny, but exhaustion had caught up with her. Sleep had been a hard enough taskmaster of late, what with the prowler situation and David's mood swings to figure out, and all, without adding to the mix lying awake at night imagining...well, the *sinful* things she'd like to do with Mal Quarrels. "I'm sorry, that sounds—"

"Honest."

"—like a two-year-old."

"Most grown-up two-year-old I've ever met."

He breathed. She breathed. Eyes—hazel and black— connected, exchanging a meaning, awareness, intimacy and knowledge that their minds fought.

And lost.

Outside the cocoon around them, someone cleared his throat. Someone else started talking—Meg, Alice, Twink, Grace couldn't even differentiate between her sisters' voices at the moment. A chair rubbed across hardwood, knives, forks, spoons clashed with dinnerware. Twink retrieved her plate from the kitchen, someone else passed the salad; the lull in the dinner conversation subsided, filled by family trying hard not to recognize something Mal and Grace would have denied. The sliding screen door to the deck where the children ate at the picnic table groaned open.

"Mom, can Rachel and Pris spend the night so we can stay up late and do a fire in the fire pit and tell ghost stories and roast marshmallows?"

"Mom, can Chris, Nathan, Ben and Jonah stay, too?"

"*May* they stay." The response was automatic, a spell irritatingly, needfully broken. Too much, too soon—especially when never would have been time enough.

Couldn't feel this way, she thought, dragging her attention out of the enchanted void. She could almost feel the vacuum *pop* when her eyes unlocked from Mal's. Couldn't.

Wouldn't.

"No, Mom." Phoebe said, correcting. "Can, can, *can.* Will you and Aunt Meg and Aunt Alice and Aunt Twink *let* them. *Can* they stay, are they able to, will you *allow* it?"

"For the weekend, Mom." Ethan, bargaining. "Get a good start on the summer."

"Keep us out of your hair." David, sweetening the deal. "So we won't be bored."

"The summer hasn't even started and you're already worried about being bored?" Why didn't Mal stop looking at her? Why couldn't she stop feeling his eyes on her? Why did it please her to have him looking at her like she was the rarest thing in the world? Whatever "rarest" meant. Rarest idiot. Rarest most hideous thing. Rarest hunka-hunka burnin' love.

No, that was him.

Oh, Lord, she'd lost it completely. Why could a certain look in a man's eyes reduce a reasonably mature woman to juvenile hormonal shreds in a heartbeat?

Ah, yes. Heartbeat, that was the answer. Bang, bang, bang. *Slow down,* she advised her thrumming pulse. *Take care.*

"Please, Mom." Erin at her most sweetly, youngest child-ly ingratiating.

"Please what?" She couldn't remember what they'd been talking about.

"Mom." Exasperated. Who could blame them? "May we please have everybody spend the weekend."

"Fine." Grace nodded, blinking, not entirely sure what she'd agreed to. Still, anything to distract them long enough so she could get a handle on this thing jumping up and down in her pulse. Anything to fill up the house with noise and distract her from thinking these things she was feeling. Anything to keep her from falling prey to her hormones, should the opportunity arise.

And long-past experience warned her that if she didn't guard her hormones with her life, they'd not only find the opportunity, but create it—without first consulting her about wisdom or her druthers.

Funny, the things children were good for. Especially when she'd spent a goodly portion of her marriage arranging kid exchanges with her sisters on weekends so they and their husbands—she and her husband—could fall prey to their hormones in peace.

Around the table her sisters exchanged knowing glances. Their husbands took immediate advantage of the situation and said yes to their children visiting Aunt Grace for the weekend.

Then they left.

Hurriedly.

Before the cleanup.

Amid whispered exchanges of stopping off for champagne and strawberries and seeing Grace sometime Monday morning instead of Sunday night.

Before Grace came to her senses and changed her mind.

With a strong sense of misgiving, Grace looked at Mal, who still seemed a tad stunned by something only he could define—or not—and waved goodbye.

It promised to be a long weekend.

He helped her clear the tables, rinse and stack the dishes, load the dishwasher and sweep the floors after the dogs took care of their part of the after-dinner crumb cleanup.

Normally, *Afterdinner* was the children's domain, but tonight was special: they had company and she needed to work out what was ailing her, rinse it clean with dish suds, pine cleaner and a vigorously wielded broom.

To no avail.

He helped because it was the polite thing—the right thing—to do. And because his mother had taught him, macho man or no, to always do what was polite, right. He'd grown up long ago, but he was still his mother's son, a product of his upbringing and the lessons of his youth.

He also helped because he needed to be near Grace and that bothered him the way nothing had in a very long time.

Something had happened to him during their exchange at dinner. Something gut-deep and wrenching, nerve-deep and painful—something that squeezed the breath out of him, life into him, sucker-punched his senses.

She bowled him over, struck him dumb, left him unable to think. He was a Marshal In Pursuit, and she was a Mom With Kids. He had no business dreaming of her, wanting her, and he knew it. His head knew it. Logic knew it.

But his heart, soul and body knew something else.

He was afraid of being betrayed by what they knew.

He hoped that betrayal was inevitable.

They were, neither of them, used to thinking about anything with such exasperating solemnity when a sense of humor would have sufficed.

The sound of children's voices erupted from the living room, laughing, arguing. Someone plunked a record on the stereo; amid gleeful shouts of "Wait, listen, this is what my mom and dad used to dance to," the strains of Three Dog Night singing "Jeremiah was a Bullfrog-Joy to the World" could be heard. Grace's fingers twitched around the broom handle, her feet itched, her body pleaded to sway, the words bounced into the back of her throat pestering to be belted out.

She'd been little more than a toddler the first time she'd heard this piece and her sisters still laughed about how she used to start to sing, wiggle-butt and twirl every time they played it—on purpose so she would, of course. It was an embarrassing memory, one she wouldn't like shared with, say, Mal, for example, but the music was still impossible to resist. Without invitation, the broom started to sweep in time to the beat, her feet and hips took up the rhythm, the words slid out under her breath.

"If I was the queen of the world..."

"'If I *were,*'" Mal corrected, his own body not unaffected by the music—which surprised him, because he didn't dance. He never danced. He hadn't danced, except at the occasional annual tribal gathering, since he was seventeen when, in order to get into Livvi's pants, it had almost been required. "And it's 'king,' not 'queen.'"

"Maybe for you," Grace sang, dancing out to the kitchen sink to grab the dishrag and toss it to him. "But there's no percentage in a woman wanting to be king, so why sing it? Queens are better, anyway. Table," she said in between song phrases, swaying past him. "Needs to be wiped."

He caught her about the waist, startling her and shocking himself, swung her into dance steps he wasn't even aware he knew. She stiffened then relaxed in his arms, snagged in the moment, enjoying herself.

He was big, square-built, solid; an immovable wall forming to fit her, laughing down at her, light on his feet—and hers. She knew if she stayed where she was, she wouldn't want to leave.

She didn't pull away.

She wasn't tiny, but his size made nearly two of her, yet she fit him, slipped easily into the crook of his arm as though born to be there. Her eyes were vividly green at the moment, bright and warm on him, liquid with laughter. He knew if he didn't let her go, he'd be in trouble.

He held on.

Curiosity did, indeed, burn the cat.

The music changed and slowed. Smokey Robinson and the Miracles singing "The Tracks of My Tears." Old songs, easy to dance to.

Easy to get caught up in.

He pulled her closer than he should have, drew her into the steps, against his chest. Her hair smelled of sunshine, shampoo and spaghetti, homey and oddly seductive; her face was warm and tangy with the scent of summer and cooking and woman when he ducked his cheek near her shoulder. Her laughter brushed his mouth, breath teased his ear; her breasts rose and fell against his chest. He could feel the rhythm of her heart tattooing his, changing his tempo to match hers.

His gut sank and twisted, pulse pounded, jeans grew painfully small.

His hold on her tightened, greedy. He made a half-hearted grab for his emotions, but they evaded him and suddenly he was no longer in charge of them, no longer keeper of his soul. She was.

A fast twirl, out of step with the music yet somehow at one with it, brought his thigh between hers.

Contact.

Laughter stilled.

He watched her eyes widen, darken, catch fire, then grow wary—all in the space of a breath. He saw her think about it, but she made no move to pull away. And he didn't let her go.

She belonged right where she was. He knew it. She knew it.

Her eyes denied it.

His swore up and down it wasn't so.

But it was.

Her arms slipped higher around his shoulders, hands slid beneath his hair, firmed at the back of his neck. Her cheek fit neatly into his shoulder, his settled lightly along the back of her head.

They danced.

Again the music changed. More sixties Motown weaving summer evening spells: Percy Sledge, "When a Man Loves a Woman."

In the distance there were children, their voices raucous, argumentative, teasing, laughing. Grace heard them only vaguely, lost on the periphery of her senses, as though they belonged to someone else. It had been forever since they hadn't come first, forever since she'd felt like this.

She'd never felt like this.

I'm sorry, Phil.

Hunger, deep and fierce, gnawing at her bones. Pleasure, sweet and lingering, full of anticipation. Languor and vitality, serenity and fear—quixotic emotions, lost and found in the utopia of a moment, in the penetration of long-forgotten senses, in the uneasy sensation of coming home.

His skin was warm to her touch, smooth and male, gloriously different from hers. Her fingertips reveled in the feel.

He smelled of hard work and masculinity, spicy, foreign to her senses, sexy. She breathed him in, let him wash through her lungs, tasting his scent in the back of her throat, relishing the flavor.

His hair was heavy silk over her arms, on the backs of her hands, a curious, unfamiliar but not unpleasant weight—something she could easily get used to. She moved restive fingers, felt the strands slide through, thick and glossy, wondered dreamily what his hair would feel like splayed across her bare breasts, brushed over her nipples, tickling her thighs. So rich, so silky, so...

Erotic.

Her breath caught, belly warmed, breasts tingled with suggestion, imagination. Her fingers tightened in his hair. Want, simple and complex, nipped through her pulse, spread wanton channels along her nerves, fluttered in her lungs. She had children, she was a grown-up, she should be beyond indulging in high school fantasies during a single dance—however impromptu. However momentary.

But she wanted to.

She breathed deep and let the music do its work and indulged, snugging herself deeper into Mal's embrace, Mal's presence.

Mal's body, hip to hip, belly to belly, breast to chest with hers.

Of their own volition, his arms contracted around her, hands slid down her back to her hips and lower, pulling her against him, trapping her safe inside the halls of danger. His lips brushed the back of her head, grazed down, parted and moist to her nape, supped gently.

A soft sound got away from her: pleasure.

His tongue slipped past his teeth, traced errant patterns toward her ear. Awareness buzzed through her, made hungry, stabbing forays into her breasts, her belly, between her thighs.

Again that soft sound escaped, more urgent this time; his mouth became more reckless, tongue more rapacious, hands more bold, cupping her buttocks, pulling her tight against the aching hardness behind his zipper. Lost in the music, the spell, the moment, she arched her neck into his mouth, turned her face slowly toward his.

His cheek was hot against hers, his mouth voracious and inviting. She wanted it on hers, now, this instant, without further ado, wanted thoughtlessness and total sensual devastation and plunder.

His.

And hers.

He wanted it, too. Here and now. There and then. Whenever and wherever, so long as immediately was involved.

So long as Grace was involved.

Close but no cigar.

There was a sudden, spine-chilling, music-ending nails-on-blackboard screech of a diamond needle ruining vinyl, then the spell-breaking crash of whooping, hollering children through the dining room and out the deck door.

"C'mon, Mom, John's back, time to start the fire!"

Blinking, muzzy, they came back from the place of no tomorrows into the reality of day's end still meshed fast together, thigh and hip, belly and loin—dirty dancing blatantly symbolic of other joinings, not-so-hidden desires.

"Oh, my God," Grace said.

Mal's expletive was far more self-directed and far less polite.

Grace shoved a disbelieving hand through her hair. "Oh, my God," she repeated.

Mal sagged against the dining-room wall and cursed himself straight to the point.

Grace made incredulous you-me-we motions with her hands. "Did we just, almost—"

Mal shoved hair out of his face, rubbed his jaw. "Oh, yeah."

"You mean, I—you—we?" Grace's hands worked.

"Oh, yeah." Mal nodded. "Any time now."

"Oh, my God." Grace grabbed hair in her hands, looked at the living room, the deck, Mal. "With the kids right there and—"

"Yeah." Mal nodded, flabbergasted. It was all he could do. "Right here, right now, with witnesses and everything."

"Oh my Go—"

"Don't say it."

"What am I doing?" She punched the heel of her hand at her forehead. "What was I thinking? God, I can't believe what I did."

Mal shook his head. "Me, neither."

"I mean—" Grace looked at him. "No offense, but what do I know about you? You could be diseased—"

"I had a physical three weeks ago. I'm not diseased."

"And for all you know, *I* could be diseased—"

"You give blood every eight weeks. You're not diseased, either."

"And the kids—" She stopped suddenly, attention arrested. Turned. Looked hard at him. "What do you mean, 'you give blood every eight weeks so you're not diseased, either'? That's my private business and we don't know each other anywhere near well enough for me to share that kind of personal stuff with you, so how would you know?"

Oh, hell, he'd screwed up now. *Think, zipper for brains. How do you know?* Had it. "Parish blood drive." Thank you, God. "Two weeks ago. I was behind you at the check in tables when they asked when was the last time you gave."

She gave him withering scorn. "In case you hadn't noticed, you're hard to miss. I think I'd remember if you'd been anywhere near me at the time. They'd have had to wash me out because my blood pressure would've been too high for them to siphon blood from me that day."

He grinned and relaxed abruptly, charmed. "Really?"

"You—" She stared at him, mouth working, at a loss for words. "This doesn't bother you at all, does it?"

"Well, truthfully, not as much as it did before you told me what I do to your blood pressure. Some, but not as much. Being out of control bothers me, but not the actual event itself." He shrugged. "Actually, I kind of enjoyed that." He considered it a moment, decided on honesty. "A lot."

"You are truly some blessed piece of God-turned work."

He scratched his ear, ducked his chin modestly. "So they tell me."

"I can't believe this." She tossed her hands in a gesture of frustration. "You know what? You don't need me for this conversation. You can have it all by yourself. I don't need me for this conversation because you know what? It didn't happen. None of it. We didn't dance, we didn't *almost,* there were no children, there is no me. I'm a figment of my own imagination and this fantasy is getting out of hand. I'm out of here. See ya."

It was only three strides to the deck door, but she didn't take them fast enough. Mal was behind her, pulling her back around, all at once dead serious.

He looked down at her face, the unprotected eyes, generous mouth, revealing features that haunted his dreams. He was using her, lying to her, living on her land to serve his own ends—guard her and her kids, yes, to serve his conscience while he kept an eye on Gus Abernathy as Dunne-bait, but using her, nonetheless. His sensibilities and libido were tangled up in her. The lines between who he was and who he pretended to be were blurring—because of her—and that was dangerous to both of them, all of them. He owed her a warning.

But one warning was all he had in him. After that, they were each on their own.

"It happened, Grace," he said quietly. "Three times, almost, since the night before last, before we knew each other at all. Don't turn your back on it or it'll happen again. Don't let it sneak up on you. I want you, you want me, but this is not what I'm here for, it's not what you need. It's not what you deserve. I'm a big-time flash in the pan—just ask my ex-wife—and there are sparks between us. Wouldn't take much to start a fire that'd burn everybody—you, your kids, me—so don't bury your head in the sand and pretend *It* didn't or *It* won't. It did happen. It will."

He touched two fingers to her cheek, looked out at the yard, the dogs, the children and Gus Abernathy piling wood into the fire pit for a bonfire. Brought his gaze back to her. Helpless. Vulnerable. Despairing. "God help me, Grace. I want it to happen. With you."

Then he was gone, out the door, off the deck, across the yard with the children: laughing, teasing, accepting the hatchet from John Roth. Splitting kindling with quick, powerful strokes that rang in Grace's blood. Handing the hatchet to Ethan and showing him how to wield it safely, properly.

The way any father might.

The sting of some nameless thing started behind Grace's breastbone; she covered her mouth with a hand. Confusion...heartache... Hope. No, God, it was too soon, she couldn't be seeing what she thought she saw. It was only the light, the emotions of the moment, the way she was looking at him, what she wanted from him. She didn't know him, she was looking for excuses for her behavior, for the way she felt, for the things she wanted. It wasn't rational. It wasn't right. In fact, it was damned stupid.

And not only that, he was hiding something from her, to boot.

She swallowed, eyes on Mal. Oh, he thought he'd distracted her with that charming Mr. Arrogant act, then with his candor and vulnerability—and he had—but she was a mother, and being distracted wasn't the same thing as forgetting that someone had managed to sidestep a question she wanted answered. It only postponed the inevitable answer.

The way, she realized with a sinking certainty, anticipation, fear, that the other things he thought abandoned had only been postponed.

Temporarily.

Lord above, she thought bleakly, she had impressionable kids, she couldn't behave the way Mal made her want to behave. She should ask him to move out, rescind his meal privileges, avoid him at all costs. Because, God help her, no matter who he turned out to be underneath all that sidestepping, no matter what he was hiding...what he wanted to happen between them?

She wanted it, too.

Chapter 8

The days moved forward with tantalizing slowness, filled with eyes across the parcel of acres, across children at the breakfast table, dinner table, through her office door.

Angus Abernathy—aka Grace's good friend, John Roth—unwitting catalyst to these events, number one on William Dunne's hit parade and Mal Quarrels's "to do" list, became a bystander in the plot of William Dunne's making, of mere cursory interest to Mal who'd begun to have trouble remembering his own name when he was in proximity to Grace.

He couldn't get enough of being near her, found himself manufacturing reasons to delay heading back across the field to his apartment every night. Helping the kids with the dishes. Walking around the neighborhood with Grace by his own invitation "to get an idea of where he was living," while the kids rode their bikes in circles around them in the road, Rollerbladed with hockey sticks and tennis balls, practicing puck control and feints. Building birdhouses and bird feeders with her, Abernathy and the kids. Doing things, he told himself, not just to be near her, but because it was his self-appointed job to stick tight so he could better watch over her and the kids—and Abernathy.

Found himself relaxing and enjoying himself with her, laughing at her dry views of an increasingly absurd and demented world.

Found himself growing hungrier for a taste of her by the day. If they'd ever wound up alone together, he didn't know what might happen, knew what he dreamed. Knew he was glad that the opportunity to have to resist the temptation she presented didn't arise.

Didn't think he'd have been able to resist temptation no matter how hard he tried.

Not a healthy state of affairs by any stretch of the imagination.

But even in the midst of personal confusion, the urgent, uneasy sense of time running out for all of them lay constantly at the back of his mind.

There'd been no further prowler incidents—largely because of his presence in the old barn, Mal had no doubt. Still, there was something…a sensation of being watched, of something he'd overlooked, of something…

Indefinable.

He knew Book was nosing around, checking him out, but Book didn't bother him—yet. He'd assuredly wind up paying for Book's questions at some point, but that would be then. This was now and he couldn't worry about *might be's* with so many more immediate concerns on his mind.

No, whatever nagged his subconscious was something far more sinister, dangerous. He had a feeling…

Ah, screw it, he had a feeling. Period. Whatever it was, he couldn't identify it—he hated that. Good visceral instincts were his bread and butter, but when the hunch was only a vague gnawing in his gut, he had a tendency to wonder if he shouldn't simply pack in his badge and invest in a crystal ball, for all the good they did him.

The other thing that bothered him was that he'd begun to like and respect Gus Abernathy, to find Grace's attitude toward Gus as John Roth contagious. He wanted to trust the man because she did, and because the man who watched over the books for so many local nonprofit human-services organizations for an almost nonexistent salary seemed to be trustworthy—a far cry from the agent who'd bent under the pressure of having to bear the financial burden of a dying parent and had embezzled money from the mob during an undercover operation three years ago.

It bothered Mal that Abernathy was unwittingly being used as bait at the end of a line he dangled. It would certainly ease his conscience to tell Abernathy what was going on and enlist the former agent in catching Dunne. From all reports, Abernathy had been a crackerjack "sting" operative—but all Mal had to go on in that regard was Abernathy's past performances when the going got tough: Abernathy disappeared. Mal couldn't afford to lose him and, in consequence, Dunne, again. Too much depended on Dunne going down. Lives, jobs, reputations.

Grace.

Damn, doing his job was one helluva lot easier when the people he dealt with had no redeeming features.

Mal sighed. His job, he reminded himself, was to keep his distance. His career was to *be* involved, but not to *get* involved.

Without involvement, his whole life was in question.

Which brought him back to Grace.

He hoisted a case of canned peas out of the back of Our Lady of Roses' pickup and headed into the center to pile it with the other grocery cases in the hall outside Grace's office. Her door was open. Inside she stood with her back to him, chatting animatedly while she packed a couple of grocery bags full of nonperishable foodstuffs, formula, baby food and diapers for a stringy-haired, overweight woman with a baby on one hip and a dirty-faced toddler clinging to her oversize T-shirt.

He witnessed this scenario played out in the center anywhere from six to twenty-five times a week and Grace's nonjudgmental matter-of-fact handling of the people who came asking for help never ceased to amaze him. *He'd* want to ask them why they didn't do something to better their situation, help themselves. *He'd* want to preach something about available programs, ways out of the pits, see evidence of industry, job applications, demand family counseling, drug rehab—anything to ensure the children he saw come through here wouldn't end up inheriting and perpetuating an overburdened welfare system simply because it was all they knew how to do. He'd want to see immediate commitment to change, current progress, reasonable growth. Grace asked for nothing, offered only example, gentle guidance toward some of the city's self-realization and transitional housing programs, encouragement and support.

Who she was disturbed him more by the minute.

He knew he had to address this thing that shouldn't exist between them. Knew that if he did address it, there was no guarantee he'd be any more useful in his quest to stop William Dunne from killing again than he was now. Knew with every passing day how much more he stood to lose if he addressed it and discovered Grace was not as absorbed as he in the longing of eyes that had begun somehow to ensnare his heart, become essential to his laughter, his being.

He was not a man who had ever in his life sidestepped trouble, but he found himself sidestepping double time every twist in his heart, every sinking in his gut, hardening of his loins, roar of his pulse that occurred when he was momentarily alone with Grace—and it was never more than a moment, big families being what they were—when their physical paths crossed and some grazing touch occurred.

He could feel her in the sun burning on his skin, in the sweat of the summer, in the all-engrossing sear of desire that invaded his dreams and threatened his sleep, his awake. She was a blister rubbing him raw behind his zipper, a hole opening in his soul; the harder he tried to ignore the symptoms of his impending overthrow, the worse they grew.

She made him hot—scorched his shorts—pure and simple. Only, the way he felt was anything but pure and the tangle of encroaching emotions was a helluva lot more complex than simple.

In short, he was one sorry excuse for a wedlock-born bastard and he knew it.

But the up side was, he was too distracted to remember he hadn't smoked a cigarette in thirty-seven hours, fifty-six minutes and eighteen seconds.

Nineteen . . . twenty . . . twenty-one. . . .

Across the field from him, Grace had her own mind-boggling heart-thumping distractions to deal with—and all of them were named Mal.

At twenty-one, not quite out of college, she'd leaped into life and her own perfect romance-novel into-the-sunset marriage, absolutely certain of her own—and Phil's—invincibility. Nothing frightened her. Not four kids in six years, not the cost of raising and educating them, nor the daunting fact that every time she thought she'd finally juggled the family budget to make ends meet, it seemed as if somebody moved the ends. Not the debt of an out-of-their-price-range house, or monstrous insurance, grocery and utility bills, increased taxes, or constant veterinary visits to care for the unending parade of stray and injured animals who found the path to their door—and used it—and stayed. But Phil had been alive to help cope with things then. That had made all the difference in the world.

Phil's two-year battle with cancer had changed everything. Almost overnight, experience made the big things she used to blithely take for granted scare her, made the tiny details that used to make her nervous old hat. Moments became too precious to waste, hours too long to think about all at once.

Time, of course, had allowed her—all of them—to grow used to living with Phil's approaching death. Long hospital stays prepared them for what it would be like to not have Daddy at home anymore, taught the children what it was like to have one parent trying to do the work of two. Taught them what to expect—and not expect—in terms of parent participation in their lives and how expectations could be dashed if they pinned too much hope on singular demands.

David and Phoebe had learned young how to care for their younger siblings, how to cook and help clean and who to call and what to say if Daddy had emergencies in the middle of the night. Ethan and Erin had learned at an incredibly young age that they were each responsible for their own behavior, no one else, and that Daddy being sick meant that Mama couldn't always be where they needed or wanted her to be. All four children had learned early to be self-sufficient and independent, how to depend on one another—and how to close ranks against well-meaning outsiders when the need arose. How to be open and accepting and generous with themselves and their hearts when they could have learned how not to trust anyone with their hearts or their emotions again.

Grace credited close family ties—her sisters, their husbands and children, her mother, in-laws and a wealth of... colorful and, mildly put, eccentric but always loving relatives—for abetting her children's adjustment to life after Phil. As for herself . . .

She'd grown up a lot in the last ten or twelve years, but especially in the three since Phil had died, learned how to complicate her life in new and interesting ways. Learned never to assume anything, never to challenge "worse," because just when it became obvious that things couldn't get worse, they always did.

She'd never allowed people too close easily. She appeared open and outgoing, big-hearted and hospitable, but it was a front, a cover to hide the fact that she never let people nearer to her private self than the most available exit, rarely let anyone in farther than the front door. She kept her lives separate: work was work, family was family and never the twain shall meet. There were people she knew she could count on if the need arose, but she counted on other people as infrequently as possible, preferring a kind of autonomy to the investment of heart, soul and energy necessary to maintain two-way relationships. She was adept at being an all-weather friend, but unskilled at accepting all-weather friendship in return, preferring to retreat and close ranks than to share burdens she erroneously felt were better borne alone.

Her reaction to Mal, the desires he evoked—both physical and emotional—stunned the socks off her. She had no idea how to handle her feelings for, about, him— although she handled him well enough. But the key to that was simple: flippancy kept people at a distance, she'd learned that a long time ago. Give better than you got, but no less than you expected in return. If you didn't appear to take yourself seriously, other people wouldn't either. If you didn't let them see how you felt, chances were you wouldn't be forced to deal with your sentiments in front of them.

But he was getting close. She was letting him near. Couldn't seem to help herself. Couldn't seem to avoid it.

He confused her. He made her laugh. He liked the kids for just themselves—she hadn't figured that one out yet, but she would. He tortured her libido. Three nights ago it had been that dance, the unnamed "almost" that kept her awake and followed her to sleep and woke her up wringing wet and aching, sent her to look wistfully across the yard at his windows, tempted, wanting.

When she'd finally gotten up the nerve and the time and gone down to the police station to file a report on the assault in Our Lady's parking lot, he'd dropped what he was doing and gone with her, "as a witness who could give a description of the perp"—and he'd done that. But what he'd really done—both literally and figuratively, and despite his own apparent discomfort at having to give his name and address to the officer who took her report—was hold her hand, bolster her ego, her nervous system, make her feel as though she wasn't in this—or anything else—alone.

Dangerous sensation, that.

With Mal's description, it hadn't taken the police long to find her mugger. When they did, it was Mal who drove her down to the lineup, who identified the suspect when she wasn't sure, signed the complaint and drove her home—after stopping first because he "wanted a piece of pie." Then he'd bought her a cup of tea and slid into the booth beside her, telling her not to worry, she'd done what she had to do, the courts had it now and he'd do his best to make sure they kept this guy jailed until the whole thing was finished.

Offering her simple closeness while she gathered her shaking insides together enough so neither her co-workers nor her kids would ever guess how difficult it had been for her to face that man again—however anonymous she'd been—through the two-way glass.

She owed him more than she cared to admit or he'd accept for that.

Last night it was Mal, Phoebe and Erin sitting on the deck energetically discussing nothing in particular over tall glasses of milk and those damned Double-Stuf Oreos. The girls were showing Mal how to eat their favorite cookies properly by unscrewing them and lifting out the cream in order to eat the chocolate pieces first, the filling last. Mal had countered by instructing them in his version of the proper eating of Oreos, which was to leave the cookies intact but dunk them in the milk. David and Ethan had come along at that point with a few gross suggestions for variations on the theme—which, naturally, Mal had to top—and the five of them had sat out there giggling and laughing, swinging their feet and making a joyful, royal mess Grace had irritatedly assumed she'd have to clean up.

Except Mal and the kids had cleaned up their own mess and Grace's grand funk had deepened.

She didn't want him to play with her kids and be considerate because she didn't want to like him. He would get called back to his job somewhere in the Badlands, or find one in law enforcement someplace else and he would leave and the kids would be devastated. She would be devastated.

It was too late. She already liked him. She was already devastated.

Why on earth couldn't Mal just be someone nice and uncomplicated for whom she felt absolutely nothing but friendship like John?

When she went out to do the grocery shopping, she bought condoms.

She didn't mean to. Sex was not—had not been—part of her life for years, consequently birth-control devices were not at the top of her list of things to think about. And perhaps she was jumping the gun a bit, considering the fact that they hadn't actually even kissed, but, well, since when did immediate necessity have anything to do with what she kept on hand as precautions? Bandages, sunburn ointment, stuffy-nose medication, non-aspirin pain relievers, condoms—they were all the same thing, weren't they? Just in case of illness or accidents?

She'd always believed in better-safe-than, and in panicking first and laughing at her foolishness later. And Mal Quarrels panicked her by looking at her, by being. When she wasn't busy simply getting to like him a lot, she was busy wanting to lie down and be ravished by him at the first available opportunity. Which was stupid, sophomoric and completely beneath her advanced age and maturity, especially for a mother trying to live a good example for her kids, but...

Damn, she hated that word. But. *B-U-T.* A big word for only three letters. A lot of consequences behind but. In fact, "but" carried so many niggling ramifications that Grace had long been of the opinion that instead of the road to hell being paved with good intentions, she was pretty darn sure it was paved by "buts."

But realizing that fact did nothing to change the situation of the moment.

So, anyway, there she was in the pharmacy section of Meijers and there they were in all their colorful, intimidating glory right across the aisle from the antacid she was out of, and...

It happened. Her mind, being the reprehensibly undisciplined creature it was, saw the condoms and immediately turned to fantasies of Mal in various states of undress. A whole bunch of what-ifs suddenly crossed her mind, and *bang!* She panicked. What if they danced again? What if the children weren't around to protect her from herself? What if she just completely lost her mind, got Mal to kiss her and things escalated from there? What if she wasn't as mature as she kept reminding herself, got up out of bed in the middle of one of those dreams, sleepwalked the three acres to Mal's, climbed in bed with him and ravished him—and he didn't stop her? What if she . . .

Oh, Lord, she couldn't even think it. "What if" panic was a truly aberrant thing.

But it was also exciting.

Grace made a face at her reflection in the stainless-steel sign racks fronting the antacid bin and knew she'd gone round the bend.

Furtively she glanced across the aisle at the shelves housing the moral conflicts between safe sex and self-control, hypocrisy and wisdom, planning and guilt in bright packaging showing pictures of silhouetted couples, Aztec warriors, Trojan conquerors. She'd never actually spent any time in front of this display before—four kids in six years, who'd bought condoms? And when she and Phil had made the decision after Erin was born that four kids was plenty, Phil had done this shopping while Grace had toured the tampon aisle to acquaint herself with all the new technology in feminine monthly protection that she hadn't really had much occasion to need in years. This was . . . different.

This was embarrassing.

I'm not embarrassed, she told herself. I can do this, it's just another product like canned spinach and you never buy that without reading the label first.

Right. Suck it up and get on with it so you can get out of here.

Okay, let's see, what did they have? Plain, ribbed, scented—no, not scented, she was allergic—colored, contoured, receptacle end; latex, lambskin—forget the lambskin, too porous and accident prone—lubricated, dry; with spermicide—definitely—without spermicide. Most effective when used with a spermicidal cream—oh, yuck, she didn't even want to think about that. Move on! Pinching, non-pinching—they didn't say, so how could a woman tell? Phil had always complained about them pinching—

Oh, Lord, what was she doing? Contemplating sin and disaster, that was what, and using her experiences with Phil to abet the process.

I'm sorry, forgive me, I can't do this . . .

Averting her eyes, she shoved her grocery cart forward past the waiting area in front of the pharmacy section of the store, through the line at the bottle return and halfway through toilet paper on her way to eggs—and stopped. Bit the inside of her cheek and glanced back. Hesitated. Breathed.

It was, she decided dubiously, all in how she looked at it. Perspective with a capital *P*. Condoms were merely another hygiene product like douches or ear drops, peroxide or Epsom salts, and she never questioned the wisdom of having them around the house simply because she didn't use them very often. They were in her linen cupboard almost as a hedge against needing them. So, if she bought the condoms, it be would kind of like the way a recovering alcoholic might keep a bottle of Jack Daniel's underneath the kitchen sink as a reminder . . .

Oh, hell, this was stupid. She was having this debate with herself in the first place because Mal, bless him, made her feel reckless and unlike her grown-up self, and therefore, the adult thing to do would be . . .

She did a quick about-face, slipped back to prophylactics, grabbed the smallest, most promising-looking box of ribbed, latex, spermicided, lubricated, contoured birth-control aids she could find in two seconds and returned to toss them nonchalantly—it was a lie—into her cart and finish her grocery shopping without meeting anyone's eyes. Her body, her responsibility, her protection. Period.

Just in case.

At home and at work, across the acres, the table, through the open doorway, the tension bunched like the tornado season, lying in wait to catch them unaware.

Chapter 9

Thursday, 7:30 p.m. Waterford Mott playing fields. Phoebe's softball game.

"Pop it! Pop the helmet, Stasi, get in front of the plate. That's it! All right, you got her. Way to go. Nice play, ladies!"

Clapping and hooting, Coach Witoczynski stalked the fence separating the team enclosure from the playing field, eyes roving over her outfielders, noting the placement of her infield players. Beside her, notebook in hand, Assistant Coach Witoczynski—otherwise known as David— paced, a constant stream of muttered advice filling his mother's ear.

"Phoebe needs to arc her pitches more."

"Her pitches are fine. Nice speed, not too flat, hittable and she's throwing strikes."

David snorted. "Yeah, right. Rachel does better." Never give your sister an inch, even when she's not in earshot.

"Rachel pitches next inning."

"Good." A critical study of the field. "Sarah T.'s too deep off second, you needa move her over."

"She's playing where I told her to play for this batter."

"She'll never get to the bag in time when the runner comes down from first."

"That's why Brynna's set to move over from shortstop to back her up."

"Yeah, but—"

Grace listened to David's voice grate and squeak slightly the way it had off and on for the past week, already most of an octave lower than it was barely three days ago. Her baby was growing up: his thirteenth birthday was next week. Five days until she had her first teenager on her hands.

Lord have mercy on our souls.

And she was buying condoms.

Guiltily, she glanced across the field at Mal, to whom she'd extended a nervous invitation to Phoebe's game after assuring and reassuring herself that asking him to her daughter's baseball game did not constitute a date, nor any kind of romantic involvement at all, was, in fact, perfectly innocent—no matter how uninnocent she felt with those things at home tucked under her mattress just begging her to get close enough to Mal to need them.

Oh lordy, lordy, she needed to have her mind examined for slow leaks because all her good sense was evaporating from somewhere. Would bathroom caulk fix the brain drain the way it did the tub? If she hired a traffic cop for her thoughts, would he or she be able to get them flowing in more than one direction again, instead of down one Mal-fantasy path after another?

She snorted at herself. Probably not. Simple human vagaries of thought being what they were, a traffic cop wouldn't fit inside her mind. It was crowded enough in there, as it was.

With a firm yank, she brought her brain back to the game.

"Sarah oughta be there." David still harping on her coaching techniques. Never let it be said that her first-born knew when to let a subject drop if he could nag her to death with it. "That's where she's paid to be."

"She's not paid to be anywhere, she's out here to have fun. If we can win in the bargain, great, that's my job. Which means, I want her where she is, not where she should be."

"Fine. It's a bad spot, but all right. What about Sarah Roberts, then? She should be at first base, not right field—"

And on it went. Grace did things her way and David knew better. Same old hammer-and-tong parent-teenager song—Witoczynski verse.

Watching them from the spot where he'd been drafted to fill in as right-field defensive coach—after extensive grilling by David to ascertain his qualifications—Mal grinned. If he'd ever talked to either of his parents the way David spoke to Grace, he'd have gotten his mother's heavy platinum wedding ring upside the head for the impertinence Grace took for granted. Of course, as she'd told him earlier when he'd half-jokingly said something to her about David and his many opinions, she never had to guess where she stood with David or what he was thinking. Hopefully, that meant he would continue to communicate verbally with her when he was the worst part of fifteen through seventeen.

Mal had laughed and told her it was a nice dream, but not to count on it. Teenage boys had a habit of straining family ties simply for the sake of straining something. Grace had sighed heavily, clunked her forehead on his bicep and prayed aloud for strength.

Mal had looked down at her honey-gold head and felt something inside him constrict. She and the kids had shanghaied him to be a defensive coach, assuming he'd participate as though he was part of the family. Roth—no, Abernathy, damn it . . . hell, what was going on? It wasn't like him to confuse the role with the real man—had told Mal they'd done much the same thing to him, only he'd wound up co-coaching Ethan's team with Grace's niece, Becky's husband, Michael.

In a kind of mental aside, Mal cringed. The woman had too many relatives to keep straight and they all showed up wherever the others were—usually unannounced. Still . . .

He felt himself smile slightly, his eyes drift half-closed, savoring the moment when Grace laughed wryly, squeezed his arm and went, at the umpire's beckoning, to call the coin toss. There was something about her, indefinable, special, that spoke to him alone—that spoke from him to her alone.

They were too aware of each other, too unaccountably comfortable together, too . . . ready to court trouble. It was simply a matter of time and timing. He recognized the symptoms in her, knew she understood them clearly in him. And if her players hadn't swarmed off the field at the moment she returned to begin the game, he was pretty certain he'd have made a fool of himself offering Grace whatever strength he had, plus . . . hell, plus whatever anything he had in exchange for one moment holding her, one kiss: here and now, there and then, whenever and wherever she chose.

Just one.

He was too old to believe that one kiss would be enough, no longer naive enough to think that he could kiss her or seduce her or whatever and get it out of the way, that's it and that's that.

She was the kind of woman who got under a man's skin in a heartbeat—and did it while he was watching, and with hardly any physical contact at all. Wisdom dictated he avoid her like the plague, but he had the heart-tight, despairing feeling that this feeling...this...whatever it was had nothing to do with wisdom, went much deeper and had the potential to be far more destructive. This was his heart finding its way home, his spirit coming to rest, his soul encountering peace.

And not wanting to leave it.

Whatever she'd be willing to part with one of, that's what he wanted and to hell with the consequences, tomorrow's desires, next week's needs. A moment wouldn't be enough, but if that's what he could get, why, he'd take it.

And may God have mercy on children and fools.

With difficulty, Mal pulled his awareness away from Grace, turned to track the rest of the family around the field: Phoebe in her element on the pitcher's mound, looking confident; Erin, her baseball cap skewed sideways so a portion of her bangs stuck out above the plastic adjustment strip and the bill kept the sun off the left side of her neck, posted in the stands with her grandmother, Julia Brannigan; Ethan trooping up with John—no, Gus. Oh, hell, had he started to believe the lie?—from the finish of his 5:45 game on another of Mott's ten softball fields; David no longer glued to Grace's side, off on the sidelines with the team's co-coach warming up Alice and Gabriel Book's daughter, Rachel, who would pitch the next inning.

Alice Book in the team enclosure, bench-momming the five players who weren't on the field at the moment.

Gabriel Book down the third baseline acting as the team's left-field defensive coach.

Gus Abernathy—got it right that time, maybe he hadn't lost it yet—at the left-field fence, appearing a tad uneasy, consulting with Book about something.

Book glancing casually toward the metal stands where the team's supporters sat, attention sharpening almost imperceptibly on something or someone he saw behind the stands.

Sweat trickled down the back of Mal's neck beneath the weight of his hair, caught in the rise of hackles. Premonition, intuition, sank like lead in his gut, tripping the threat indicator.

Instinct sent him along the baseline toward home plate, every sense alert; training made him appear relaxed, aimless, a man stretching his legs waiting for the action on the field to require his attention. Sunglasses hid the sudden keening of his gaze, prevented his eyes betraying the adrenaline jolt through his veins when he caught sight of a lone, neatly dressed man watching the game from the shadows of the trees bounding the southwest side of the field behind the backstop. The intruder seemed familiar. By itself, that meant nothing; without a good view of his features, however, Mal could suspicion, but he had bupkis.

No, something else about the guy didn't set right: he didn't cheer, didn't smile at the girls' occasional bloopers, didn't even seem to see the game. He was too smooth, too casual, too carefully blended to his surroundings, too hard to get a clear picture of, too uninvolved. There was too little emotion about his shadowy features and he was too still.

Too professional.

Exactly the sort of person Dunne used to hire to do his dirty work for him.

Not a parent, not with a family. Doesn't belong here.

His gut would have told him that if Book's and Abernathy's reactions hadn't already. Cops' instincts were the same no matter what branch of law enforcement they worked for. Some were merely more finely honed than others.

He saw some fine awareness prickle across Grace's face, saw her take her eyes off her players and glance at Book,

Abernathy, him, read their wariness. Watched the mom instinct kick in, the immediate question written on her face, directed not at Book or Abernathy, but automatically at him. As though she could count on him to understand, take care of things.

Hoped she could.

Problem?

He shook his head once, negative. Hoped he wasn't wrong.

She cocked her head, followed the direction of his interest, found what he'd seen. Sucked in a breath and brought her gaze back to Mal. Quirked an eyebrow over her sunglasses that stated as clearly as words, Check him out?

Already going, Mal gave her a clipped nod and started off the field through the opposing team's enclosure without stopping to wonder why Grace wanted the stranger investigated. Coach Witoczynski took her responsibility for her players seriously and there were too many mild-mannered perverts out there trying to get close to preteen girls for him to wonder. Parental paranoia was a given.

Out of the corner of his eye, he saw Book headed off the field, too. At the same time, Phoebe pitched a third strike to end the inning and the opposing team's players flooded onto the field, frustrating Mal's progress; Book had the same problem in reverse when Grace's team swarmed off the field, crowding through the gate ahead of him.

Abernathy appeared behind the backstop, hesitated, scanning the trees. Mal looked. The man who didn't belong was gone.

Thursday, 10:37 p.m.

Home. Kids reading in their rooms, on their way to bed, light from their reading lamps shining softly through the miniblinds in their windows. Grace out in the yard alone, trying to wind down. The scent of damp lilacs was strong along the back of the house. Laughter and occasional splashes two yards down around a lit pool. Bug-zapper hanging from the porch next door *zzztt*-ing every few seconds, frying bugs. Dogs and cat scattered across the deck, beneath the trees in groaning, panting lumps, cleaning themselves, snuffling after night crawlers and crickets: everything right in their world.

Across the yard, a light on in Mal's kitchen, the strains of something bluesy but indistinct drifting out his open windows, his solid silhouette backlit in his open doorway as he leaned against the jamb.

Air soft and warm on her skin, slightly sticky with humidity; night quiet and dark, seemingly serene and unthreatening. Standing in the darkness watching fireflies flash their mating calls, wondering which were the mimics pretending to call mates only to attract prey to kill and eat, Grace didn't feel unthreatened. She felt vulnerable.

That man at the ballpark had spooked her in a way she couldn't define; turning to Mal for security the way she had instead of depending on herself only added to her sense of peril. She didn't want to feel what she felt, didn't want to do what she knew she'd have to do soon, didn't want...

She hugged her arms around herself, shivering from something other than cold. She didn't want a lot of things, but she'd be damned if she'd waste the night or weaken herself by listing them all now.

"Grace."

She started at the sound of her name, even though beneath the hum of insects and her thoughts, she'd heard the catch-tear of his feet through grass left to grow too long. His voice was soft, rough, sent an electric thrill down her spine. She wanted, she needed . . . to ignore him.

To respond.

"I'm here."

Her voice held a quality of inevitability and invitation, despair, sadness, need. She'd turned to him earlier when she was worried, not to her friend, Abernathy, not to her brother-in-law, Book. To him. Malcolm James Quarrels. The urge to protect her had been—was still—ferocious, unequivocal. He should walk away, go back where he'd come from, and he knew it. But he couldn't.

He wouldn't.

"Nice night," he said. Lame, boy, very lame. What'd you do? Leave your brain in your other head or are you wearing it in your shorts?

"Mmm," Grace agreed. Don't do this, her mind told her, Get out of here. Go in.

Stay, her heart said. Stay, stay, stay!

"Take a walk with me?" he invited. It was the safest thing he could think of at the moment.

"Yes," she whispered, half-afraid, mostly exhilarated. "I'd like that."

Together they turned and moved across the yard, close enough to touch, but careful not to. The dogs came to the fence and woofed pleadingly after them, then settled down in front to the gate to watch and wait. The cat climbed a tree and meowed loudly, but they ignored him and he subsided, slid backward down the tree and jumped on a dog. A momentary free-for-all erupted, complete with fierce dog snarls and dying cat yowls.

"Cut it out," Grace told them sternly, and after another moment of halfhearted battle, they did.

The night drew a cloak of stillness and darkness around Grace and Mal, intimate and snug, discordant and awkward. They wanted to speak, but, for the first time in their lives, didn't know what to say. They were first and foremost communicators, but of late too many things had happened too fast, too many things they couldn't share—secrets they kept from each other and from themselves.

Eyeing each other from moment to moment, they walked in silence for a way.

Grace spoke first. "Who do you think he was?"

"Who?"

"That guy tonight."

Mal shook his head. "Don't know. Wish I'd gotten a better look at him. He's got a real hinky feel. I don't like it."

"Do you think he's stalking any of the girls?"

Mal looked at her, experienced the chill of new concern chase his spine. "I don't know, why?"

Grace hesitated, shrugged. "I'm not sure, but I think he's been around before—at Ethan's games, a couple of practices. He doesn't talk to anybody, he just watches, Ethan, I think, and John... I've never gotten a good look at him, either, but he's never with anyone and he always just kind of appears and disappears—you know, odd. Nothing to nail down. But I'm sure he wasn't at our game before Ethan and John got there. He gives me the willies."

"How many times?"

"How many times has he given me the willies?" Grace gave him deadpan, suddenly feeling better. "Every time I see him. Or don't quite see him."

Mal grinned and groaned, as she'd intended, gave her tried patience. "How many times have you not quite seen him?"

"Oh." She made the word long and exaggerated, light dawning.

Mal rolled his eyes.

Grace grinned. He played this game better than the kids who'd invented it. The grin faded. Worrisome, that. Their senses of humor meshed.

She eyed him sideways, taking in the now-familiar profile, the rugged altogether sexy physique, and felt the restless, earthy buzz she'd come to associate with looking at him spiral through her nervous system, her emotions.

She swallowed and looked away, at the road, the trees bordering the cul de sac, the gibbous moon. Considered his question a moment so she wouldn't have to consider other things, serious this time. "I don't know. Three? Four? Enough so I've heard a couple of other parents comment, but I hoped we were all just paranoid. Then John said something, and Gabriel noticed him, and you—" She stopped walking inside a stand of trees that hid the tall grasses of a deer meadow within the woods at the end of the street and blew out a breath, hunched into her shoulders, troubled. "Now I still hope we're all paranoid, but I'm also..." She paused, loathe to admit it to him, to herself. Shrugged and admitted it anyway because it was true. "It scares me."

"Grace." Quietly.

He touched her shoulder; she turned to him. Not because he was there, but because he was Mal.

"Maybe I can find out who he is." He couldn't tell her he was already pretty sure he knew what the guy was if not who, but he'd promise her the earth to keep her looking at him the way she looked at him now.

"Gabriel couldn't find out anything." Warning him, not doubting him.

"Book's been out of the game longer than I have."

"He's kept up his contacts." Then in a low aside Mal almost didn't hear. "Especially lately."

Lately. Mal had a feeling he should worry about that, but he had other things on his mind at the moment. "So have I."

"None of us can even really describe—"

"Grace." He touched her jaw with the side of his forefinger, drawing her attention. "I'll find something or I'll do something, trust me." Fierce. "Either way, he won't get near you or the kids." Definite, ferocious, almost savage. "Yours or anyone else's."

Emotion peppered her nerves, fitted that nameless something she refused to define closer to the missing piece in her heart. She shouldn't fall for him. She didn't have time for him, room for him. Her life was overloaded enough, as it was.

But only a good man, a man worth a few complications, this man, Mal, would promise what he shouldn't, and mean to deliver.

She lifted the tips of her fingers to the center of his chest, looked up at him, heart in the moonlight shining in her eyes. "I do," she whispered, "trust you. I have a feeling that I shouldn't, but I do."

"Grace." Rough, ragged. And again, wondering. "Grace."

Then he lowered his head and kissed her. Gently at first, tentatively, with circumspection.

Her mouth was soft under his, malleable. Completely involved in kissing him back. He lifted his head, aware that his breathing was no longer under any kind of control, rested his forehead on hers. Her face was warm.

"You don't even know me." His voice was hoarse, raw. "I'm not who you see."

"Hardly anyone is," she returned softly, touching her fingers to his mouth. "I know I'm not. It doesn't matter."

"It should, Grace." He turned his face into her palm, brushed a kiss there. "For you, it should."

"For you, too." She took his face between her hands, brought his mouth down, skimmed a series of butterfly kisses along his lips. Each touch left them both hungrier than the last. "It should matter for you, too. But not tonight. Please, Mal. Not tonight."

"Not tonight," he agreed, powerless to deny her. Deny himself.

Then he took her mouth and stopped thinking.

Pleasure, deep and sinking, melting in his bones, turning her muscles to jelly. Hunger, hot and intimate, impatient, burning away sense and inhibition. The world was a dark void somewhere outside them, existed between them where their mouths met and clung and clashed; where his arms came around her and hauled her tight; where hers circled his neck, hanging on to him. Where their chests touched, their hearts banged, their bodies tried to get closer than was possible.

Their faces parted to breathe, lungs shuddered and trembled trying to catch air enough to calm. Failing.

Grace's fingers tunneled Mal's hair away from his face, stroked his neck, his cheek, his chest, greedy. "This isn't a good idea."

"No." His hands were restless on her back, brushing up her sides to the outside of her breasts, sliding away.

Grace pressed closer, lifting her chest, inviting his touch. "You'll leave."

"Yes."

His thumbs traced her jaw, down her throat, across the top of her breasts, around the full curve, toward the center and down away from the crest without touching. Moaning, Grace slid her hands roughly down his chest, around his sides, brushed them over his hips.

"I want you."

Groaning, Mal crushed her to him. "Yes."

Her mouth was under his, open, eager. He thrust his tongue between her teeth, marauding, taking what he was given. His thigh was between hers. Intimate. Against her. Along her mound. Bringing her thigh hard against the aching demand inside his jeans.

His hands were on her hips, rounding the curve of her buttocks, pressing her to him, rocking.

Her hands were everywhere, mindless. On him. Pulling him close. Beneath his shirt. Touching, tantalizing...torching his reason, claiming his sanity. Her breath was sketchy, gasping. Pleading.

But it was only a kiss, nothing more, a reckless, shocking, heavy-petting whim of the moment. He told himself—or would have if he wasn't so completely occupied otherwise.

In the long term it meant nothing, she meant nothing, her kids meant nothing. The fire in his blood, the craving to possess, to protect, the all-consuming necessity to have her wrapped around him, become part of her for as long as she'd have him, meant nothing.

Less.

She tightened her arms around him, angled her mouth and thrust her tongue against his, sabotaging his efforts to convince himself. He groaned and oblivion claimed him. He wouldn't do anything more than touch her a little over her clothes. He swore to himself.

He slid his tongue beneath her upper lip, drew the heart-shaped center into his mouth, teasing and suckling, the movement of his tongue across the sensitive flesh erotic and heart-stopping, hot and evocative of how he might tongue and taste more secret places, toy with the nub at her center, making her mindless, making the honey flow before he slid hard within her, claimed her...

His.

Somewhere deep, something clutched inside Grace: a thrill of fear, a single lucid recognition of danger—an eager desire to take risks, touch the peril with her bare hands, own it, become part of it—Mal.

It was not a familiar sensation, she didn't know the person she'd become in Mal Quarrels's arms, but it didn't seem to matter anymore. Lately, the familiar had taken on immense overtones of safety. Fear lay outside her everyday world, restlessness inside with her. Mal was the instigator and the balm for both, she'd known that the minute she'd laid eyes on him, known that sooner or later she'd let him—hell, invite him—to trample her defenses the way he'd already begun to trample her emotions, making a path to her soul.

Become part of her the way he'd become part of her everyday thoughts without her consent, her knowledge.

But it was only a kiss, not a commitment, not a hope. Only a kiss. She told herself—or would have if she'd been able to tell herself anything at all.

The litany pounded in her blood: take me, I want you, take me, I need you, take me, I know what I'm doing and I choose it freely....

For the moment, tomorrow's inevitable repercussions and compunctions could take care of themselves. Now was all that mattered.

Getting closer.

Getting rid of cloth trappings and restrictions.

Wrapping her legs around him.

Losing herself in him with him deep inside her.

She moaned and undulated beneath his onslaught, telling him what she wanted to share with him more clearly than she might have in words.

He was lost.

He turned her in his embrace, slipping his hands beneath her oversize cotton shirt. Aching to explore more of her, struggling to salvage his ethics—don't ravish a woman you're lying to, who's part of your investigation, even if only a peripheral part—his morals even, as he felt himself intensifying the kiss, rushing to take her deeper—

And found it was she who took him, who breathed life and strength into him even as she drew him around herself, brought sanity to the midst of his chaos. For all the wrong reasons, this was right, she was right, being with her here and now was—

Wrong.

The knowledge intruded like a blast of January wind in the Badlands: stinging, icy, full of three feet or more of drifting snow and dire consequences for the careless. If they did this here and now, impatiently, in some libido-drugged thoughtless state, he couldn't protect her from the possibility of an unwanted pregnancy, of days spent wondering whether she was or wasn't, of feeling dirty in the morning, hating herself for her rashness, for behaving like an adolescent in an adult world—hating him for things he was perfectly capable of despising himself for.

Couldn't protect himself from his own recriminations, the regret in her eyes, the loss of some special communication, special trust developing between them that meant more to him than any sex—however incredible. Meant more to him than any single moment of physical pleasure could ever mean.

For reasons he couldn't bring himself to admit, he didn't want her to hate him.

It's a kiss, it means nothing, I can stop anytime I want. He tried to reassure himself.

He lied.

It was a kiss and infinitely, astoundingly more. He couldn't stop what was happening, what they were about to commit—he tried—and what was happening between them, beyond the kissing and the groping and the clanging of their hearts as well as within it, meant the moon.

To him.

To her.

Her skin was silk beneath the coarseness of his fingers, soft and perfect. Her one-piece cotton-lycra sport bra was in the way of his exploration—a problem impatiently dealt with when he found a frayed-open seam and an eager Grace helped him tear it. A similar solution rid them of his T-shirt. Her loose, big-armed tank top was simply shoved up, out of their way. The ripe fullness of her breasts flattened against the hard planes and ridges of his chest, maddening, when he crushed her to him and dipped his head to find her throat, lifted her against him to bring her breasts closer to his mouth.

Out of control.

This was the way she'd imagined they would be, the way she wanted them to be: hot, hard, tempestuous, demanding, without patience—without time for thought or second thoughts. A blinding, brilliant burst of insane passion and satisfied cravenness in the darkness that would hardly seem real in the morning, but would feed her dreams for the rest of her life.

Take me, I want you, take me, I need you...

Out of control.

He had to stop. Now. He knew it. Had to.

This was not the way he'd fantasized they would be—he would be. Well, not the first time, anyway. He'd visualized a sunlit, quiet room with a wide bed and satiny sheets behind a locked door, hours of exploration and discovery, and time after time of driving her to the brink of delirium, pulling back and propelling her there again before finally toppling her into oblivion and slaking his own thirst in the well of her body. A long, sweaty, glistening, sense-overloading, pleasure-saturated summer affair that would bring a secret smile when she remembered him on winter evenings and would keep him company long after she was gone. After she made him go.

He moved his mouth to the top of her right breast and felt her gasp.

"Oh, yes, Mal, please...please..."

Oh, hell. He'd never been a choirboy and he was certainly no saint. If this was what she wanted...

There was only so much a man could ask of himself where the right woman was involved. Anyone else...and he wouldn't be here right now. He'd be in charge of himself—hell, this wouldn't have begun. What a revealing thing to have to admit to oneself in the middle of the most incredible...

Grace hooked a knee around his hip, bringing them as close as two people could get with denim jeans and cotton-lycra bicycle shorts between them and he groaned. Okay, so in a minute he would stop. When she quit pleading with him to continue, he would stop.

"Please, Mal, please . . . don't stop, please. . . ."

He was doomed.

He was in heaven.

He was out of his mind.

He was . . . he was . . .

Surrounded by a dazzling white alien light.

Chapter 10

It was like suddenly winding up in the middle of one of
the unmentionable Freudian nightmares his ex-partner,
Tolski, used to tell him about.

Like most of Tolski's nightmares, these truly frightful
dreams usually took place in tiny, airless interrogation
rooms, under blindingly bright lights with the mothers of
all the women of whom he'd ever had carnal knowledge
staring through the two-way mirror at him while their at-
torneys ground him to dust. Tolski, ever morbidly maso-
chistic, often theorized that hell was probably the place
you put yourself in your worst nightmares and that, if you
didn't come to terms with your dreams somewhere along
the way, was where you spent eternity.

Mal, usually tolerant of the long-winded Tolski's more
entertaining theories, had always refused to touch this
conversation with a ten-foot pole. Now he knew why. His
own pet nightmare was occurring right here with him wide
awake inside one of Tolski's dreams. Only he wasn't Tolski—he thanked God for that nightly—and the preter-

naturally bright light was, in reality, a combination of car headlights and the powerful, hand-held spot aimed at them by—

Jolting himself back to the real world, Mal abruptly shoved Grace behind him and turned, squinting against the glare. Yep. Damn, wouldn't you know. The first time he'd necked in the woods since he was twenty and along came a White Lake Township cop with a spotlight.

No getting away with things for the innocent but eternally guilt-ridden.

"What's going on here, folks?"

"Nothin', Officer." Mal played it self-consciously embarrassed but polite. Again, because of Grace he found himself lying with the truth. "Enjoyin' the moon, you know."

"Uh-huh." The cop's agreement was dry and skeptical. He moved the spotlight over Mal, looking for Grace. "Everything okay, ma'am? You enjoyin' the moon all right, too?"

Behind Mal's back—thank God his musculature was broad enough to hide her—Grace tugged her torn bra down over her breasts, making sure it caught under the fold of their weight—at last, something the sag of age and nursing four kids was good for!—so no one accidentally got an eyeful, straightened her shirt and poked her head out underneath Mal's arm. She'd be damned if she was going to feel embarrassed by this. Absolutely refused to feel humiliated for rediscovering lost pieces of herself, getting back something she hadn't realized was missing for years. She felt too good. Full-of-herself good.

Damn good.

"I was," she said flatly, annoyed and feelin' fine.

Mal nearly choked. She wasn't supposed to behave like this, he was supposed to handle this, protect her identity with her virtue and save the day. That was the man's job, right, to take the heat? Because despite her boldness in other areas, when it came to men-women-love-sex, Grace embarrassed more easily than any woman Mal had ever met. Not to mention Mal was pretty sure Miss Manners and Emily Post would have advised something besides going on the offensive when caught by a cop in a compromising situation. But then, she hadn't yet done anything he'd expected, so why should she start now? Still, even in Tolski's wildest musings things never happened this way, so why was it happening in real life to him, Mal? And when had he lost any semblance of control of this situation?

Oh, probably around a month ago, the first time he'd set eyes on Grace.

"I was," Grace continued, edging around Mal just far enough to be sure the cop saw her, but not enough so she was out from under Mal's protective, somewhat possessive arm, "enjoying the moon and this man and myself very much, thank you for your concern. And if you'd go away, I'd be perfectly willing to go on enjoying the moon and this man and other things even more than that, so if don't mind . . . ?"

The cop's light wavered over her face, dropped. "Grace?" he said incredulously.

Grace peered out at the darkness on the other side of the light. Mortification returned in a hurry. "Harry?" she asked weakly. Then, more firmly, gathering herself together and telling herself that if he hadn't turned up, she'd have nothing to feel mortified about, "Oh, for God's sake. Harry, what're you doing here?"

"Harry?" Mal asked. "You know him?"

Grace shrugged. "He's my late husband Phil's sister's husband's ex-brother-in-law."

"You're related to him?"

"Not exactly."

"Besides the multitudes I've already met, how many other people in this county are you 'not exactly' related to?"

"Oh..." She calculated. "Six sisters, plus cousins, nieces, nephews, aunts and uncles... family's been in the area for three generations... a lot."

"Of course." He'd known before he opened his mouth he shouldn't ask. "Any more of 'em in law enforcement?"

She shrugged a you-tell-me hand, "I lose track," and returned her attention to the cop. Harry. "I thought you patrolled the other side of the township."

Harry switched off the spotlight. "I was—I do. Got a call from Gabriel in the middle of shift. Told me you've been having some problems with prowlers lately, said some guy keeps turning up at Ethan's games, looks like he could be casing the kids, asked if I'd drive around and check on you. Quiet night, end of shift, sort of family—" He made an offhand gesture. "Here I am. Sorry about intruding where you didn't need me."

"Gabriel?" Grace glanced at Mal, dismayed—and ticked off. Her eyes narrowed, mouth tightened. "Gabriel." The name sounded a lot like "damn it."

"Book?" Mal eyed Grace, looked at Harry, resigned. Again, of course. What was the point of Grace's having too many meddlesome friends and relatives to keep track of if they weren't going to get in his way while butting into her life?

Harry nodded.

"Oh..." Disgusted, Grace planted her hands on her hips. The oversize armholes of her tank top sagged open and she immediately reversed tack and crossed her arms over her chest, anchoring everything. Her irritation with Gabriel remained unaffected. "That's it, I've had it."

She tapped her foot, considering options. Didn't bode well for someone, Mal decided.

"Grace." A warning.

"He's gone too far this time, Mal. He's a pit bull in the overprotective department. I feel sorry for Rachel when she starts to date. And while I appreciate the thought, I can't let him keep getting away with it, either. He's got his own family to look after."

"It was a phone call, Grace. If I knew the locals better, I might have done the same thing." A lie. He had a tendency—macho bull apple pride, as Grace had told him that first night, but there it was—to take care of things on his own without consulting anyone else. "And you have had problems with prowlers lately. There was a guy at the game. Other games."

"Yeah, well, at the moment I've got four dogs, an attack cat, you and John right in my own backyard to overprotect me and the kids, don't I? And don't—" she held up a hand when Mal attempted to protest "—don't try 'n' tell me you're not patrolling my perimeters in the middle of the night because I've seen you. John's not quite as obvious, but. Add Gabriel on top of the two of you and it's too much."

"We don't want anything to happen to you." Mal's eyes on her were intense, his voice unequivocal. Revealing. "I don't."

Emotion curled and corked inside Grace. Surprising them both, she turned her head and pressed a quick kiss into Mal's shoulder. "I'm glad," she whispered. "But we can talk about that later." She turned to Harry, evading dangerous territory, and her demeanor went from soft to ominous without transition. "Thank you for driving over, Harry, but understand...if you tell Gabriel where you found me tonight, I will personally call my sister Helen and tell her to stop by and see you at home."

"The Major?" Harry asked—although "gulped" would be a more appropriate term, if a cop who'd been decorated for heroism on more than one occasion could be accused of gulping.

"General," Grace corrected sweetly. "She's been promoted a couple times since you last saw her."

"Are you threatening a police officer, Mrs. Witoczynski?"

Grace nodded, affable. "Damn straight."

Harry winced. "Just checking." He holstered his nightstick, headed for his patrol car. "Well, have a nice night, folks. Grace, I didn't see a thing, but take the rest of it home, huh?"

"My regards to the family," Grace called after him.

Harry sketched her a two-finger salute of acknowledgment, folded his nightstick along his leg to get into the car, put the vehicle in gear and left.

Mal looked at Grace, who sagged against him in relief.

"Some reintroduction to the world of necking, huh?"

Mal snorted. Then, "What was that stuff about your sister Helen, the ... General, was it?"

"You haven't met her?"

"Alice, Meg, Twink, your niece Becky, and was there an Edith, maybe a Sam and your mother Julia in there someplace, plus a ton of kids? But nope, no Helen."

"Ah, well, then." Grace smiled, tucked her arms around his waist. "You have a treat in store for you."

Mal cupped her face. "Why do I suddenly feel threatened?"

"Helen does that to people."

"No." Mal traced her jawline and Grace's breath caught. "I meant by you."

"Oh," Grace breathed. "Mal." She faced him, bold and wary at once, her fingers twisting at his sides. "I—"

"I know." He tilted her chin, dipped his head to drop a gentle, seeking kiss on her mouth. "I shouldn't have let things get as far as they did. It's too much for one night."

"Yes." She shut her eyes, dropped her forehead to his chest. Oh, Lord, the feel of him, the touch of him...the sense of permanence and ache of transience all in one. "My fault, too. I shouldn't have...I know...how fast you—I mean, I—I mean people in general, anyone... can lose...control, but I wanted...want...and I...let myself..."

"You let yourself trust me and I let myself go."

"Yes. No. I let me go because it was you. Because...because..." She hesitated. The reasons were nebulous and full of more revelation than she wanted to handle. How she felt about him. How she could feel about him, given half a chance and very little more time. "Because I didn't stop to think. Didn't want to think. Still don't want to."

"No. But we have to."

A sigh. "Yes."

"It's a big step and you've got kids in the house."

"Yes."

"Fast and furious there'd be no time to consider consequences or regrets until later, but now..."

"Yes." Small, quiet voice. She didn't look at him. "I'm sorry."

"No, don't be. I'm not."

"But—"

"Grace." He touched a finger to her lips. "We got carried away, that's all. We came to our senses, no harm done, no..." He paused. *Regrets* was the wrong word. He had plenty of regrets about what hadn't happened, what might have happened—what he wanted to happen—but no other word described what he meant to say. "I don't want you to wake up tomorrow and feel—" his hold on her tightened "—cheap because you gave something to me—shared something with me that..." Another search for words he couldn't find. "You don't know me. You deserve more than I can... I don't want you to have any regrets because of me...especially since I can't promise you anything but.''

Grace looked up at him. Smiled slightly. ''You said that before. I don't have any...reservations...about anything we might have done, just inhibitions. And I do know you. Better than you think. Better than you'd like to believe.''

He huffed a short laugh without humor. ''No.''

''Yes.'' Soft. Definite. She touched his arm. ''You're not who you think you are. You're more than that.''

''No.'' Intense and savage.

Grace went still, withdrew half an inch. Mal swallowed, gathered her back, looked at the sky. Sometimes God had the most ironic sense of humor, enlightening people about themselves at the most inopportune moments. Like now. It was more than too many people's lives were worth, but right now Mal wanted to tell her who he was, why he was. Things about himself he'd never shared with anyone. Beg. He wasn't sure what for. Anything. Everything. Forgiveness. A stay of execution. A minute more with her.

Like the song said, he half thought he'd walk on his lips through busted glass for that.

He swallowed again, looked at the sky. The moon was high and silver. Late. They'd been out here a long time, and he still had work to do tonight, the man from the game to identify. Cigarettes to find and smoke as displacement activity. Grace to quit thinking about.

Grace...

He jerked himself back to the here and now. To Grace, still watching him, troubled. Time to quit daydreaming and get cracking.

''It's late,'' he said, looking away. ''You should go in.''

''You, too.''

She took his hand, fitted her fingers through his. The concern, the questions in her voice slid over him unspoken. An act of friendship and of trust.

More than he deserved.

"Come on, I'll walk you home."

"No." He jerked away from her, almost violent. Fought for calm. Humor escaped him. "I don't think you understand how badly I want you right now, and you at my door would tempt the devil farther than I could handle."

She was stronger than she looked and didn't let him go.

In the pit of her stomach sat the heavy, heady intuition that in one capacity or another she would willingly fight for him tooth and nail even if it meant fighting him. Long-term, short-term, romantic relationship, physical intimacy, platonic friendship...she refused to speculate on their potential together, in what direction their paths might take them, jointly or separately, but in every way that counted, he'd begun to mean the earth to her and that was enough to send her barreling into uncharted territory—for the moment.

"Then you walk me home. Say good-night at the door. See me in the morning. Go on a little closer to each other than we were before."

He eyed her, bemused, astonished. He'd offered her a way out, practically threatened her with the singular carnality of his immediate desires so she would go, but instead of turning tail the way she should have, here she was burrowing in. "You are extraordinary, you know that, lady? What do you want from me? What the hell am I going to do about you?"

"Nothin' I don't invite," Grace assured him, positive. She took a step and tugged gently at his hand. "Come on. Home. Bed. Our separate ones."

"Grace—"

She faced him on tiptoe, but still wasn't tall enough when he held himself away; caught a fistful of his hair and hauled him down for a brief, telling kiss. "Trust me," she said. "You won't get away with anything I don't want you to get away with, and I'll trust you not to try to get away with anything neither of us is prepared to deal with at the moment."

His hands made their way to her waist to hold her, support her, independent of his commands. "What if what I'm not prepared to deal with at the moment—or ever—is simply you being you?"

She grinned. "Ready or not, here I am." Caught his hands off her waist and tugged, inching backward out of the trees and onto the street. "And no matter how scared I am of the possibilities you represent, there you are, too. We have to make the best of that, because stay or run, there's no way out." Then softly, almost in aside. "For either of us."

"I could leave. Move out. Be gone."

"You don't run away from things if your life depends on it—"

Oh, God, she did know him.

"You won't leave."

"Grace." Quiet, wry, aching with laughter and need. "Damn it, Grace."

She gazed up at him with a woman's faith, a woman's pure knowledge, steady and serene, heart in her voice, soul in her eyes. He should never have looked at her that first time. Seen her. Listened to her.

"Walk me home," she said.

Helpless to do otherwise, Mal grasped her hand and went with her. He'd learned something damning about himself, inexorable about her, out here tonight: in the long run, Grace would go where he led only if she chose. He would go where she led because he had to, he wanted to.

Because in the end, if he didn't, he'd wake up one morning and find himself lost.

He was lost already.

He said good-night to her in the breezeway—a swift, self-conscious clasp of hands and parting; his sudden choice to return and haul her up and kiss her senseless while she kissed him crazy, then slowing to a lingering, real promise of good-night—and let himself out the back to cross the acres between his residence and her home.

And spent most of his journey away from her looking back.

Four people besides Grace watched him stride through darkness alone:

Phoebe and David, upstairs in their separate rooms, wrapped in their separate feelings—Phoebe full of a twelve-year-old girl's romantic plans for the mother she loved and hated to see lonely; David full of a thirteen-year-old boy's mixed emotions of selfishness and selflessness in his need for his mother's attention, the desire to cut his apron strings without losing hold of them yet and the sense that his role as the man of the family was about to be usurped and he didn't intend to let go without a fight. To anyone, no matter how much he liked Mal. Or wanted a father to talk to. He glanced worriedly at the damp sheets stuffed beneath his arm, trying to figure out how he could slip them into the wash without his mother being the wiser, and where to hide them in the meantime, especially now.

From the shadows of his balcony, Angus Abernathy, who wished more than ever that he really was John Roth, observed Mal go with a sense of bitter irony, knowing from the sheaf of papers in his hands that he wasn't the only one of Grace's tenants who'd started out lying to her. Wondering how to protect Grace from the consequences of her overly generous, righteous nature when it came to her wanting to do the right thing no matter what—or who—it cost. Hoping that what he saw developing between Mal and Grace was the genuine article, and that the weight of revelations he would soon entrust to Mal in hopes of safeguarding Grace would not be misplaced.

A quarter mile away, in the middle of a stand of trees bordering an empty field in the middle of a state recreation area, the hit man from Phoebe's and Ethan's softball games who'd been hired, not by Dunne to kill Gus, but by the Mafia to kill Dunne, was hidden high in an elm tree deer blind, telescopic sights of a sniper rifle trained on the activity at Grace Witoczynski's house. Paid only to hit William Dunne, he remained uninterested in anyone else, sitting unhindered by thought or conscience in a tantric sea of emptiness and calm, waiting for his target to arrive.

Soon, his instincts told him. Very soon.

When the twenty-two bullet hit him with a quiet zap behind the left ear, he had less than a millisecond to realize his instincts about where to find William Dunne had been absolutely right.

And then he was dead wrong.

Dead.

Chapter 11

Unable to sleep, Grace prowled the dark house aware of every creak and shiver of settling floorboards, of snoring dogs, of the cat, Fred, skulking through the rooms on his self-appointed quest to keep the world safe from marauding earwigs, escaped rolypolys and the ever-light drawn moths—leaving the more dangerous mosquitoes strictly alone.

Across the backyard, a single dim light burned in the window over Mal's sink, somehow beckoning and warning at once.

Arms crossed, Grace stood hipshot against the deck doorjamb, looking through the screen, conscious of how close he was, how far away... of how much he'd come to mean to her in too short a time. Of how badly she wanted him with her, in her, the scent of him on her skin, left lingering on her clothes, her sheets; the intimate, absolute knowledge of *him*—the feel of him, weight of him, touch of him—tarrying in her memory for as long as she could make it last. Whether he, himself, lasted with her beyond the making of the memory or not.

Of how easy it had been to slip a few condoms out of the box under her mattress and tuck them in her pocket, how simple it would be to cross the yard and invite herself into his domain, his bed—if he would have her—choose to be with him, if only for a few hours of this single night. To choose...

She hesitated, watching the yard, not quite sure what she meant to choose, aware that however she sliced it, risk was the name of the game: risking rejection, risking involvement, risking eventual heartbreak... And then, of course, there was the biggest risk of all: the risk of letting the moment pass unpursued, of wagering nothing, and then winding up spending the rest of her life wishing she'd taken the chance on the moment, on herself and on Mal, when she'd had it.

Doing nothing and winding up with nothing was more than she was prepared to risk.

Heart resolute, pulse shivering with expectation, soul serene, she slid the screen door open and stepped onto the deck. Behind her, the dogs came awake woofing at the sound of security breached, settled when she informed them who she was. Above her an aluminum lawn chair rattled and John appeared at his balcony.

"Grace, is that you?" He sounded tired.

Grace sighed. Scumped again. "Yes."

"D'you mind if I come down? I need to talk with you."

She looked at Mal's light, up at Gus. "Can it wait, John? I was just—"

"I wish it could wait, Grace, but it can't." Despair and resignation. "It's important."

Grace slid her hand into her pocket, felt the condom packets, eyed Mal's light a half-relieved *rats!* and nodded.

"Sure, John, no problem. I can't sleep, anyway. Come on down. Let's talk..."

Anger, deep and enervating, such as she'd known only once before in her life—that night a little over three years ago when it seemed Phil had deliberately quit trying to live and decided to simply let go and die—soaked every nerve, jammed every pore. Anger at herself, at John, at Mal, at the world and its insanities, its apparent need to create victims—innocent and otherwise—to take prisoners in order to feed itself and prosper.

Her fists clenched, crushing foil packets in one hand, the box she'd taken them out of in the other. Her heart made aching leaps, lungs quivered painfully inside her. God, how could she have been so stupid? So blind, so irrational?

So hopeful.

She looked at the box of condoms in her hand, and her mouth twisted, mocking her. Protection. Yeah, right. Protection from what? Sexually transmitted diseases? Probably. Pregnancy? The odds were good. From stupidity where her emotions were concerned? No. Protect her heart from liars and other madmen who'd rented space there? Uh-uh, not a chance.

She threw the box hard across the room at her wastebasket. Missed. Picked it up and squashed it between her palms. How naive could she be? How dim-witted to think these little pieces of shaped, plastic-wrapped rubber could keep her safe from someone like Mal. What had she called him that first night? A big old playful tomcat with nothin' but fun and mayhem on his mind. And she... Oh, God, she *cared*.

A lot.

A tiny moan of pain escaped her throat before she could call it back. Her heart hurt, her lungs hurt, her pride hurt—and it wouldn't hurt half so bad if she hadn't only just realized she cared...obviously a whole lot more than she should. She'd crawled all over him tonight. She'd have bedded him if she'd had half a chance. She'd have put her heart in his hands and begged him to keep it if he'd let her. And he'd lied to her. She'd offered him her trust from the beginning and he'd lied. Her kids' lives could be in danger because she'd trusted him and he'd *lied*.

Her kids, damn it. Her *kids*.

Bleakly she stared at the black night eyes that were her windows. God, oh, God, what was she going to do?

The phone beside Mal's bed rang at a quarter to five in the morning.

Standing sleepless and fully clothed at the window where he'd stood since leaving Grace at twelve-thirty, he held the same cigarette he hadn't yet gotten around to smoking because he'd been too busy daydreaming about Grace's mouth and the comment she'd made to him that first night about what kissing a smoker tasted like to a nonsmoker. What other people thought never used to make a difference to him, but now...

He'd also spent the night trying to convince himself that just because he'd only given Grace ninety-five percent of the truth about himself, it didn't mean he was a lying, conniving bastard even when his job sometimes demanded he behave like one. Really.

Exactly what he was, if not a liar, he couldn't say, but what he had learned about himself during the wee hours was far more disturbing than naming himself a liar could ever be: he and Grace hadn't even done *the deed,* but he already knew he'd passed the point of no return with her. Where she was concerned, he was no longer in control of his own destiny. Life had become very simple, really, boiled down to one incontrovertible fact: without Grace, he had no destiny. With Grace . . .

God, he couldn't even think about that. She came with a lot of baggage—kids, pets, relatives, her own life—and he'd barely learned how to cart around his own.

Which was as far as he'd gotten in the self-search when the phone interrupted him. He eyed the ringing instrument with dislike. No good news ever came by phone prior to 10:00 a.m., so if someone felt the need to call before then, the news was invariably bad. He waited until the sixth ring to pick it up.

"Meet me," the voice of his case contact said and the connection broke. No time to say "I got other things to do," no time for anything but compliance.

"Screw it," Mal muttered, in a mood to be at odds with the world, especially *his* world, and cradled the receiver. Before he could lift his hand, it rang again. He jerked it to his ear. "What?"

"I seen him, man, I seen him." Tigger, talking fast, higher than the proverbial and twice as anxious as Mal had ever heard him.

"Where'd you get this number?"

"I ain't. Some dude where you say t'call says hol' on, 'n' I wait, man, and I ain't got time fo' t' wait 'n' finally it ring again 'n' I *seen* him."

"Who?"

"That otha dude you lookin' fo', man, I seen him plain an' I want mo' money for this one, lots mo'. Don' need do this, baby, not no mo'. Ain't worth it."

"You saw Dunne?" Sharp, hard, attention focused.

"Man," Tigger moaned, "don't tell me his name, don' wan' know, but it's him, man. You say I see him I call, but this be it, we square now, we done. Ain' doin' no more for you."

"Where?"

"Man's a stone killer, I seen him do it, jes' walk right up and *pop* behin' the ear an' it done. Don' wan' him seein' me, I got t' go, you got do this man, take care-a it an' get me my money an' I outta here. I meet you—"

"*Where*, Tigger? *Where* did you see him?"

"Oh, man, *here*, where I am now, out the recreation area. Highland Rec. He do some dude in a tree then he—" There was the sound of nervous gulping and skittering, and Tigger's whine went up a notch. "Oh, man, oh, man, he comin' out the woods, I gone, you meet me, I gone—"

A click, a moment's dead air, then dial tone.

Mal stared at the receiver in his hand and felt the adrenaline rise, the fear settle deep and steadying. For Grace, the kids. For himself only because after a long night's thought, he knew that what he needed now with her, with them, was something he might just have run out of.

Time.

All right, okay. He ran his hands through his hair, gathered it together at his neck and looped it into a knot, out of his way. Then he unlocked a drawer in his nightstand, reached way back and untaped his gun from the solid top of the drawer's slot. Time to go to work and make it count.

Options . . . the way he scored it, he had three: one, he could meet his AC—Agent in Charge, who was also his case contact this time out—as commanded, find out what was important enough to call him out of undercover for; two, he could head out to Highland Recreation and look for Dunne and Tigger, who were both undoubtedly long gone by now; or three, he could stand here and try to figure out how to get Grace and her kids out of here without telling them why they had to be sent to a safe area for an unspecified amount of time, and without alerting

Dunne, Abernathy or anyone else to their going. And, given it was Grace, he figured he had about as much chance of getting her out of here without lengthy explanations as he had of roping the moon without a spaceship.

Gotta do somethin', his pulse whispered. *Three things to do, start somewhere.*

Okay. All right. Best thing to do would be to start where he knew he could accomplish something: call number one, his agent in charge. That would give Tigger enough time to get to their prearranged meeting place. It could also give Dunne enough time to find Abernathy at breakfast with Grace and the kids...

Mulling over his options, he checked his weapon's load, made sure the safety was on and clipped the gun in its holster to his belt at the small of his back underneath his T-shirt and a leather vest. Then he collected extra bullets from the small canister at the back of the high cupboard over his refrigerator. Rattled them in his hand while he made his decision.

Hell, no choice. He had to get Abernathy out of here first, then meet his AC, then find Tigger.

He dumped the bullets in the pocket of his vest. And God help him if he'd called it wrong.

Erin was sitting in the driveway putting on her Rollerblades when, less than fifteen minutes later, he vaulted the gate and headed for the steps up to Abernathy's apartment.

"Hi," she said cheerfully.

Mal stared at her. "What are you doing out here by yourself at this hour?" What if Dunne saw her? What if... He shook off the chill of panic. "Do you know what time it is?"

"Putting on my skates and it's almost five-thirty."

"Why are you putting on your skates at five-thirty in the morning? It's hardly light."

"I know, that's why I turned on the outside lights. I have to take my Delta test this morning. I have to practice."

"You're practicing for a Rollerblade test at five-thirty in the morning?" This was stupid. He had to get out of here, but he couldn't leave her out here by herself knowing Dunne was in the area. *So pick her up and tell her to get her butt in the house,* he told himself. Simple.

Or at least, it should have been. And if Erin were a little boy and less her mother's daughter, it undoubtedly would have been. But she was, and it wasn't. "Can't you practice for your roller-skating test later?"

"Ice-skating test, and no I can't. I have all my other patches and I want my Delta patch, but it's harder and you don't get much ice time unless you pay extra for it so I'm practicing on my blades." She put out a hand for him to help her up. "I can't practice later 'cause that's when my test is, so I have to practice now. Mum says if you want something, you have to be willing to work hard and sacrifice for it, an' if you want it badly enough to work for it, there's probably not too much reason you won't get it, and I want to skate and get my patch. At least," she amended, "that's what I want right now."

"Ah," Mal said. Wasn't much else he could say. He frequently hadn't known quite what to say to Jennifer, either, when she was eight and full of the same graveness and indecipherable logic that filled Erin now. "Does your mother know you're out here?"

"No, but she won't care so long as I stay in the driveway 'n' wear my knee pads." Positive. Questioning. "What are *you* doing up so early? Most people stay up late and sleep in in the summer—Phoebe likes to sleep late but I like to get up—especially if they don't have to work."

"I have to work."

"Not till eight. I know, 'cause you drive to work with my mum sometimes."

"Well, right now I have to work with John."

"Oh." She screwed up her face, rolled a pace and did a practice turn in the driveway. Skated wobbly crossovers back to Mal. "If you have to work with John, how come you don't even know he's not home? He had to go to Lansing or someplace, and he won't be back till next Tuesday, or something—I think."

The nag of paranoia started along the back of his neck. "Are you sure?" Sharper than he'd intended.

Erin nodded, troubled. "Is something wrong?"

With an effort, Mal checked his sense of things going wrong in a hurry and shook his head. "No. No, darlin', everything's fine. I just...need to talk with him, that's all."

"Oh." Satisfied that all adults were as inexplicable as her mother, Erin skated a few feet, put out her arms for balance and, concentrating hard, completed a tight, one-footed direction switch. "He came down and talked to Mum real late last night an' I heard him. I was sleeping before that, but the dogs woofed and woke me. Phoebe heard, too, she wasn't even in bed. They talked a long time." She peered sideways at him with little-girl shyness and unknowing insight. "We heard your name a couple times."

"Did you?" The question was out before he could stop it. Damn, you'd think he was back in junior high, getting his friends to bring him up in conversation with some pretty little thing whose name hadn't mattered since about two months after he'd first heard it, finding out for him what she thought of him. He didn't have time to go through adolescence again—especially now. He had to go. He had to get Erin out of here. He had to make sure she and her siblings and her mother would be safe.

He had to go.

Erin was nodding at him, important. "I don't know what they said about you, but Phoebe went out on the steps, so she might."

"It doesn't matter what they said." Impatient with himself for caring. "It's not polite to eavesdrop." Sanctimonious lip service, and he knew it. If he hadn't grown up eavesdropping on adults, he'd never have learned half of what he understood now.

Which was beside the point when it came down to his immediate objective: getting Erin out of the driveway—which didn't feel the least bit safe to Mal at the moment—and getting on with finding Dunne, since Abernathy was conveniently unavailable.

And hopefully, as far as the Witoczynskis were concerned, that meant Dunne was out of town by this time, too.

He prayed.

"Listen, babe—"

"I'm not a 'babe,'" Erin said firmly, all at once grown-up and definite about it. "Unless you want me to call you stud."

"Pardon?"

"Don't call me *babe,* it's sexist."

Oh, God. Women's lib had hit the third grade. He didn't have time for this, no, sir. "Okay, then, Erin, I'm sorry. I didn't mean to be sexist, I was just calling you the same thing I call my daughter. Now—"

"You call your daughter 'babe'?"

What had his mother said to him once? Never plan on hurrying when talking with a child; they'll only make you wait. "Yes."

"Oh, well, that's all right then. My mum calls David 'babe' sometimes, too. And Phoebe is Peaches and Ethan is Hon and I'm Darlin', but if you want to call me—"

"Erin." Firmly. Taking control. "Erin, what I want is for you to listen to me."

"Okay."

"If you're sure it's all right for you to be out here this early practicing for your test, that's fine. But why don't you go out in back on the deck where it's nice and smooth like the ice rink and practice there. You could let the dogs out with you so they won't go crazy and wake the rest of your family. Then when you're done practicing, you could leave a couple of them out and take the rest in."

"Why?"

Never leave room for the *why's*. He'd forgotten that part of parenting. "Why?" All right, he asked himself, why? "Because...you've been so busy lately with baseball and everything that I think they've been lonely and they want your individual attention. You know, special time you can spend with each dog alone."

"Oh." Wisely. "Like Mum does with us sometimes when she's been really busy, taking us shopping or to breakfast, or something?"

"Exactly."

"Okay."

Wonderful child, agreeable child—so long as all her questions were answered. She headed for the breezeway door and Mal turned toward his motorcycle. He should have realized that despite the difficulty, she'd been convinced too easily. There was a clatter of Rollerblade wheels on blacktop and Erin slammed into his back. He swung around to catch her before she fell, but not before she grabbed hold of his belt to steady herself. His holstered gun unclipped from his pants and hit the ground.

Erin reached for it. "You dropped—"

Cursing himself for not bothering with a shoulder holster, Mal got to it first. "I'll get it." He covered the gun with a big hand, hoping she hadn't recognized what it was. "Are you all right?"

She looked up at him big-eyed. "Is that a gun?"

He sucked in a breath, let it out slow. "Yeah." *Damn.*

"Why do you have it?"

"I'm . . ." No good explanations except a piece of the truth. "I'm a policeman, kind of, like your Uncle Gabriel used to be."

"And you have to carry the gun when you're a policeman?"

Mal nodded.

"Like my friend Allison's mom always has to carry one 'cause she's a sheriff?"

Another nod.

"Does my mum know you have it?"

"She knows I've been a cop."

"Oh." She mulled that over. Decided to accept it. "Do you hurt people with your gun?"

"Oh, God, honey, no. Not if I can help it."

"Have you ever hurt anybody with it?"

He looked at her, dead serious. Dead truthful. Shook his head. "No. I went to school to learn how to be very careful with it. I've had to pull it a few times when I'm working, but I've never shot anybody, and I've never had to shoot *at* anybody, either."

"That's good." She was equally serious. "We have DARE officers come to school to teach us classes about no drugs and next year we're going to have GREAT classes to teach us about how to stay out of gangs, too, so I know a little about why police officers carry guns—"

"That's good," he said, but she wasn't finished.

"Because they told us, and they say they'd rather not, but that most cops don't have to . . ."

Mal could see her digging for the word.

". . . don't ever even have to *discharge* their weapons . . . mmm . . . *in the line of duty,* that it's just a . . ." Her mouth worked while she thought. "Just a *precaution.*"

"That's right," Mal agreed. "Most don't."

"Good." Satisfied. She turned to skate away again.

"Wait a minute," Mal said.

She did one of her practice turns, cocked her head to look at him. "What?"

"Didn't you come back to ask me something?"

She stared at him, puzzled, then light dawned. "Oh, yeah! Well, I was just thinking," she said, "that if John's not here, you don't have to go to work with him, so maybe you wanted me to make you coffee and you could drink it and watch me skate so I could practice like I'm in front of a judge."

"Ah." From guns right back to skating. He couldn't shift gears that fast. "No, I wish I could stay for coffee and see you skate, but I can't. I thought, as long as I'm up, I'd go in to Our Lady and finish up a couple things I didn't get done yesterday that Father Rick wants done before Mass this morning." Hell, now he was lying to a child. Would it never stop? "Give me a rain check?"

"What's that?"

Mal grinned. At last, something he knew that this eight-year-old didn't. "Make me coffee some other time?"

"Oh. Okay." Erin nodded, cheerfully accepting, and skated away. "I'll make it for you when you get bac—"

Something scraped in the driveway. Mal swung Erin on her skates behind him and looked—to find Grace in front of him, expression icy.

She knew.

He read it in her stance, her eyes, the unsurprised look of loathing she cast at the weapon still in his hand—the mocking, dismissive glance she swept over him. It was a warm morning, but the air chilled instantly; he felt the freeze to the bone.

"Hey, Mum!" Erin, bright and giggling, enjoying the ride Mal had unexpectedly given her. "What are you doing up—"

"Erin, go inside." Her voice was quiet, emotionless; her eyes on Mal were flat and lightless.

"But I was just—"

"Inside."

"Going to practice—"

"Now."

"Skating on the deck."

Grace looked at her. Hands on hips, Erin glared back.

"I'm taking my *test* this morning, Mum."

If you want it, work for it. How many times had she told her children that? How could she take what Erin was willing to work for from her just because—

"Fine." Grace nodded. "On the deck, then. But stay there or in the house and let the dogs out with you."

Erin viewed her with disgust. "Mal already said that," she told her mother and skated away.

The breezeway door shut behind her.

A moment later, Mal heard the clump of her skates on the deck boards, then the slide of the patio door opening and the dogs woofing as they crashed outside, Erin's laughter as she talked to them. For a second, he shut his eyes and listened. If he forgot, for the moment, who he was and what he was supposed to be doing, the racket in the backyard almost sounded like home.

Or might have if he didn't have the weight of this gun and the knowledge of its uses in his hand and Dunne loose somewhere too close to this family he cared more about than he should.

For longer than he should have, Mal stared after Erin, avoiding the inevitable present—Grace; remembering Jennifer at Erin's age, Ethan's age, realizing how much he'd missed by not being there anymore by the time she'd hit Phoebe's age, David's age. Hoped . . .

He glanced at Grace and hope died aborning.

"I know who you are." Her voice was even, dead quiet. The calm before the hurricane and twice as devastating.

His mouth worked, heart filled with an intolerable ache. Eyes on Grace, he hiked up his shirt and clipped his gun to his belt once more.

"I figured."

Didn't matter what he'd hoped, he knew; she already understood in exactly what kind of heel she'd placed her trust—the man he wasn't, but would have given his eye-teeth to be. With her. For her.

You don't belong here, his mind whispered, adept at sabotage as he'd trained it to be. He'd known for a long time that if the worst was to be said, he'd say it to himself. *It's a pretty picture, but it's not for you.*

Not for you.

"That's all you've got to say?"

Bewilderment mixed with her anger. She wanted something he wouldn't give her: excuses. At the moment, last night was simply history, a moment out of time, past tense and long over now. He knew it, she knew it.

Damn it.

"What else can I say, Grace?"

"Tell me why. I want to understand. What's the attraction? What's so important? I don't care, tell me anything. Tell me I'm not just some cheap trick—"

He sucked in air, stung. "You're not."

"You say that like you mean it," she said bitterly.

"I do."

"Then *tell* me—"

He bent to unlock his motorcycle, concentrating on anything but the pain of self-betrayal he heard in her voice. "I can't, Grace. There are a lot of things I'd like to tell you, but right now I have to go to work and I don't have time."

"No," she said mockingly, "of course not. Lies are a shortcut. Truth takes too long."

"Grace—"

She held out a fist. "I bought these—" she opened the fist to show him the flattened condom box "—because I wanted—with you—I've never...done anything...like this...and now you—" She stopped, slumped, exhausted; this was a cheap shot and she refused to let herself pursue it.

Deliberately, she closed her hand and drew herself erect, catching a fistful of dignity and hanging on to it for all she was worth.

Mal looked at the box in her hand, looked at her face, felt the ache in his chest gain greater foothold, threaten to overwhelm him.

There was so much more to her than met the eye.

"Grace, I—" He swallowed.

She waited, but he had nothing to offer except the same platitudes that hadn't worked with Livvi, and so, sure as hell, wouldn't suffice with Grace.

"I have to go," he said, not looking at her.

"Me, too," she agreed and, without a backward glance, did.

Mal watched her back, the long unfettered stride that had struck him the first time he'd seen her, and he wished...

Nothing, he told himself savagely. *Don't think. Go to work.*

No longer looking back at a life that wasn't his, he bleakly rolled the Moto Guzzi down the driveway. Climbed on and stamped harder than necessary on the starter.

Went.

Chapter 12

She knew more than she wanted to know.

She didn't know enough.

She knew too much.

God, Mal, who are you? What have you done?

It had been a rough morning.

Watching Erin practice spins on the ice, Grace sat behind the windows in the small cafeteria at Lakeland Ice Arena trying to wake up—and warm up—by sipping at her second large cup of the inky black coffee she'd come to regard as disembalming fluid, aka the staff of life. Around her, other skating parents chatted, watching their daughters leap and spin, their sons run hockey speed drills. Behind their custodial eyes, dreams of Olympic gold and glory lay packaged in encouragement and criticism, in frustration because the parent couldn't get out on the ice and just *do it* for the child.

Backed by the filtered noise of ice machines and mingled voices, the silence was almost deafening.

Tiredly, Grace cupped her chin in her palm and rubbed her eyes. Her heart wasn't in this today, her mind wasn't on Erin. Last night and this morning sat heavy on her soul, weighted by discoveries and disclosures she'd rather have left suspected but unconfirmed. A little about Mal, a lot about John, some things about herself she'd prefer not to believe.

Things Erin had asked about Mal, John had told her, Gabriel had said.

Things that Mal had all but admitted.

Things she'd gone to discuss with him—to confront him with—only to have him walk away, duty-bound. *Honor*-bound by some macho male code of ethics, damn it.

Damn *him*.

Things she couldn't deny she'd already half suspected. Especially since he'd half alluded to them himself last night.

Be careful what you wish for...

The caution hung in the air like the odor of spilled milk in a carpet on a hot day.

She moved restlessly on the picnic-table bench, easing the tension in her back, staring through the heavy Plexiglas at Erin's bright mint and purple figure on the ice. Peering, as it were, through a keyhole at the face of her daughter as Erin accomplished her special dream; watched while Erin discovered her own individual talents—as was a parent's right and privilege. But lately it had also become an obligation. A job.

A chore.

Self-recrimination reared its ugly head. No excuse for what she'd done, what she still felt. With Mal, for Mal, because of Mal. *No* justification. None.

At all.

To each thing a season went the song, the Bible verse, the adage. And it was true. But it was also true that the seasons sometimes encroached on each other, changed without sharp delineation, bled into each other like sunshine and shadow, like watercolors in rain.

She felt guilty—and frustrated and angry with Mal who, she'd just discovered, wasn't who she wanted him to be—because, where he was concerned, her needs had begun to conflict with her children's, their needs occupied nearly every waking moment, and David's needs ...

Oh, Lord, David's needs. Like the tourism ads for Texas claimed, a whole 'nother country.

And Mal, damn him, was a whole 'nother continent.

"Grace." His voice was above her, quiet, raw.

She looked up and the breath in her lungs fibrillated nervously, her palms began to sweat. Oh, Lord, there he was: Mal "Too Sexy For His Shirt" Quarrels.

Mal "The Liar" Quarrels.

Mal—who - she - couldn't - forgive - herself - for - still - wanting - needing - caring - about—Quarrels; Mal—who - she - didn't - think - it - would - have - taken - much - more - provocation - for - her - to - fall - in - love - with - if - this - hadn't - happened—Quarrels.

Resolutely, she picked up her copy of *A Coach's Guide to Slowpitch Softball for Kids* and forced herself to ignore him, to read. He sat and covered the pages with a hand, weighted the book flat to the table.

"Grace, you and the kids have got to get out of here."

She eyed him, jaw set. John—she'd long suspected that wasn't his real name, but now she knew for sure—had said the same thing last night. But his saying it then hadn't made her feel the way Mal's saying it now did. Worried rather than merely concerned. Frightened rather than distantly afraid. Absolutely aware that waiting until Sunday morning before driving the kids up to Jones Lake outside Grayling to leave them for a week's camping with

Twink, Edith, Alice and their families, while she came back home to work until next weekend the way she'd planned, was out of the question.

They, not she—she had too many obligations, had decided too long ago that to run from fear was no way for her to live—had to be gotten out of here now, today. She knew that. Stubborned it through for a minute, anyway, so Mal wouldn't think she was doing what he said because he said so. Because she was angry. Because the urgency she heard in his voice seemed unreal to her; little in her experience had ever been so urgent.

And so he'd know she made her own decisions.

Always.

About everything.

"Who are you to tell me my kids and I have to do anything? What gives you the right to put them in jeopardy in the first place?"

"That's why I'm here, to make sure—"

"Don't give me that bull. You're here to do whatever it takes to catch some killer who should never have been let loose just because some prosecutor wanted to know what he knew and dealt for it—and don't *tell* me that's not how you bastards work, because it is, and *don't* try to tell me the bunch of you couldn't have figured out someplace other than my kids' home to fix your damned screwup, either."

"Grace—"

"And don't *Grace* me. Don't anything me. All I want right now is for you to go to hell, Mal Quarrels. Who the hell do you think you are, anyway?"

"The guy who wants to keep you safe."

"The guy who lied to me, you mean."

"That, too."

He eyed her steadily, without apology; she looked away first, at the ice and Erin. The anger stung like bile in her throat, making it hard to swallow, to breathe. The fact that she wanted him to hold her and lie to her to make it better stung far worse.

"I suppose you're going to tell me you're only doing your job." God, it *hurt*.

"I could. I *should* only be doing my job."

"Are you?"

"Doing my job?"

She looked at him and her mouth worked. She nodded.

His turn to look away. "Trying to protect you is part of my job. The way I feel about you isn't."

"Then what is it?"

He turned to her, eyes intense and haunted, face haggard. She hadn't slept much last night, but he hadn't slept at all.

"Nothing I can change or control." He made a move to touch her fingers, withdrew it, unsure if she would let him. Looked through the Plexiglas at the ice. "Nothing I want to."

She stared at him, the raw honesty, the plea for clemency he didn't even know he wore. *It's all in how you look at it,* she'd told the kids more often than she cared to count. *What you say to other people, what you do, it's all tangled up with how you see yourself. How you want to see yourself.*

She'd said it to try to explain away unkind things said by classmates, rival coaches, siblings—tried to stress that there was always more than one way to look at a thing, more than one way to hear, to listen. More than one point of view. That if they were happy with themselves, if they did their best to always try to do the right thing, then what other people said or thought about them didn't matter.

And now here she was throwing her own words back in her own face.

Swallowing, she looked at the hand Mal didn't touch, at his face, remembered the hunger, the physical honesty between them last night. Remembered the things he'd said without lying, the things he'd tried to warn her about himself.

Remembered what she'd decided he was worth.

Damned herself for remembering and not being able to look away from what she saw.

"Devil take it," she muttered and, laying caution on the altar of the to-hell-with-it gods, covered Mal's hand with hers. "Tell me," she said softly.

"Grace, please." He tried to pull away; she held on. Damn it, he was nearly twice her size. Why did she make him so weak?

Because he wanted her to hold on, he didn't want to let her go.

He shut his eyes and swallowed, looked at her. "There's no time."

"Tell me," she repeated, and this time the softness was edged in steel, fierce and undeniable. Not asking him to deny what she knew about him, but to confirm it so they could move on.

Mal studied her, jaw working. Knew she wouldn't move until he told her, stubborn woman. Phenomenal woman. Capitulated.

"How much do you know?" he asked.

She eyed him steadily. "I know that a man whose name is not John Roth is being used as bait to catch a killer in a joint operation between the U.S. Marshal's Service and the FBI. I know that this killer and the man who's not John were both part of the witness protection program for a time."

"I know—" she made an off-hand gesture "—that John made a lot of noise when he left for Lansing to go over the books for one of the state's charitable camps this morning, hoping this killer would follow him and stay away from the kids and me. I know he doesn't want anyone between him and this guy and how to get hold of him if this man comes here looking for him. I know that he doesn't want a repeat of what happened with his ex-partner and this guy on Long Island a couple years ago and that he'll be back tonight."

She drew a breath, let it out. Looked him in the eye. Mal felt his gut tense.

"I know that you're an employed U.S. marshal with special duties and a special classification, not a laid-off South Dakota cop."

"Grace—"

"I'm not finished." Her hand tightened painfully on his, her mouth twisted. "I know how angry I am with you for not trusting me with your truth the way I've trusted you with my kids and their lives, but I also know that how I feel about you is a lot more complicated than a simple explanation and a quick heave-ho will satisfy. So there we are. I may know a couple other things, too, but I'd rather you tell me the rest. And make me believe it."

He stared at her, coming to grips with what she knew, what she needed to know. The silence between them was deafening.

"You don't ask much," he said finally.

The ghost of a smile haunted her eyes and mouth; she slipped her fingers into his hand. "You knew I wouldn't," she returned.

"True," he agreed. His laughter was wry and self-mocking. Part of her appeal for him was that she was an unbreakable, get-involved, never-back-down, give-what-she-got, bust-a-guy-in-the-chops-when-he-needed-it-but-hang-on-tight kind of woman. Exactly the opposite of Livvi, a hundred and eighty degrees removed from the kind of woman he'd always thought he wanted.

God, had he been wrong.

"So?" she asked, expectant.

He turned his palm up and squeezed her fingers.

"So," he acknowledged, sucked in a breath and told her.

Quietly, tersely. From the beginning. William Dunne. Dead witnesses. Leak in the department. Gus Abernathy. Seeing her. The gut recognition that she was…special. His growing concern for her and her children. The hit man at Ethan's game. What he'd felt with her last night. Talking with his case contact this morning only to learn that the trickle-down theory of information passing hadn't trickled down to him in any timely fashion at all. Being told that the suspected department leak had been killed mere hours before he was to be arrested. Learning at the same time that Dunne had eluded the agents sent out to apprehend him and was now either on his way to Michigan and Grace's house or had already spent several days casing the neighborhood.

Eyes black with fury, he told her about the dead hit man Tigger had called to tell him about. About Tigger seeing Dunne in the area. About finding Tigger bleeding to death in the field where they were supposed to meet. Tigger identifying Dunne as his killer before he died with more courage than he'd lived.

Mal's own anger over having had to use a seventeen-year-old boy's addictions against him, and his guilt that because of him Tigger had died. His gut-deep fear for Grace and her kids and his need to get them away from here so he wouldn't lose any of them. Because if anything happened to any of them, especially Grace, he didn't know what—

"I passed!" Erin's skated feet clomped gleefully over the rubber mat between the ice-rink door and the table where her mother and Mal sat. She waved her Delta certificate and patch in Grace's face. "See?" she crowed. "I'm so happy! It says, 'Excellent, much improved, a pleasure to work with, very talented. Recommend moving Erin into the advanced classes.'"

She plonked herself enthusiastically onto the bench beside Grace. "Isn't that cool? She thinks if I work hard and go to competitions that I could even go to the Olympics! Hi, Mal, did you see me? Did you? I was *good*. I'm glad I practiced!"

"You are terrific," Mal said solemnly, and meant it.

Grace eyed Mal, her daughter in dismay. The urgency to get her children out of here was uppermost in her mind, but this other thing had to be dealt with . . .

"The Olympics?" she asked. "You're eight."

"I know." Erin nodded. "That's why it's so good. I have eight years. That's *lots* of time to get even better than I am now."

"Oh, God," Grace groaned, mentally toting figures for coaches, costumes, skates, International Figure Skating Association dues and fees, special tutors to keep up Erin's studies . . . There wasn't a chance in hell she could afford it. Not one. Lord, why couldn't her kids have simple dreams, inexpensive dreams . . .

She glanced at Mal. He nodded. But she'd have to discuss practicalities with her daughter—and her financial consultant—later.

She turned to Erin. "Look, darlin', get out of your skates and let's hit the road. We'll talk about the Olympics later. I've got a surprise for all of you when we get home."

"What is it?"

"When we get home," Grace said firmly, and, Erin's half-tied shoes and all, they went.

"No problem," Alice said half an hour later when Grace called. "Matter of fact, Gabriel just made the same suggestion, only he included you coming up tonight, too, instead of waiting till next week."

"No, thanks, Allie, I appreciate the thought, but I can't. I don't get a paycheck if I don't work—and I've got a few other things to take care of, too."

"Mal?" Alice guessed.

"Well," Grace hedged, looking across the bed at her closed bedroom door, on the other side of which Mal waited. She turned back to the phone, noncommittal—even to herself. She was still mad at Mal, right?

Right?

"Well . . ."

"That's what I thought." Alice laughed. "Be careful, but enjoy."

"Take care of my kids," Grace advised her sweetly, "or they'll take care of you." She hung up to the sound of Alice's laughter.

"You're not staying here." Mal's voice behind her was flat and emotionless, provoked.

"I believe I closed the door when I came in here," Grace retorted, startled. "Even the kids knock before barging in."

"Sue me, I'm not a kid—"

"No? Well, you're behaving like a—"

"—and you're old enough to figure out that—"

"—possessive idiot and treating me like—"

"—if anything happens to you, what happens to—"

Grace clamped her mouth shut and looked at him. "I'm staying and that's flat," she said resolutely.

Equally resolute, Mal jutted his jaw and brought his face down level with hers. "Then you better make room in the house because if you're stayin', I'm moving in."

Into this decidedly unadult standoff, Phoebe and Erin marched, shoving the door open hard enough that it bounced off the doorstop and slammed shut in Ethan's face.

"Hey!"

Furious, he clonked it back open, stormed into the room and, at the sight of his mother, visibly bit back the comment he'd been about to make to his sisters. Maintaining a reserved distance, David followed him.

"Why'n't ya pay attention to what you're doing?" Ethan asked.

Concentrating on Grace, Phoebe and Erin ignored him.

"Erin says," Phoebe began, "that you told her you had a surprise for us all when you got home."

"You did," Erin agreed, definite.

Grace drew a breath, eyeing the children, Mal, gathering a moment to shift gears. Damn the man, anyway. What was it about him that rattled her normally collected self to such a degree? And why did she let him get to her like that?

Because, she realized with a start, this was her *bedroom* and the condoms she hadn't had with her last night and intended to throw at him this morning were right *there*, back in place beneath the upper left-hand corner of her mattress and she was thinking . . . and *her* kids were in the room and the whole thing was just not . . . just not . . .

Something she was the least bit prepared to handle.

"How," she asked, mustering an enthusiasm she was unnerved to discover was real, "would you like to go up north with Aunt Alice and Uncle Gabriel tonight instead of waiting until Sunday?"

"Oh, *man*," David burst out, disgusted.

"Without you?" Ethan asked, anticipation evident.

Bright-eyed, Erin and Phoebe bounced beside him, excited and expectant. Grace eyed them, dismayed. Their enthusiasm about being without her for a week bothered her almost as much as hers about being without them for the same period. Maybe it was time they all—including her—left the nest.

Just for a while.

She grinned and nodded. "Without me."

"Yeah!" Phoebe, delighted.

"Cool!" Ethan, the same.

"*Way* cool!" Erin, jumping up and down and doing her impression of her favorite television character, Nickelodeon's Clarissa, from *Clarissa Explains It All.* "I have to pack!"

"I'm not goin' anywhere," David said flatly, "tonight or Sunday, so you can just live with it."

"David," Grace exclaimed, but her son had already stomped out of the room, punching whatever came to hand on his way through the living room and up the stairs. The house rattled when he shut his bedroom door. *"David!"*

She stared after him, bemused, for almost three seconds, then the morning and all of its complications hit her and annoyance woke with a vengeance.

"David, God bless it, get back here. What the heck's your problem? You never want to stay home and then when I say you can go—who the hell am I talking to, you're not even in the room."

She turned to Erin, Ethan and Phoebe. "Get packed," she said and headed after David, muttering as she went. "I didn't sign on for this, I don't want to do this, I do *not.* First you want to play ball, then you don't, then you want to coach, now you think it's babyish, this morning I find your sheets in a wet lump in a corner of the basement behind the water softener, now you've got *this* bug in your ear and I do *not* have time—"

"Grace." Mal caught up with her.

"What do you want? I've got a crisis on my hands, kids to get out of town, an almost-thirteen-year old who's lost his mind and you're in my way. Go away."

"Did you say you found wet sheets?"

"Yeah, so?" Belligerent.

Despite himself, Mal swallowed a grin at her imitation of Mother Bear Protecting Her Cub. Sheila behaved the same way with his nephew.

"So," he said, working hard to keep the humor out of his voice, "so trust me. He doesn't want to talk to you right now."

"Of course he does. I'm his mother. He talks to me about everything."

"Not everything."

"Yes." She was adamant. *"Everything."*

"Including, er—" he dropped his voice so three pairs of big, listening ears couldn't overhear "—nocturnal emissions?"

"Pardon?" Grace asked, blinking.

"Wet dreams," Mal said succinctly.

Grace's jaw dropped. "You're kidding."

He shook his head. "Wet sheets behind the water softener? I don't think so."

"He won't even be thirteen until Tuesday."

"Some guys mature faster than others." Mal shrugged. "Happens in its own time."

"Now? It has to happen now? I don't have time for this now. *He* doesn't have time for this now. Oh, crud." She looked up the steps. "What do I know from wet dreams? Phil was supposed to take care of this. Aw, damn. I better go up and talk to him so he knows it's okay—"

Mal stopped her. "Let me."

"But I—"

"Trust me," he repeated.

"I did," she said smartly. "You blew it."

He looked at her.

She sighed, not quite apologetic. "I know," she said. "You had valid reasons, and sometimes questions of trust and betrayal are a matter of how you look at them rather than of what your emotions think."

He touched her cheek. "Thanks."

She nodded, eyed him darkly. "That doesn't mean we won't talk about it later, you understand, but right now, like you said, we have to get them—"

"Gone." Mal nodded, heart lightened, gut knotting all at once. "Don't worry. He'll go." He started up the stairs, turned back to her. "Oh, yeah. Why don't you send Ethan up, too, and we'll take care of the whole thing at once."

Grace nodded, still discombobulated by her sons actually growing up instead of this just being another unreal page in the *What's Happening To My Body: Boys* book she'd forced herself to read—and tossed aside, and forced herself to pick up again even though she *wasn't* ready for this point-blank version of the Facts of Life from their point of view. The girls' version of the same book had been hard enough to deal with. She turned, only to have Mal call her back one more time.

"And by the way..." His turn to look ominous. "After I'm done here, you want to talk to me about the things I've done?"

She nodded, wary.

"Fine, we'll talk about 'em. *After* you listen to my version of why and how we're getting you out of here, too."

No way was she about to let him have the last word. "We can talk," she said evenly, gently. "As long as you know that the only place I'm going from here is to work on Monday morning. Can't let a bunch of jackasses decide how I live my life."

Then, before he could ruin her exit, she was off the steps, calling to Ethan and the girls, deaf to the explicit profanity Mal delivered after her.

David's room was dim, the shades pulled against the daylight. To one side of the covered window, he lay facedown on the top bunk and didn't look up when Mal entered, shutting the door behind him.

"Hey, Dave."

"Go away."

"Nope." Mal sat down on the bottom bunk of the untidy set opposite David's. Ethan's personality to a tee, just as the carelessly neat trim of David's bunks matched him. "Came to talk."

"Hope you like talking to yourself, 'cuz I got nothin' to say."

Mal shrugged. "I don't mind if you don't."

David didn't move. "Long as you don't talk about me apologizing to anybody for anything 'cuz I'm not sorry and I won't say I am."

"Got it," Mal agreed. He let the silence collect for a time.

Impatient as well as stubborn, David propped his chin on his hands and stared at the blinded window. "I thought you came to talk."

"Thought I'd wait for an invitation."

Trying to seem as if he wasn't, David peered at him sideways, almost intrigued. "My mother never waits for invitations."

Mal gave him rolled-eye wry. "Your mother is her own invitation."

A stifled snort didn't quite sound in David's throat. He tried not to grin, but for a young man with a sense of humor despite his age, it was difficult. "Are all women as volatile as she is?"

Mal's turn to snort, covering laughter that David would even know, let alone use the word *volatile*. "Only the interesting ones."

"Then I'm never getting married."

"Too soon to say never," Mal advised. "Women like your mother have many, er, *redeeming* qualities."

"Like what?"

That put Mal on the spot. He couldn't very well say, "she's one hell of a kisser, and, boy, does she ring my chimes" to the woman's not quite thirteen-year-old son, now, could he? "She found your sheets behind the water softener—"

"Aw, *man.*" As incriminating a nonadmission as Mal had ever heard.

"—and didn't say anything about it."

"Then how do you know they were there?"

Logical children were a pain in the butt. "She muttered it on the steps after you stomped off here. I heard her."

David buried his head under his pillow. "Aw, jeez."

"You want to talk about it?"

"Not really—"

The door banged open and Ethan entered, planted himself in front of Mal. "Ma says you needa talk to me 'n Dave."

"Mmm," Mal agreed.

"'Bout what?"

"Things that will happen to your body in—"

"Aw, man." Ethan gave him disgust. "I already know about that stuff." He flopped onto David's lower bunk, and made snoring noises. "Boring."

"What stuff do you know about?" Mal's patience did him credit; his thoughts, however, were more along the line of feeling some awe that after dealing with this crew for the last thirteen years, Grace's sanity was still more or less intact.

Ethan turned over, sighing. "In a couple years, I'm gonna want to start looking at naked women in nudie magazines and then I'll have sexy dreams and pee in my bed like—"

"Shut up," David said, starting to get hot.

"—Dave has."

"Shut up!" David bellowed, hitting the boiling point before he even had a chance to simmer.

Ethan slid around to peer up at him, overly well informed. "Then why did you get up in the middle of the night and start swearing to yourself about everything being wet and have to change your sheets and your gym shorts—"

"I did not!"

"Did so."

"Shut up!"

David angled himself over the side of his bed to grab his younger brother by the shirt, haul him into pummeling range. Fully prepared, Ethan grabbed back and socked David first. Mal separated them.

"Hey!" he thundered. "Knock it off."

They barely paused to look at him, intimidated almost as easily as their mother.

"He started it." Ethan.

"Make him shut up." David.

"You shut up."

"Both of you shut up," Mal said firmly, dumping them each on their respective bunks, and wondering why the *devil* he'd felt the need to come up here in the first place to try to make David feel more comfortable with the realities and practicalities of puberty simply because he remembered how uncomfortable and embarrassing it was like to be where David was.

Because, he realized with despair, with hope, they were part of the package that was Grace and that's all there was to it. Not to mention, that no matter how terrific it was to have Jennifer as a daughter, he'd always kind of...wanted a son—he glanced at Ethan—or even two.

God help him, he'd lost his mind.

Dumbfounded, he eyed Grace's boys—sitting on their beds, making rude faces and expressive gestures at each other behind his back—and swallowed a chuckle. At them and at himself. Amazing, the things one learned about oneself when one least wanted to.

"All right." He cleared his throat. "First, let's get one thing straight. Nobody is peeing in anybody's bed. Peeing, sexy dreams and nudie magazines have absolutely nothing to do with wet dreams. Second, this is how this is going to work. I will speak to you about wet dreams and what to do about them when there's nothing you can do about them, then you may ask questions, then I will answer them and you will listen attentively without making faces at each other or snide remarks, or anything...."

Forty-five minutes later, when Twink's van—Alice's car was too small to carry four extra kids and their luggage—pulled into the driveway to collect the Witoczynski crew, David bounded down the steps two at a time, grabbed Grace in a none-too-gentle bear hug and bussed her hard.

"See ya, Mum."

"Yeah—huh? Hey!" She caught his arm and pulled him back to hug him. "You the same kid who told me he wasn't going anywhere an hour ago?"

"Ma." Pulling away, rolled-eye embarrassment. That was then, this is now and never the twain shall a boy be reminded of by his mother.

Grace lightly cuffed the back of his head. "Behave yourself and have a good time. Don't worry about anything, hmm?"

"Ma-a." Two syllables, more rolled eyes and an I-gotta-go tug.

Grace squeezed him one more time "I love you" despite his efforts to escape.

"Bye, Mum-mum." Erin wedged herself between them for a quick kiss and hug. "See you, miss you, love you."

"Love—"

"Love you, Mom, see you next week." Phoebe, piling in for an instant then dashing off.

"Take care—"

"Mom!" Ethan, grabbing her around the waist in a smaller version of David's hug, but holding on a little longer. "Love you, bye!" Then, aside to his brother, "D' ya get the extra washcloths?"

David gave Grace a peck on the cheek and Ethan a light shove. "Yeah, now shut up."

Ethan, always bolder than he should be, shoved his taller, older, weightier brother back—and ran. "Make me."

David dashed after him. "I will, you little weasel—"

"Hey." Grace went to the door and shouted after them, "Behave!"

Twink poked her head out the driver's window while they loaded up. "Don't worry, I'll sit on 'em if I have to."

"Just get 'em there and back in one piece," Grace called.

She waved them down the street and out of sight. Turned back to the house, sighing. In the yard around her, quiet reigned where once ran chaos. Mal awaited her in the doorway, surrounded by four forlorn-looking dogs and one wild-eyed cat. She approached him filled with a sense of trepidation and anticipation.

"What did you do to David?"

Mal shrugged and held the door open for her. "I told him what my mother told me."

She slipped past him. "Oh?"

"Sure." He grinned. "Just like women do, use layers to absorb."

"Excuse me?"

Mal's grin broadened; he shut the door before the cat escaped. "I told him to wear skivvies under his gym shorts and that if he was still worried about his sleeping bag getting wet, to stuff a washcloth or some toilet paper down his trunks, too."

Grace viewed him, astonished. "That works?"

"Uh-huh."

"Well." She was suitably impressed. "I'd never have thought of it. Too simple, too practical. My mind runs to more elaborate solutions."

"Mmm," Mal agreed, facing her. "I noticed that about your mind—" he slipped his hands along her jaw, beneath her hair, cupping her face "—how you like to complicate things when you aren't going straight to the heart of a matter."

Grace placed a hand on his chest, holding him away, wanting to draw him close. "Mal..."

He shook his head, silencing her, dead serious. "I'm taking a page out of your book, Grace. Straight to the heart of it."

"I won't leave." She tried to lift her face out of his hands and pull away, the way David had, end this conversation here. He held on. The way she had last night, earlier this morning. "I won't run. I can't."

"I know."

His eyes seemed to hold her breath, govern her ability to breathe. She felt breathless and giddy when she should have been angry. At least still mildly teed-off. "And you can't get rid of me by tossing me over your shoulder and carting me away to someplace you think safe just because you're bigger than I am."

"I know that, too." Half a smile sketched his mouth. "I note you didn't also say I'm stronger than you."

"That would be foolish to admit—whether it's true or not." She tucked her hands around his. "And you believing you are would be even more foolish."

"I'm not foolish." He spread his fingers, let his thumbs graze her mouth. His eyes were hungry, his lips were close. "Except about you."

Chapter 13

"Mal," Grace whispered, but that was as far as she got before his mouth closed over hers.

The kiss was long and complicated: gentle, achingly tender, demanding, giving . . . loving. A place to build the fire, rather than the fire itself. A commitment, rather than merely a promise. An emotion without words, a prelude and a quest.

A request.

He lifted his head. His eyes on her face were dark and liquid. "You have to get out of here."

She looked at him, eyes soft, belying the mind behind them.

"This is your plan?" she asked dryly. "Kiss me silly then tell me to go and I'll do it?"

His grin was sheepish—and hopeful.

Grace rolled her eyes. "Boy, you really don't know me at all, do you?"

"No. But I sure as hell want to, and if you stay, I may never—"

A Certain Slant of Light

Grace turned her back on him, moved to arrange scattered pillows on the couch, fold the cotton throw someone had used and left on the floor last night. "If I go, you may not get to, either." She looked over her shoulder at him. "But if I stay, we have now, without kids or other distractions. Later is a gamble, no matter how you stack the deck."

"Grace—"

"What do you think?" She placed the throw on the back of the couch, moved on to turn and fluff cushions. Busywork. Anything to occupy her hands. Keep them away from him. "Do you think this guy—Dunne, is it?— do you think he's going to walk up, knock on my door and take me hostage when I answer it until Gus Abernathy shows up? With you here, and God knows who else out there watching this place, patrolling the neighborhood, you think he's that stupid?"

"No." Mal's voice was taut, hard, passionate. He crossed the room, caught her shoulders and spun her to face him. "I think he's that bold, and I think he's that smart, and I think that the reason he's loose is that too many people—including the U.S. attorney you referred to earlier—underestimated his capabilities."

He shook her once and let her go, stared out the big front picture window. "William Dunne is not like other people, Grace. He didn't get to be head of the one of the biggest Mafia family operations on the East Coast because he was afraid to kill off his competition and risk big." He looked at her, troubled. "He hasn't stayed alive all this time when his higher-ups want him dead because he's stupid."

Grace studied him, dazed by something that hadn't occurred to her before. "You're afraid for me."

"Damn right."

She swallowed. That put her stubbornness in a whole new light. It meant she had to explain to him things she'd barely had time to explain to herself.

"I'm afraid for you, too," she said finally, softly. "That's part of the reason I sent the kids up north with Gabriel, Mal—" her turn to catch his arm, make him face her "—with *Gabriel* who's got the paranoid instincts of a she-bear with cubs. He'll pay attention to who's skulking around and he'll keep them safe."

He stared at her, light not quite dawning. She dropped his arm and turned away.

"I *know* Dunne's not stupid, Mal. I figured that out last night when John told me about what almost happened to his friend three years ago, when he told me how Dunne offered up his...I don't know, his friends, co-workers, bosses, whatever you want to call them, in order to beat the judicial system. *That's* why I have to stay, do you understand?" Passionate. "*I'm* the reason John stopped running and took up residence here, he reminded me of that last night when I was blasting him to bits, damn him. I'm the one who told him that if he didn't stop running and face whatever was chasing him—even when I didn't know specifically what it was—he was going to wake up one morning old and alone and the people who'd cared about him along the way weren't going to be able to reach him."

She paused, reaching for air, for reason, watching the thoughts collect in Mal's eyes.

"Don't you see?" she asked. "I'm like you, I don't have any options. I *have* to stay because, knowingly or not, I'm the one who started this. I'm afraid for you and for my kids. Because if I go hide someplace and Dunne's looking for someone John cares about to use to get John to do whatever he wants John to do and he doesn't find me, what stops him from going after my kids, my sisters' kids, my sisters, or anybody else I care about? You? I care about you, too. That's what happens when you walk into people's lives, Mal, or hang somebody out as bait. They get involved, whether you intend them to or not and there's no way to keep it clean. None.''

Her jaw was squared, her face determined. He stared at her, stunned, defeated. Instinctively or logically, she'd thought this whole thing through further than he had. Nothing he could say or do would change it now.

He'd thought he'd covered all the angles, seen all the possible sides, but she'd come up with one that hadn't occurred to him at all. By staying here in full sight, she was like the mother bird pretending to have a broken wing, leading the predators away from her nest. Even if he forced her to go, took her away in chains, she'd find a way to come back because, as she said, from her standpoint and for the sake of her children, she had no choice.

And now he didn't, either.

"I guess you'd better shove over," he said, grimly. "I'm movin' in."

It was a quiet day, filled with sun and zephyr breezes, idyllic in every aspect save the single dangerous one that sat foremost in Mal's and Grace's minds—right beside the thing they both wanted most: each other.

Beside other needs, the danger of Dunne paled, became almost preferable to the peril they represented to each other. They'd made emotional admissions, confessions they couldn't take back, but weren't quite ready to stand by. They needed each other in ways less basic, more intricate than the mere physical, but caving in to those needs, their more primitive desires, seemed a long way out of the question—like inviting a tornado into the midst of a hurricane and hoping for the best.

Awkwardness set in where they hadn't been awkward before; getting it right this time meant the world.

They were aware of each other more than ever. Yesterday's thoughtlessness was past, tomorrow was uncertain, and even later today was iffy in the extreme. *Now* was what they had, and *now* was the thing they weren't sure how to deal with, how to approach.

When Grace got out the tractor to mow the lawn, Mal quit working on his motorcycle, went inside where he could see her but not be near her and called Jennifer—which worried his daughter, because her dad usually called her in the evenings when the rates were down and they could spend time. He assured her everything was fine, that he'd only called because he had a moment and she was getting darn hard to reach on a weekend night. She snorted, but didn't press. Then, beyond learning she was well, Mal barely followed what else she said. His mind was occupied elsewhere, outside, with Grace.

Thinking that the spot out there among the trees, where the yard dipped and was hidden and private from the everything else around it, would be the perfect place to dump her off the tractor and love her until neither of them could move and they had to simply lie there in the sun-dappled shade, bodies entangled, drowsing together until their strength came back—and he could love her again.

Imagining what it would be like to have those long legs of hers wrapped tight around him, holding him in.

Imagining what it would be like to bury himself inside her, lose himself in her depths and not resurface until at least a week from next Thursday, when it would surely be time to get lost in her again.

Imagining what it would be like to become part of her, integral to her life for the rest of time the way he had the uncomfortable, despairing feeling that she'd become critical to his well-being, his sanity—only he was going to wind up being too backward to admit it in time and end up losing her, if not to Dunne, then to some nonessential piece of himself. Like pride.

Tortured himself by imagining what it would be like to simply wake up to her face every morning, get into the same bed with her every night—and he hadn't a clue, at the moment, how to make that imagining be true.

It was much the same for Grace.

When Mal fixed lunch and brought it out to her after she'd finished with the lawn, she sat as far away from him on the deck as was politely possible. To be any closer meant to want to reach out and touch, to pick up her napkin and wipe the dab of mustard off the corner of his mouth, to taste away the strawberry juice that stained his lips, to...

She shocked herself with the intimacy and brazenness of what else she wanted to do with Mal, to Mal. She'd been married for better than nine years, for Pete's sake. She'd always assumed she and Phil had explored all the physical realms of pleasure. Which meant that nothing she could imagine should shock her.

She'd thought.

But it did. And not because it was more erotic than anything she'd imagined before, anything she'd done with Phil—although it was both—but because somewhere between yesterday and right now, the things she wanted to commit with Mal, the temptations she wanted to give in to, the completely private territory she wanted to explore with him no longer had anything strictly to do with sex.

They had to do with love, with commitment. With expanding her horizons to include him despite his profession and her knowledge of the mortality rate on law enforcement—she forced herself to think the scary word—*marriages*. Despite the complications even getting distantly involved with him had already entailed.

He would be, she realized, bemused, worth *all* the complications she could dream up and those she couldn't—in spite of his macho, overprotective drawbacks.

And because of them.

She shut her eyes and let the pictures collect.

She could imagine growing old with him.

She could imagine making love with him when she was eighty.

She could imagine raising her children and baby-sitting her grandchildren with him.

She could imagine a life full of bad jokes and disagreements and political disputes and discussions and making up and waking up with Mal Quarrels.

She could imagine...

Sudden laughter sent a piece of inhaled strawberry down the wrong pipe and nearly choked her.

"Grace, are you okay?" Alarmed, Mal was up and across the deck, arms around her waist.

"Fine," she wheezed, laughing harder.

Mal squatted in front of her, still concerned, but also suspicious. "Are you dying or laughing?"

She chortled. "Both."

"I see." He shook his head. "No, I don't. What's so funny?"

"Ah, Mally, Mally, Mally." She brought the laughter under control and patted his cheek. "If I told you, you'd get embarrassed."

"If I remember correctly, you're the one who gets embarrassed, not me."

She let her hand settle on his shoulder. Of their own volition, her fingers moved to twist in his hair. She loved his hair. "Maybe when you're old and gray."

"Grace."

Laughter sputtered in Grace's throat, her eyes sparkled. "Trust me," she said.

"I do," he told her, serious.

Laughter died, replaced by something infinitely more wondrous. "That's good," she whispered and kissed him.

He tried to pull away, too aware of the situation, the moment. Too full of want to simply kiss her this time and let her go. "Grace..."

She thrust her fingers into his hair, anchoring his face between her hands. Turned in her chair to plant her knees more comfortably on either side of his waist. Kissed him again.

"Shut up and keep trusting me," she murmured.

He struggled with his conscience, his desires, how quickly she moved from moment to moment—collecting them almost the way a squirrel collected nuts, attracted most by those that were most portable—and caught her hands away from his face. If this was what she wanted— *please, God!*—there was nothing to stop him here from giving in to her, from taking her...no patrolling cops, no inquisitive kids... But, no matter how badly he wanted this, wanted her aggressively, tractably willing in his arms, he had no intention of going blindly where she led without first finding out if she knew where she was going.

He shouldn't do this. It went against principle, against the code of conduct that allowed him to maintain his distance and do his job effectively—except where Grace was concerned. With Grace he'd long since discovered that his principles had been sidetracked, his code of conduct rewritten—not compromised—to include her. But it had to be a choice. *Her* choice. His own choice had been made for him the first time he'd seen her better than a month ago.

For this moment, for them both—but especially for Grace—he wanted nothing but pleasure between them: no second thoughts, no future recriminations, only memories fully aware and deliberately made. Choice, not chance, for her. For him. Because for him, she was his choice.

"Grace, don't." He pushed her back in her chair, held her hands in her lap. "Stop. Look at me. Do you know what you're doing? If we start, it'll be too hard for me to stop this time if you don't. Please know what you're doing."

"I know what I'm doing, Mal." Her eyes filled with light, her generous mouth curved in invitation. "I know what I'm doing. I'm making a choice." She lifted his hands to her mouth, planted a kiss in each of his palms. Looked him in the eye. "I'm choosing you."

He stopped breathing, waited. Impatiently. Hoped. Against hope.

She didn't disappoint him.

"Take me to bed, Mal," she whispered. "Please."

Her mouth was a hot wet invitation, a hint of secrets and pleasures to be revealed. He took it roughly, parting her lips with his tongue and stabbing inside in an act of possession she met with eagerness and hunger, her own act of possession when she took his face between her hands to draw him closer, deeper, sent her tongue plunging on its own marauding mission into his mouth.

He groaned, a dark sound full of craving.

For her.

She whimpered, an impatient song filled with need.

Of him.

Kneeling on the deck between her legs, he hooked his hands underneath her knees and pulled her toward him. Moaning, she wrapped her legs tight around his hips and linked her ankles, looped her elbows around his neck and hung on. He slid his hands beneath her buttocks and rose, carrying her into the house, into her bedroom, came down with her onto the bed. Raised himself on his hands to look at her.

Her eyes were half-closed, dreamy, filled with something that he knew was only for him; her lips were plump and moist, ripened by his desire, curved with pleasure. Beneath her T-shirt, her thin cotton bra, her nipples already beaded: an offering, a request. She slid her hands down his chest and, amazed, he felt his own nipples tighten in response, beyond his control. It was a first for him. He was a man who controlled his own destiny, controlled both the pleasures he took and those he gave. Livvi had expected him to take the lead in the bedroom as well as other places, expected him to use her to pleasure himself as well as expecting him to pleasure her. Grace, it was perfectly clear, intended to participate, share the lead . . .

She flexed her legs around his hips and arched against his arousal, rocking while she worked her fingers into his waistband to untuck his shirt, shove it up his chest for him to catch and discard while she unsnapped his jeans, peeled down his zipper and shoved aside his shorts to take him in her hand.

He shuddered and groaned, pressing up into her palm, felt her fingers encircle him, contract-release-contract, slowly, steadily, exquisitely. Felt himself stretching and swelling in response, while the slim semblance of control he'd had only a moment ago slipped further.

Grace, it was abundantly clear, intended not only to share the lead but impatiently take it. His weeks of anticipating what it would be like to have her where she was right now would be all over for him in seconds if he didn't do something to distract her from what she was doing *now*.

"Grace." He caught her wrist, held her hand still. "You keep that up and this'll be over before it starts."

She stared up at him, eyes wide and dark in the heavy afternoon light. "I just want you to—"

"Yeah, but I want *you* to, too, *with* me." He loosened her fingers from around him, raised them to his mouth to graze the sensitive pads with his tongue and lips before kissing them, one by one. "It's not a contest, darlin', and it's not one-sided. I'm just ready faster, is all. Let me catch you up with me."

"But—"

"No 'buts', Grace." He was definite. "Not this time." His fingers on her skin, smoothing her T-shirt slowly up her midriff, were equally definite. Sensuous...calming...stimulating. Gentle. "I want to enjoy you—us. Take our time the first time."

She swallowed and shut her eyes, moistened her lips, uncertain. Throughout her body, every nerve and pore reached for his touch, clamored for more of this lazy, completely unrelaxing adventure, but her mind didn't have a clue how to do this. At least not this way.

She'd known one man, and that man had known one woman—her. They'd been young together, learning... the ways and means...the "what went where and why" together, experimenting, exploring...but there had always been a point beyond which Phil had never...been willing to go. She'd been the one who'd usually had to take charge, initiate the act; he'd been the one to set the pace. Without lingering.

She'd loved Phil to distraction, felt complete as his wife; she'd never doubted that. But there were things she hadn't learned—fantasized, yes, but fantasy was a place that existed only behind her eyelids, had never had a place in fact.

Mal was a fantasy—her eyes drifted the length and breadth of him—a gargantuan daydream in every respect, she'd decided that the first time she'd laid eyes on him. But now he was flesh and bone, too, and what he wanted from her, she didn't know how to give him. Share with him.

Dry-mouthed, she collected her legs and curled onto her side, away from him, and gave up the last greatest secret she possessed.

"I don't know how," she said.

He stilled, astonished. "You don't know *how?*" Another first among the many he'd already experienced with her. Grace Witoczynski knew how to do everything—or so she was adept at making people believe—and what she didn't know how to do, she brazened through so anybody watching couldn't tell the difference.

He slid up beside her on the bed, rested his hand at her waist, fingers splayed over her bare stomach, thumb easing beneath the edge of her bra elastic. Tread gently, instinct told him.

His instincts rarely lied.

"Don't know how to what?"

"Do what you want." She swallowed again, breath catching, and shivered slightly, head dropping back against his shoulder when he let his hand drift farther up her side, farther inside her bra to tease the underside of her breast. "Let you love me. Slowly or—*ooh*—" A moan when his fingers framed her breast, brushed lightly at her nipple. "I like that," she murmured, then tried to complete her original thought. "I don't know how to let you slowly or fastly—*mmm*—" Another caught breath when he released the three hook-and-eye catches at the back of her bra and trailed his hand back around to cup and squeeze, dragged it down her belly to hike her buttocks tight against his loins. "Or any—" He drew her upper leg back across his hip, traced high up the inside of her thigh and rocked her against his erection. "*Oh*, Mal, that feels good, but you're making it hard to think. What are you doing?... Or any...*mmm*...speed at all. I never—we didn't—I always—I don't know how."

"Sure you do." His voice was a low murmur in her ear, his mouth a hot, wicked tease along her neck.

She shifted, helping him hike up her shirt so he could whisk it off. "I don't."

"You do. It's easy." He hiked himself up to spoon himself tighter along her back, tucked his thigh between hers and twisted a bit to weave a track of biting kisses over her shoulder, down her side while his fingers loved and played, teased and tormented. He turned her upper body toward him.

"No, I don—" He laved his tongue over her nipple, mouth closed on it. Suckled once, gently, then drew hard. *"Oh!"* Her heart pounded, her breathing went rough.

Mal lifted his head. "Like that?" He dipped his head, still watching her face, made a lazy tour of her breast with his tongue, flirting with her nipple without touching it.

"Yes." She arched into him, clutched at his head, offering, begging for relief. "Mal...oh, Mal...Jiminy Pete...please...I don't—"

She gasped and bucked against him when he brought his thigh hard up into the apex of her thighs, tucked his hand intimately over the quickening center of her need and rocked her. His arousal was hot and thick at the waistband of her shorts, against her back.

"You *do*," he growled. "Now shut up and let me."

"Do it for me," she muttered and, twisting toward him, framed his face in her hands and captured his mouth.

Darkness swirled around them, blocked out everything but the lost world they built between them in the center of her bed.

His skin was smooth to her touch, hard and sculpted around muscles that didn't quit, a sensation all its own. His hair was long and in the way, a scintillating, unruly third hand with a mind of its own that got caught between them, interrupted but didn't stop deep, fire-building kisses—a silky magnet brushing her breasts and leaving them hard and aching, her gasping for more.

He turned her onto her back and slipped between her thighs.

Her skin was velvet beneath his calloused fingers, her breasts of a softer fabric still—silk and cream overflowing in his hands. Her legs were as long and agile as he'd dreamed—which she demonstrated when she dragged the soles of her feet up the backs of his legs to his waist, snagged her toes inside his jeans and, with a little weight-shifting by Mal, worked them off his hips and shoved them down past his knees so he could kick them onto the floor. It was a difficult feat, what with her whispering filthy nothings in his ear and him laughing as hard as he was and breathing raggedly at the same time, but they managed.

Then there was only her baggy cotton shorts and thin cotton underpants between them.

She, of course, wanted them off now. He stopped her from tugging at them by capturing her hand and sandwiching it between them against his belly and growling, "Slow down, let me," in her ear.

To which command she capriciously responded by dragging her tongue around his ear and nibbling at his lobe while she turned her hand palm up and slid her thumb over the moistening tip of his sex.

His turn to want her out of her pants *now*, her turn to chuckle wickedly, nip his ear and murmur, "Ah-ah-ah, slow down, let you."

To which he responded with a profanity that sounded a lot like a prayer and a deep, drugging, no longer playful kiss that curled and coiled through Grace's blood like flash fire, ran roughshod through her senses. When he rolled onto his back and pulled her astride him, she settled above him, a flushed rose and silk phoenix rising in the flames.

His hot, black eyes found her beautiful; his hands rocked her hips, made her arch her back and sway forward, brought her breasts to his rapacious mouth. Gasping, greedy, she placed her hands on either side of his head and undulated her hips while he suckled and laved her, stroking him, stoking him through the two layers of dampening cotton until they were both harsh-breathed and mindless, rough with need.

"Grace." Groaning, he lifted her off him, snagged his fingers in the waistband of her shorts and tore them down her legs. "Where are they?"

She was already reaching for him, angling underneath him. "Where are what?"

"The condoms." He was in pain from the pleasure, nearly bursting. The feel of her was more than he'd imagined, the desire greater than any he'd known, his need for her a sharp insatiable hunger he'd long ago stopped believing he'd ever feel for anyone. Stopped believing it was possible for him to want to feel for anyone. "Please. Where...I...need you. Need...to protect..."

"Oh. Oh..." In her frantic desire to mate, to cradle him inside her, become one with him, she'd forgotten there was anything else to think about, any needs other than this. "I'm sorry. Wait..."

She braced her heel and shoved herself across the mattress, fumbled along the edge of it until she came up with the crushed box. Dropped it in her haste. Mal scooped it up, tore open the cardboard and dumped the contents on the bed, grabbed up a set of connected packets and separated them, tossed the extras aside, started to rip into the one left in his hand. Grace captured his hands, stopping him.

"Wait," she said.

"Not anymore, can't wait anymore. You'll kill me."

"Wait," she repeated and took the condom from him, tore it open with her teeth. "This is my protection as well as yours." She pulled the coin-rolled bit of rubber out of its package and, eyes on his face, placed it over the tip of his arousal. "Let me."

He made a thick, guttural sound of concurrence and thrust once, heavily, into her hand, hurrying her when she unrolled the bit of rubber over him. Then he hauled her underneath him and caught her hips, she wrapped her legs around him and they joined.

"Finally," Grace breathed, adjusting her hips to accommodate him.

"Pardon me?" Mal jacked himself up on his elbows, withdrew a bit then drove himself deeper into her.

She arched her throat and smiled blissfully, tilted her hips and tightened long-denied muscles around him, urging him deeper still. "I said, it's about time you got here and it sure took you long enough."

He grinned, drew back and reentered her in a slow delicious glide that she met and milked. They had about a minute and a half before he burst his seams if she kept doing whatever it was she was doing to make the fire in him burn this hot, but if she wanted to waste it talking, who was he to try to stop her?

Besides, he knew how to shut her up if he really wanted to. But first there was something he wanted to know.

"It took who long enough?" he asked—although "rasped" would be a more accurate description, because her hips were moving in time to his, meeting him, drawing on him and he was slowly losing whatever grasp he had on the situation at hand.

Fine with her. She'd lost her grasp on it long ago.

"You," she gasped. "If you really want to talk about it—*ohh.*" A sigh, a plea when he began to drive faster, harder, deeper. "Oh, Mal, yes...please...*please.*"

"I don't want to talk about anything." His breath was a harsh song in her ear. "Except..."

"Except what?" She was breathless, abstracted, her pulse seemed to be up around three hundred beats a minute and the unopened condoms were sticking her in her left lower cheek and crackling every time she moved. "If you want a coherent answer, you'd better talk fast because in about three seconds—"

"What were you laughing about at lunch?"

Ah-ha! Success. She pulled the damned condoms out from under her hip, prepared to fling them across the bed while still concentrating on the exquisite sensations Mal was arousing deep inside her. "Laughing?"

"At lunch. You said it would embarrass—"

The condoms rattled in her hand. "Oh, that." A breathy chortle escaped. "You're sure you want to know? Now?"

"As sure as I am of anything at the moment."

"Well..." Another gasping chuckle, another crinkle of prophylactic wrappers. She held them up for his inspection. "Well, I was remembering I had these under the mattress and I was thinking about, um, that song, you know, the one The Fabulous Thunderbirds did a few years ago called—"

He caught on fast. "Oh, hell. No, don't say it."

"Called, um, 'Wrap It Up, I'll Take It'..."

"Oh, God."

He was strangling and dying and in heaven all at the same time and she was no help, dancing those damned things around like puppets while she sang that damned song in the lowest, sexiest contralto she could manage, *"Wrap It U-u-up...",* and it was all his own fault. He should have known better than to ask at a time like this.

Shaking with laughter, he buried his face in her neck and fought for control. It wasn't all that funny, really, he assured himself. It was just her singing in his ear, making up the words as she went along, suiting them—as it were—to the occasion, and if he didn't stop her soon, she'd be the death of him. Okay, all right, he had it now.

He raised himself on his hands, in control and intending to stay that way—and collapsed again when she winked up at him and said, "See, I told you, you couldn't take it," and went on singing. No siree, nope, never had he ever met anyone quite like Grace Witoczynski before.

She was one of a kind, unique, and right now, he had her. She was his.

The sudden, insistent knowledge stirred emotion deeper than laughter. His. He heaved himself up to look down at her in awe, and whatever she saw on his face quieted her more quickly than him picking the condoms out of her hands and flipping them to the other side of the bed, or the lingering kiss he planted on her mouth.

She touched his cheek with suddenly shaking fingers. "Mal..."

He bent, brushed his lips over her temples, her eyes, cheeks, nose, before dipping once more to take her mouth.

"Mal."

One more time he smiled that bemused half smile down at her and shut her mouth with his. "Shut up and let me love you, Grace. Love me."

Then he moved and she bowed into him, off the mattress, crying out. "Yes, Mal. I do...I do..."

And then there was nothing but that incredible light-filled darkness, that place with neither face nor name where shattering and splintering did not mean breaking apart, but mending, joining, becoming one. When Mal lunged hard into her one last time and went rigid above her, Grace was already at the edge of the canyon ready to fly with him into whatever piece of eternity they could find together.

Whole.

Chapter 14

The afternoon passed, became evening, turned to night and still they loved, coupling time and again with passion and tenderness, haste and fever, laughter and silliness and uninhibited enjoyment.

Whatever emotion preceded and accompanied it, the result was the same: the need would not abate. One joining led to the next; one appetite appeased created another. They loved and ate and loved and dozed and loved and loved and ate, touching the while, holding and caressing, sharing.

What should have been enough wasn't. What would have been more than sufficient for anyone else was barely their beginning.

Grace had never experienced anything or anyone like Mal in her life. All she knew was that a day that had begun by standing her on her head inside out and going downhill for a time from there, had turned into a burst of joy, a time to cherish, a giddy roller coaster she wanted to ride forever—or at least for a few hours more, and Mal...

For Mal, Grace was a revelation beyond supposing, a carnival death-drop, a skydive with a chute that refused to open until after he'd plummeted five hundred feet past the safe zone—and then she was the one who opened his chute and lifted him and dropped him in water way over his head and remembered to bring the life raft with her when she finally fell in, too. He couldn't get enough of her. And he understood, with trepidation but not surprise, that no matter how much of her he had, it would never be enough.

Beside him, Grace lifted herself on an elbow and whispered his name, "Mal."

That was all it took. He turned to her smiling and cradled her head, drawing her into his kiss, his arms, while she drew him into her body and took them both home.

It was light outside once more the next time Mal came back to himself, chuckling out of his sleep.

He'd never felt quite so pleased with himself before in his life, quite so satisfied, so...sated. And it wasn't even with himself, really, it was Grace. Amazing Grace, astonishing Grace, incorrigibly creative Grace, who lay sprawled across him in un-Grace-ly silence—asleep, judging by the weight of her—who made him feel so fantastically, primitively...complete. Exhausted. Alive.

Male.

Again that pleased-with-myself chuckle, the sensation of being full to brimming and content beyond anything anyone deserved. Astounding how a liberated, abandoned woman could make a man feel.

Especially if she was the right woman.

He hiked a couple of pillows under his head, smoothed a few damp curls from the corner of Grace's eye. Incredible how he felt about her. Protective. Even more so than before. Possessive. She was his, he'd staked his territory in the most primal way he knew and the sooner every other man in existence was aware that Grace Witoczynski was off-limits to anyone but him, the better. Possessed. He was hers and if he'd had any doubts about that before, he didn't now.

She'd told him in so many words, more than once. She'd shown him in a hundred minute ways—and her falling asleep on top of him was only the latest and one of his favorites. His most favorite, however, and the one that had sent him to sleep and brought him awake laughing was his memory of Grace joyously singing him her private pun-filled version of the Fabulous Thunderbirds' song.

Oh, yeah. There was nothing like creating a private joke and loving an incredible woman to settle a man's soul.

Sighing, he closed his eyes and gathered Grace close, careful not to waken her. He could get used to this. Coming to bed with her. Being there when she woke up in the morning. Watching the concentration on her face when she read the paper, the pleasure she took in her first morning cup-a, the sloppy, totally engrossed way she mowed the lawn.

Her laughter and the firm, warm, lunatic way she handled her children. Her children themselves . . .

The grin came, slow and appreciative. Yep, no doubt about it. She was pretty damned special, his Grace, pretty damned remarkable, a woman he'd go to hell for and someone he could truly—

Love.

His eyes popped open. Whoa, what was that? Who'd said that? Love? Nah, not him. Love . . .

He felt Grace shift and sigh, settle more comfortably atop him and that fierce place next to his heart where his soul seemed to lie opened wide and refused to close. Her place, he realized with something like consternation, no one else's. Never had been, never would be. Just like that, without a by your leave, she'd moved in where she belonged, opened the shutters, tossed out the clutter, polished the windows until they gleamed and put up her sign. *No Vacancy,* it appeared to read. *Under New Management. Watch for Renovations,* and he had nothin' to say about it.

Didn't really, he admitted to himself with some astonishment, want anything to say about it. Except to ask Grace to stay and then do whatever it took for him to work it out from there.

Love? he asked himself, looking at her, the wild honey hair so much shorter than his, the generous mouth, the features that seemed animated even in repose. And the answer came back: Yeah, well . . . okay. Maybe.

No, not maybe, the sign in the window seemed to flash. *Yes.*

He gulped, feeling the rush of panic, the slow spread of peace, and clutched Grace tight. *Yes.*

Yes.

Oh, God, he had to leave. Because for the first time since Jennifer's birth, he had something in his life he couldn't afford to lose.

"Mal?" Muzzy-eyed and delectable, Grace lifted her head and looked at him. "Is something wrong?"

"No." He shook his head, hoping the panic didn't show. "Nothing. Why?"

"Because you're squeezing me to death."

"I am?" He loosened his grip. "Sorry."

"No problem." Sighing, she stretched against him, rested her chin on his chest. "I kind of like it."

"Being squeezed to death?"

"Being squeezed by you."

Panic disappeared, replaced by the lazy, arrogantly male complacency she roused in him. He cupped the back of her neck. "Yeah?"

She strained forward to reach his mouth. "Yeah."

The click of two car doors and the sound of voices outside the open windows forestalled the natural course of events. In an instant, Mal was all law enforcement personnel, out of bed and on guard, checking. A car and a small truck he didn't recognize sat in the driveway, and a fuzzy-haired mid-fortyish woman with military bearing and a good-looking man about Grace's age approached the breezeway door. The woman bore a decided genetic resemblance to Grace.

"Who is it?" Working a T-shirt over her head and adjusting a pair of sweatpants, Grace came up behind Mal.

"Don't know. Man and a woman. She looks a bit like you. Is that—"

She couldn't help it. Grace took one look and panicked. "Helen."

She ran a hand through her hair, turning wildly, looking for she had no idea what. Escape, probably. "Oh, damn. Oh, God. Oh, holy—for the love of Pete, what's she doing here with a man who's not her husband? He looks like her husb— Oh, horse hockey." She slapped her forehead with the heel of her hand. "That's his *brother*. She brought him for *me*. Somebody—probably Twink, I'll kill her—told her I was going to be home alone for a week without the kids and didn't tell her I have company and so she decided—oh, *God,* for a Catholic, she's the biggest yenta you'd ever *not* want to meet and she's made *me* her next project. Damn, damn, *damn*. What time is it? Seven o'clock. *Seven* o'clock? In the morning? What the hell is she doing— It doesn't matter. Maybe we can pretend I'm not home, d'you think—"

"Yoo-hoo, Grace."

Helen waggled her fingers at Grace's bedroom window and Grace knew she was doomed.

Telling Mal he'd better get some pants on and muttering unkind epithets about déjà vu and certain members of some people's families, she banged her head on Mal's upper arm while he did his best not to laugh at her until the doorbell rang.

Mumbling, "Oh, God, I need a drink," she eyed Mal gloomily and went to answer it.

"Grace!" Helen bulldozed her way into the house and hugged her youngest sister when Grace opened the door. "How you doin'?"

Not known for mincing words among her sisters, Grace gave Helen a cursory hello-pat on the shoulder and viewed her blackly. "To what unfortunate set of circumstances do I owe this unexpected annoyance?"

"Gracie, Gracie." Sadly, Helen shook her head, eyeing Grace with disappointment. "Such a greeting—especially when you know I only ever have your very best interests at heart."

"What the hell are you doing here at 7:00 a.m.?"

"Did you say a.m.?" Some tut-tutting while Helen glanced at her watch and hauled the man who appeared to be her brother-in-law out of the breezeway and into the house. "It's 7:06 *p.*m., Grace. Where have you been? Edith said the kids were gone for a week, so this is Jed, my brother-in-law. He's only in town for the weekend, but I thought you should meet him, go out, get to know each other—"

Grace clenched her teeth. "Even if I don't *want* to? No offense, Jed, your brother's a terrific guy when he keeps her—" a thumb-jerk at Helen "—in line, and I'm sure you are, too, but, you know, you're really just window dressing so she can come around here and stick her nose in my life whether you or I want her to or not—"

Wait a minute. She stopped abruptly, nonplussed. Had Helen said p.m.? It was evening? You mean she and—a half-guilty, half-delighted glance toward the bedroom— had been in—another glance—a day and a half?

The cat-with-cream grin came before she had any idea it was there. Well. Well-well. She'd been enjoying herself—*him*—even more than she'd thought.

She drew herself up and glared Helen straight in the eye. "I have a guest," she said firmly, "and I'm loving every moment I have him to myself and I'm *not* ready to share him with *any*body yet, so *go away.*"

"But, Grace." Wounded. "What about Jed—" She stopped in midword, jaw dropping open to her chest.

Barefoot and bare-chested, jeans mostly zipped but not snapped, Mal padded into the room carrying a tall glass of ice and liquid, stopped close behind Grace and nuzzled her neck. Glanced assessingly at Jed and caught her chin in the crook of his thumb and forefinger and turned her so he could kiss her. Announcing claim. Thoroughly. Lazily. Possessively.

"Mmm." The sound purred in the back of Grace's throat when he released her. Eyes half-closed, she touched her tongue to her lips, savoring the loitering taste of him.

"Your ice tea, m'lady." Mal placed the glass in her hand and dropped another lengthy kiss on her mouth. His eyes were glazed and intense when he lifted his head. "Nice," he murmured. "Very nice. You going to be long?"

"Uh-uh."

"Good." He brushed her mouth with his thumb. "I'll wait."

He padded over to the picture window and, staring out but casting occasional glances at Grace, settled himself comfortably to do so.

Sighing deeply, Grace shook herself back into the moment and returned her attention to Helen. If it was possible, her third-oldest sister's jaw had dropped even farther, and she stared disbelievingly from Mal to Grace and back. Irritated by Helen's continued presence, Grace eyed the glass in her hand, eyed Helen. Reached out a

forefinger and shoved Helen's mouth firmly closed,
hooked that same finger in the front of Helen's blouse and
dumped tea, ice and all down her sister's cleavage. Helen
snapped something inelegant and jumped a foot, glow-
ered at Grace. Behind her, Jed backed into the breezeway, laughing. His brother had tried to warn him about
the Brannigan girls, but he'd been too caught up in his
sister-in-law's enthusiastic description of her sister to listen. Helen glared at him, too.

"Time to chill down," Grace advised her coolly. "Go
home and take a warm shower with Nat. This one's
mine."

"I can see that," Helen said, shaking the ice out the
bottom of her shirt. "Congratulations."

"Thanks. Now go home."

"I will after you introduce me to—"

"Grace." Mal's voice was sharp and sudden, cutting
between the sisters.

Instantly on guard, Grace turned to him. "What?"

"Where're the dogs, and whose truck's in the driveway?" He'd seen it when he'd first looked out at Helen's
arrival, but had been too preoccupied with Grace to really notice it.

Looking around her for the beasts, Grace joined him at
the window. "I'm not sure. I think I recall getting up to
feed them and let them out at some point, but if we let
them back in, or they barked about anything, I don't remember. I think we were kind of—" she colored, peeked
self-consciously at Mal "—busy. Helen, that's your car,
right? Did Jed drive himself or come with you?"

"With me." Helen joined them, too. "I think I heard
the dogs way out in back when we pulled up. Sounded like
they were locked in somewhere. Why?"

The same thought occurred simultaneously to Mal and
Grace. Of one mind, they swung around, looked out the

back window at Mal's apartment. The sound of Grace's dogs barking was faint but distinguishable.

"Judas," Mal swore and headed for the bedroom at a run.

Grace went after him, frightened.

Mal jerked a shirt over his head then jammed his feet into socks, pulled his gun and shoulder holster out of a boot, checked the load and slipped the weapon into the holster, snapped the holster shut and pulled it on at the same time he stepped into his boots.

"Mal."

Mal didn't look at her. "Is John's car in the garage?"

"I'll check." She went to see. Called back, "It's there."

"Good." Hauling on his leather vest, Mal came out of the bedroom and headed for the breezeway door. "Maybe I can—"

"Look, there's John," Helen said. "Do you want him? John," she yelled. "Hey, John! Who's that with him? What's he doing? It looks like he's got a gu— Hey!"

She fell back into Jed when Mal suddenly yanked her away from the window and shoved her toward the breezeway, grabbed Grace and dropped to the floor, covering her a bare second before the picture window shattered, spraying glass all over the living room. A second bullet hit the wooden window frame. Then there was the heavy roar of a truck engine and the screech of tires backing out of the driveway.

Mal heaved himself up off of Grace, doing his best to ship the glass fragments covering his back away from her. He had to go. He had to make sure about her, first.

He bent to her, dumped the glass off the backs of his hands before he touched her. "You all right? Grace, please. Are you—"

"Fine." Her voice was shaky but clear. Amazing. Her brain felt frightened numb. She took the hand he offered, hauled herself to her feet. Eyed the thin trails of blood on his arms and the backs of his hands with horror. "God, Mal, look at you—"

"Scratches, nothing serious." He took her hands. "Grace, I've got to go, that was Dunne. Are you sure—"

"I'm sure. Don't go. Let someone else—" The plea was selfish and futile, she knew it. Clamped her mouth shut. Hard as it was to do, let him go.

Mal took a last look at her. "Stay here. Call the police—call Harry. Tell 'em—" He rattled off the license number of his cycle, what he'd seen of the number on the truck. Made sure she had it.

"I do," she assured him, but he was already gone.

Gut twisting, she heard the Moto Guzzi rumble to life, listened to it thunder down the driveway. Knew suddenly that there was no way in hell she could let him go out after Dunne alone. Figured that a big bright red Suburban driving at high speed would be a lot easier for the cops to spot than simply Mal on a motorcycle chasing some nondescript mud-coated four-wheel-drive Jimmy with a killer behind the wheel. Didn't matter that she hadn't a clue what she would do if Mal caught up with Dunne and she caught up with Mal. The only thing that mattered was being there when he did, no matter what.

Her truck keys and license were on top of the television with a pen and labels for some VCR tapes. Not even stopping for shoes, she snatched the stuff off the TV and headed for the garage.

"Call 9-1-1," she ordered Helen, pausing to jot down the plate numbers Mal had given her plus the number on her Suburban. "Tell 'em you're General Brannigan. Throw your weight around, I don't care, but make 'em get hold of the U.S. Marshal's Service or the FBI or Gabriel or somebody federal and give 'em these numbers and tell 'em they've got an ex-Fed who's been kidnapped by William Dunne—"

"The mob guy?" Helen asked, dumbfounded.

Grace nodded, but didn't stop. "—who's armed and dangerous—" God, that sounded melodramatic, even if it was true. "—and a marshal with his butt in a sling out there by himself in pursuit and that if they don't get him some help, I will personally—"

"Yeah, yeah." Helen nodded impatiently. "We'll all go. Let me at the phone. Hey, wait. Where're you going?"

Grace shrugged. "After Mal," she said and was gone before a gaping Helen could stop her.

Muttering something about how *some* women—especially her sisters, first Alice, and now Grace, for heaven's sake, who was doing things even more idiotic because of Mal than Alice had done for Gabriel—didn't have the sense of self-preservation God gave *flies* when it came to *some* men, Helen stomped off to find the phone—after first turning around and sending a terse, "Go get 'em, Grace," and a silent thumb's-up after the Suburban Grace was backing out of the driveway, and deciding she really had to find somebody to replace Grace's front window before all the flies who had more sense than most Brannigans came in to roost.

Which left Jed sitting somewhat dazed in the breezeway by himself trying to figure out exactly what truly horrendous thing he could do to get back at his brother for introducing Brannigans even remotely into his life.

Chapter 15

There wasn't time to be afraid.

Her teeth felt dry and she could almost feel her eyelids sweating, but beyond that, fear was absent, lying in wait for later feasting. The only thing she thought about was finding Mal.

She gunned the truck, fishtailing around the tight curves—the only way in or out of the private subdivision—and sped up on the flats, eyes peeled, intent on wishing Mal just *there* ahead of her, or around the next turn. At each press of the accelerator, the old Suburban shuddered, protesting the abusive speed.

Around her the evening lengthened the shadows, the sun intensified in color and brilliance, blinding as the spinning earth sent the light toward the horizon. A few trucks and cars passed, heading toward home. She nearly met one or two head-on on the narrow zigzags, was glad of the Suburban's high underbelly and heavy suspension when she turned out and ran it tilted sideways along the drainage ditch to avoid the seemingly inevitable collisions.

The slim cloud of lingering dust kicked up by Mal's motorcycle was a tease drawing her on. She would find him because she had to. At the moment, nothing else mattered.

A mile or so ahead of her, Mal's thoughts were similar, focused with his eyes on the dust fog in front of him. The roar of the Moto Guzzi between his knees was familiar, exhilarating, but it wasn't enough to cover the thud of his heart, the adrenaline-enhanced pound of his pulse in his ears. He was so pumped, he had adrenaline in his bootstraps.

Beneath his breastbone the fury was intense, a grinding fist filled with anger and exigency to catch and destroy Dunne, make sure he could never again aim a weapon at Grace, erase a kid like Tigger as though the boy had never existed. God, Jennifer and his nephew were both only two years younger than Tigger had been, David was catching up fast and Phoebe was bang on his heels. Even if not for Grace, something had to be done for the kids.

He knew that getting rid of Dunne would not eliminate the dangers faced by his nearest and dearest teenagers, encountered by Grace in dark parking lots where he couldn't always be to help her out, but it was a strike he could make, one menace he could confront so they wouldn't have to.

The haze kicked up by Dunne's truck thickened around Mal. His lips drew back against his teeth in a smile that was mostly snarl. *Getting close.* He flattened himself over the gas tank and gave the Moto Guzzi all the speed he could.

* * *

She could hear sirens somewhere far away, but they didn't seem to be getting any closer.

Trying to keep the Suburban out of one of the abundant local "wetlands," Grace jerked the wheel hard to avoid a pair of deer leaping suddenly out of a cornfield. The truck lurched up a high grade and through the flimsy livestock fencing bordering an empty field. The view was a thousand times better than the one from the road—no curves, trees or hills in the way. Wresting control of the transmission from the jouncing-their-own-way wheels without slowing appreciably, Grace leaned into the steering wheel and stared ahead, impatient for some sight of Mal. She wasn't disappointed. Two curves up the road, he and his motorcycle were a slim speck in the dust; a few feet ahead of him, Dunne's truck fishtailed back and forth across the road barely under control.

Teeth bared in determination, Grace gunned the truck across the field at top speed, heedless of ruts, rocks and other impediments. Stones pinged off the Suburban's underbelly, weeds caught and tore in the carriage.

Mud flew from under the tires where the ground was soft, speckled the windshield so thickly she had to switch on the wipers and the squirters at regular intervals. It didn't matter. She was closing on Mal, ready to do whatever she had to simply to make sure he'd be around for years to come, to be with her, help her deal with whatever came along.

To love.

Something caught in her throat, perhaps frustration, perhaps something harder and more fierce. Her eyes stung and blurred, but the truck vents were open and the dust was intense.

Come on, damn it, she thought at the truck. *Come on. He's mine, I just found him. Nobody's taking him from me yet.*

Down on the road Dunne braked suddenly and swerved his truck sideways across Mal's path. Grace saw Mal attempt to avoid the collision, saw the Moto Guzzi skew sideways and tip, skid out behind Dunne's vehicle and go down, snaking at skin-ripping speed along the rough dirt and gravel road with Mal underneath it. Then Dunne reversed, put it in drive and careened away, sideswiping the motorcycle a crunching blow as he ripped past it.

Someone was screaming. Grace only realized it had to be her when her throat went raw and the screaming turned into a croak. Heedless of consequences, she powered the Suburban toward the roadside ditch, jounced through and onto the road, slowing only when she came abreast of Mal.

His left arm was a torn and bloody mess embedded with gravel, and the left leg of his jeans was shredded, but he was already removing his helmet and kicking out from under the Moto Guzzi when Grace pulled up beside him. He took one look at the mud-coated red vehicle and Grace didn't have to hear what he swore to know what he said.

Eyes tearing—this time without any made-up excuses even occurring to her to justify the tears—she leaned across to unlock the passenger door, shove it open. Limping, Mal hoisted himself into the front seat beside her.

"I thought I told you to stay home."

"Yeah." Grace nodded and reached across to touch his face, laughing shakily and brushing away the tears at the same time. "Good thing I'm hard of hearing sometimes, huh?"

"No," Mal snapped. "The point here is to grow old *with* you, not *because* of you." But then he shut his eyes, caught her fingers and planted a kiss on her knuckles. "Still, as long as you're here," he suggested, "punch it."

Grace nodded and, sniffing once, brushed the back of her hand across her nose. Took a deep breath. "Buckle up," she advised Mal and stamped the gas pedal to the floor.

For a moment, the Suburban's engine bucked and shimmied, sputtering in minor rebellion. Then it caught and held and the truck leaped forward in pursuit of Dunne.

It didn't take long to find him.

About a half mile ahead of them, he'd turned off the road and was jolting through the dried-mud ruts of a poorly marked, heavily wooded side track. Grace kicked in the four-wheel drive and bumped after him.

Branches scratched the paint, rocks flew up and dented the side panels, put a spiderweb break in the rear passenger window, but they were gaining. Grace had the Suburban practically riding Dunne's bumper when the track abruptly widened and the two vehicles exploded into a grassy meadow. Dunne immediately took on speed and pulled away, veering onto what looked like a private landing strip. Was a private landing strip, judging by the small blue and white plane coming to a stop at the end of it.

Beside Grace, Mal had picked up the cellular phone and was shouting something—at her or into it, she couldn't tell which over the whine of the truck and the roar of adrenaline in her ears. All she knew to do at the moment was drive and dodge, wheel and swerve, and make sure she stayed close to Dunne.

A few feet from the plane, Dunne braked to a stop and jumped out of his truck, dragging Gus—John? Grace couldn't remember who he was anymore—out with him, turned and opened fire at the Suburban. Swearing, Mal dropped the phone, popped his seat belt and pulled Grace's head down, angling in front of her to grab the steering wheel and maintain control of the Suburban.

"Brake," he shouted, scrambling to get his feet over the console so he could do it himself.

Tangled up with him, Grace did her best to comply.

Too late. A bullet punctured the Suburban's grill and the radiator ruptured in a hissing blast of steam. A second shot blew the right front tire out from underneath them and the Suburban listed wildly in that direction and pitched sideways, coming to rest up to the wheel well in a hole a bare dozen yards from Dunne.

One gun held to the back of Abernathy's head, the other extended at arm's length and aimed at the Suburban, Dunne forced Gus, in front of him, around his truck and screamed at Mal and Grace to get out and keep their hands where he could see them. When they didn't immediately comply, he fired a single shot into the windshield that grazed the dash and embedded itself in the seat just above Grace's head.

Grimly, Mal removed his own small second pistol from the pocket of his vest and tucked it into the small of his back.

"Stay behind me," he told Grace tightly. "When I say go, you drop and get under the truck and stay there no matter what until I come for you. And don't selective-hear me this time, Grace, understand?"

"Yes."

"Okay." Mal squeezed her hand, let her go. "Here we go."

He kicked open the passenger door and eased himself into the open, hands wide at his sides. Grace followed, mimicking him.

"Stop there," Dunne ordered when they were about five yards from the Suburban. They did, Grace almost hidden behind Mal's back. Dunne motioned her sideways, out where he could see her. "Take your weapon out and throw it away," he told Mal. "Two fingers, easy."

Mal did as he was told.

"Take your vest off," Dunne said. "Slowly. Get rid of it."

Chest tightening, Mal removed the vest. The next command was the one he dreaded.

"Pull up your shirt. Turn around slowly." Dunne smiled at the little pistol tucked against Mal's back. Motioned Grace over to get rid of it. "Now step back."

Gaze jerking from Mal to Gus to Dunne, Grace did what she'd been told.

In front of Dunne, Gus watched her, face a mask of apology and futility. This wasn't supposed to happen. He'd done everything he knew how to keep her out of it and here she was, anyway, up to her neck and sinking. He looked at Mal. Understanding passed between them. Whatever happened to the two of them, Grace would go out of here alive. They would die making sure of it.

Behind Dunne, a man in a sport shirt and slacks climbed out of the plane, approached. Stopped beside Dunne, hands at his sides. An automatic handgun dangled from his left hand; his right hand lay awkwardly flat against his leg.

"Mr. Dunne."

Dunne nodded, didn't take his eyes off Mal.

"Mr. diSalvo sends his respects, Mr. Dunne. He hopes we can work this out here rather than taking any extra baggage back. He asked me to handle the arrangements here for you."

Dunne smiled slightly, took a half step back without losing contact with Gus. "Good."

Sport Shirt raised the automatic, motioned Gus away from Dunne, jerking his head in silent command for him to join Mal and Grace. From the corner of her eye, Grace saw Mal tense and shift his weight toward her. Gus crossed the space between them, halted before he reached them and turned to face Dunne and Sport Shirt.

"Look," he said to Sport Shirt, "you're here for me, not them. My guess is there's no extra money in it if you do them, too, so why not let them go. You've got a plane, you're in the air and out of here before anyone even knows you've been. You kill one dirty ex-Fed, who cares? You kill a marshal and a female civilian with kids and your bosses won't thank you. It won't be worth it."

"That would be true," Sport Shirt said, "if I'd been paid for you." He straightened his arm until the automatic was aimed directly at Gus's head. His right hand came up slowly, behind Dunne. "Move back," he ordered Gus.

Gus took a step. Behind him, Mal also took a step, toward Grace and tensed to leap. Sport Shirt's right hand stopped at Dunne's shoulder, rested companionably beside Dunne's ear. Dunne smiled, waiting.

In the distance rose the sound of sirens, approaching. The plane that had never stopped idling began to move slowly down the runway toward them.

"Time to go, Mr. Dunne," Sport Shirt said, and pulled the trigger of the twenty-two caliber pistol that had been hidden in his right hand.

Within minutes, the field was a scene of chaos with local, state and federal authorities all converging on it at once. Apparently, when General Brannigan spoke and Mal Quarrels let people know where he was, authorities listened.

Dunne lay dead where the mob hit man had shot him then jumped aboard the taxiing plane. Mal had reached Grace and taken her down about the same moment the bullet entered Dunne's skull. He'd come up with the gun he'd tossed in her direction and had begun firing at the departing plane at the same time Gus dived for Dunne's weapon and did the same. The exercise had been one of futility, but still, they'd made the effort. The plane was gone by the time the first Oakland County Sheriff's four-wheel-drive Jimmy burst into the field.

According to Mal's contact agent, FBI intelligence had learned—a little late—that not one but two contracts had been taken out on Dunne. The second had gone into effect immediately after the first hit man had been killed. Dunne had believed he'd made a deal with one of his former bosses to bring Abernathy to them as a goodwill offering in return for his own safe conduct back into the family and his old stomping grounds. But Dunne's higher-ups had decided a long time ago that the former capo was too much of a wild card to leave around loose and had gotten rid of him.

Gus Abernathy was debriefed as the civilian, John Roth, his statement was taken and he was ordered to be available for further debriefing should it be required, then released, free of his past.

Finished with the man who would now be officially listed as John Roth, Mal Quarrels's case agent attempted to question Mal, but Mal didn't hear him. He was much too busy holding on to his heart and she was equally busy getting lost in his arms.

Chapter 16

He asked her to marry him in the emergency room while the resident was cleaning the gravel out of Mal's arm and leg.

It was a proposal full of grimacing and sucked-in breath, because his scrapes had had enough time to dry out and stung like hell when the doctor swabbed them out to debride them, but Grace wouldn't have traded it for anything.

They'd tried to get her to leave while they treated Mal because she wasn't family, but she hadn't come this far with him to be shut out now—and told them so, in no uncertain terms. In any event, Mal was in no mood to let her out of his sight for the foreseeable future. When he tucked his good arm around her waist and hung on to her, the doctors decided that, big as Mal was, exceptions were the things that made the rules, after all, and let her stay.

He proposed to her in the next breath and she accepted in terms as impassioned and unequivocal as those she'd used to tell the doctors she wasn't leaving the treatment room without Mal—conditions of the agreement to be negotiated later.

After which she informed him that he had until the end of the week to decide how he was going to tell the kids about their new stepfather. Then she took him home and kept him in bed for most of the week. Since he'd already decided to take her there with him in any event, he didn't object.

On Monday, he called Livvi and Jennifer to tell them about Grace, and ask Livvi to let Jen come East for the summer. Livvi was cool to the suggestion until she spoke with Grace. They spent an hour and a half on the phone getting to know each other—and laughing a lot about something Grace refused to tell him about until he was "old and gray," much to Mal's consternation.

But Jennifer would arrive Friday night.

On Tuesday, he requested to be transferred from the Marshal's Service—which took him out of town too much—to the local FBI office. Grace made a face when he told her, but Mal was a cop to the bone and she knew it and had made her decision to live with the man he was because that was the man she loved. But she did hope he wouldn't feel compelled to bring any more of his work home with him the way he had when they'd first met.

He grinned and told her that if he *did* have to bring his work home, he was going to tie her up and stick her in a closet before he told her about it and make sure she stayed there if it killed him. Because sure as these damned road burns hurt while they healed, if anything ever happened to Grace, it would kill him.

On Friday, they met Jennifer at Detroit Metro together and she and Grace spent a short, but awkward evening trying to figure out how to break the ice without stepping on each other's toes.

On Saturday, Twink brought the Witoczynski clan home, met Jennifer, guessed why she was at Grace's and gave Grace a hug, a big *yes* and hung out the window of the van while Rob backed it down the driveway whirling her arm and yelling *woof-woof-woof,* then asking if she could be the one to break the news to the rest of the family.

"No," Grace yelled after her.

Twink called everyone and hinted, anyway.

Grace introduced Jennifer to the kids who accepted her without much comment, ran off with her and got to know her a lot more quickly and easily than Grace had.

Sighing, she broke the news about Mal after dinner.

"I'm getting married," Grace said.

"To whom?" Ethan, polite, and obviously a changed man after a week in the woods.

Grace looked at him, wondering a) where she'd gotten him from and b) how he could possibly not have figured out that since Mal was standing behind her with his arms wrapped around her waist, it was probably Mal she was marrying.

Phoebe dealt with the situation for her by punching her younger brother in the arm. "She's marrying Mal, stupid, that's why his daughter is here." Ruined the effect by turning to Grace for confirmation. "Aren't you, Mom?"

"We're getting a *dad,* yay!" Erin, flinging her arms out to Mal ecstatically. "Now maybe Mum won't have to coach my teams all the time. It's fine when she coaches softball, but she doesn't know anything about basketball or soccer and we always lose. Do you know anything about basketball and soccer, Mal, and you won't coach my teams if you don't, will you?"

"When?" David, reserved.

"Two weeks," Grace said.

David nodded. Looked at Mal, the child who'd taking over being the man of the family without anyone but himself ever telling him to, intent on carrying out his self-imposed duties to the end.

"You like my mom." A statement, no intonation.

Mal nodded. "Yeah, I do."

"A lot?"

"Oh, yeah." Mal smiled, rubbed his cheek in Grace's hair. "More than that, even. A lot more."

"Do you love her?"

Mal nodded.

"Even though she's volatile?"

"Pardon me?" Grace asked. "Volatile? Where did you get that word? And I'm *not* volatile."

"Yes," Mal said into the back of her head, "you are. And yes," he looked over her head and winked at David, "I do. Even though and especially because she's volatile."

"Okay." David took a breath, made a decision. "You can marry her, but I won't call you Dad."

"David," Grace began quietly, but Mal stopped her so David could finish.

"I had a dad," David said, looking Mal in the eye, "and I remember him and you can't take his place, so don't try."

"No," Mal agreed. "That would be wrong. And you can call me whatever you want, it doesn't matter. *Mal* is fine, or—"

"Poppa," Phoebe suggested, eyes alight.

Ethan snapped his fingers, pointed at Mal. "Pops," he said.

"Poppy!" Erin crowed in delight, dancing across the room to hug Mal and dance away again giggling.

Mal looked at Grace. "Pops?" he asked. "Poppy?"

"You said," Grace told him, laughing, "they could call you *anything*."

"Poppy?" Mal asked, grimacing.

Jennifer got up from where she'd been sitting on the couch observing the proceedings. "Well," she drawled, moving to the edge of the group, "if you don't like those suggestions, *Dad*, they could always call you what *I* call you behind your back."

Mal looked at her. "You call me things behind my back?"

"Sure," Jennifer said, deadpan. "Doesn't everybody?"

That was the moment Grace realized she and Jennifer wouldn't have any trouble at all getting along. All they had to do was deal with a sense of humor and not work too hard at it.

"What do you call him, Jen?" she asked, grinning.

Jennifer took her time, running her tongue around the outside of her teeth before canting her head and answering, "Old Poop."

"Old Poop?" Mal, feigning outrage.

"Old Poop?" Grace, laughing and choking appreciatively.

"Old Poop!" Ethan, Phoebe and Erin, whooping with enthusiasm. "Hey, Old Poop, wanna go shoot some baskets? Old Poop, wanna take a bike ride?"

"I'll get you for this," Mal informed his daughter blackly. "Maybe not now, but someday next year when you've finally gotten your license and you're asking me for the car—"

"Hey, Old Poop," David interrupted quietly, offering Mal his hand. "Welcome to the family."

It took Mal a stinging-eyed, slow-motion moment to let go of Grace and take David's hand, but he did. Then he engulfed David in a huge bear hug and the rest of the children, including Jennifer, piled in and Mal reached out to collect Grace and ...

The evening light slanted through the trees, sparkled through the new picture window and any way he looked at it, Mal knew he was home.

*   *   *   *   *

Take 4 bestselling love stories FREE

Plus get a FREE surprise gift!

Special Limited-time Offer

Mail to Silhouette Reader Service™

3010 Walden Avenue
P.O. Box 1867
Buffalo, N.Y. 14269-1867

YES! Please send me 4 free Silhouette Intimate Moments® novels and my free surprise gift. Then send me 6 brand-new novels every month, which I will receive months before they appear in bookstores. Bill me at the low price of $2.89 each plus 25¢ delivery and applicable sales tax, if any.* That's the complete price and a savings of over 10% off the cover prices—quite a bargain! I understand that accepting the books and gift places me under no obligation ever to buy any books. I can always return a shipment and cancel at any time. Even if I never buy another book from Silhouette, the 4 free books and the surprise gift are mine to keep forever.

245 BPA ANRR

Name	(PLEASE PRINT)	
Address	Apt. No.	
City	State	Zip

This offer is limited to one order per household and not valid to present Silhouette Intimate Moments® subscribers. *Terms and prices are subject to change without notice. Sales tax applicable in N.Y.

UMOM-9265   ©1990 Harlequin Enterprises Limited

HEARTBREAKERS

Hot on the heels of **American Heroes** comes Silhouette Intimate Moments' latest and greatest lineup of men: **Heartbreakers**. They know who they are—and *who* they want. And they're out to steal your heart.

RITA award-winning author Emilie Richards kicks off the series in March 1995 with *Duncan's Lady*, IM #625. Duncan Sinclair believed in hard facts, cold reality and his daughter's love. Then sprightly Mara MacTavish challenged his beliefs—and hardened heart—with her magical allure.

In April *New York Times* bestseller Nora Roberts sends hell-raiser Rafe MacKade home in *The Return of Rafe MacKade*, IM #631. Rafe had always gotten what he wanted—until Regan Bishop came to town. She resisted his rugged charm and seething sensuality, but it was only a matter of time....

Don't miss these first two **Heartbreakers**, from two stellar authors, found only in—

INTIMATE MOMENTS®
™ *Silhouette*®

HRTBRK1

**ROMANTIC
TRADITIONS**

Patricia Coughlin

Graces the ROMANTIC TRADITIONS lineup in April 1995 with *Love in the First Degree*, IM #632, her sexy spin on the "wrongly convicted" plot line.

Luke Cabrio needed a lawyer, but high-powered attorney Claire Mackenzie was the last person he wanted representing him. For Claire alone was able to raise his pulse while lowering his defenses...and discovering the truth behind a vicious murder.

ROMANTIC TRADITIONS: *Classic tales, freshly told. Let them touch your heart with the power of love, only in—*

INTIMATE MOMENTS®
Silhouette

SIMRT7

UP IN THE SKY—IT'S A BIRD, IT'S A PLANE, IT'S...
THOMAS DUFFY'S BRIDE-TO-BE!

Years ago, a very young Thomas Duffy had found a lost girl from another planet crying in the woods. He dried her tears, helped her find her spaceship—and never saw her again.

Then one day Janella, now very much a woman, dropped from the sky into his Iowa backyard, in need of a husband.

But the last thing Thomas Duffy wanted was a wife—especially one from another planet.

OUT-OF-THIS-WORLD MARRIAGE
by Maggie Shayne

available in April, only from—

Men and women hungering for passion
to soothe their lonely souls.

The new Intimate Moments miniseries by

Beverly Bird

continues in May 1995 with

A MAN WITHOUT A HAVEN (Intimate Moments #641)
The word *forever* was not in Mac Tshongely's
vocabulary. Nevertheless, he found himself drawn
to headstrong Shadow Bedonie and the promise
of tomorrow that this sultry woman offered. Could
home really be where the heart is?

Coming in July 1995

A MAN WITHOUT A WIFE (Intimate Moments #652)
Seven years ago Ellen Lonetree made a decision
that haunted her days and nights. Now she had the
chance to be reunited with the child she'd lost—if she
could resist the attraction she felt for the little boy's
adoptive father...and keep both of them from
discovering her secret.

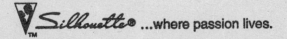

...where passion lives.

CODE NAME:
DANGER

Because love is a risky business...

Merline Lovelace's "Code Name: Danger" miniseries gets an explosive start in May 1995 with

NIGHT OF THE JAGUAR, IM #637

Omega agent Jake MacKenzie had flirted with danger his entire career. But when unbelievably sexy Sarah Chandler became enmeshed in his latest mission, Jake knew that his days of courting trouble had taken a provocative twist....

Your mission: To read more about the Omega agency.

Your next target: THE COWBOY AND THE COSSACK, August 1995

Your only choice for nonstop excitement—

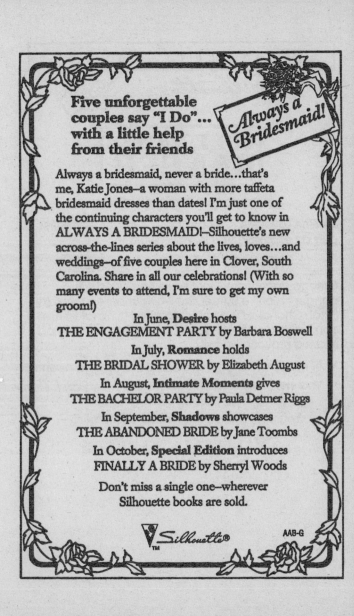

Five unforgettable couples say "I Do"... with a little help from their friends

Always a Bridesmaid!

Always a bridesmaid, never a bride...that's me, Katie Jones—a woman with more taffeta bridesmaid dresses than dates! I'm just one of the continuing characters you'll get to know in ALWAYS A BRIDESMAID!—Silhouette's new across-the-lines series about the lives, loves...and weddings—of five couples here in Clover, South Carolina. Share in all our celebrations! (With so many events to attend, I'm sure to get my own groom!)

In June, **Desire** hosts
THE ENGAGEMENT PARTY by Barbara Boswell

In July, **Romance** holds
THE BRIDAL SHOWER by Elizabeth August

In August, **Intimate Moments** gives
THE BACHELOR PARTY by Paula Detmer Riggs

In September, **Shadows** showcases
THE ABANDONED BRIDE by Jane Toombs

In October, **Special Edition** introduces
FINALLY A BRIDE by Sherryl Woods

Don't miss a single one—wherever Silhouette books are sold.

Silhouette®

AAB-G